THE REVELATION
OF BEATRICE DARBY

Visit us at www.boldstrokesbooks.com

THE REVELATION
OF BEATRICE DARBY

by

Jean Copeland

2015

THE REVELATION OF BEATRICE DARBY

ISBN 13: 978-1-62639-339-4

This Trade Paperback Original Is Published By
Bold Strokes Books, Inc.
P.O. Box 249
Valley Falls, NY 12185

First Edition: April 2015

Credits
Editor: Shelley Thrasher
Production Design: Susan Ramundo
Cover Design By Gabrielle Pendergrast

Acknowledgments

Bannon, Ann. *Odd Girl Out*. San Francisco: Cleis Press, Inc., 1957, 2001. Print.

Tim Parrish, my mentor.

Anne Notarino-Santello, my first-draft copy editor.

Dedication

For my father, James P. Copeland,
and the late Carolyn F. Copeland,
the other writers in the family.

CHAPTER ONE

S uddenly they were alone on an island of forbidden bliss.

Beatrice Darby did a double take at the sensational caption on the cover of the novel she knew right away she shouldn't be looking at. *Odd Girl Out* was its title, and she tingled as she absorbed the image of the half-naked blonde perched under it, her naughty parts barely hidden in a pile of plush pillows. She glanced around DeLuca's drugstore to make sure no one she knew noticed her ogling its cover art on the rack in the back corner.

This discovery raised the stakes in her presence at DeLuca's that afternoon in 1957 as she was supposed to come straight home from her summer job to prepare supper—a week-long penitence for skipping Sunday mass the day before to enjoy a sunny morning at Lighthouse Point Park. She and her older brother, Quentin, rarely agreed on anything except that when their mother had one of her nervous spells, and couldn't accompany them to church, they would act as each other's alibi as they pursued separate adventures in religious hooky. Her caper would've been a success, too, had their gossipy neighbor, the heathen Mrs. Pritchett, and her brood of five not been struck with that same notion.

Her heart raced as she snatched the paperback from the cluster of other tawdry romance novels on the bottom shelf. She pivoted toward the wall on the heel of her saddle shoes and began fanning through the pages.

A wash of heat flooded Laura's face. She bent over Beth again, perfectly helpless to stop herself, and began to kiss her like a wild—

"What do you think you're doing?" a woman hollered.

Beatrice flinched and dropped the book on the floor. As a woman scolded her son for stuffing penny candy down the front of his suspender pants, Beatrice kicked the book under a magazine rack until the mother-son riot ended with the mother dragging the red-faced, screaming boy from the drugstore. Exhaling with relief, Beatrice slid the book out from under the rack with her foot and poked through the pages to finish the stimulating sentence.

…like a wild, hungry child, starved for each kiss, pausing only to murmur, "Beth, Beth, Beth…"

She could hardly believe what she was reading. People actually wrote these kinds of stories? She devoured the passage, fearing at any moment she might be discovered. She wanted to read the novel from beginning to end, yet she couldn't stroll up to the counter and buy it. And if she stayed and kept reading, she would get home so late from work she would rouse her mother's fury. Before she realized what she was doing, Beatrice tucked it under her baggy blouse and headed toward the exit. She focused on the top of her outstretched hand as it was only seconds from pushing the door handle to freedom.

"Beatrice," Mr. DeLuca called out from behind the counter.

She stopped at the door, clutching the soft cover sticking to her moist stomach, and glanced at him over her shoulder.

"Your milkshake and doughnut," he said. "You haven't touched them."

A rush of heat swept up her neck and tickled her ears. "I can't, Mr. DeLuca," she stammered. "I'm gonna be late for supper."

"Well, come over here and I'll wrap up the doughnut for you."

"Oh, no, that's okay. I really need to go," she said, pulling at strands of hair from her chestnut-brown ponytail sticking to her neck.

"It'll only take a second, Bea. Take it home to your mother if you don't want it."

She flicked her tongue at the sweat mustache tickling her upper lip. What had she done? Not only had she stolen, a crime that had never tempted her in all her seventeen years, but if she were apprehended she would never be able to explain what she'd stolen. In the moment, however, the high of being only inches from a clean getaway snuffed out those inconvenient thoughts.

She shuffled over to the counter, still hugging the book through her blouse.

"What's wrong with your stomach?" Mr. DeLuca asked, handing her the doughnut in a rolled-up brown paper bag. "You want a sip of Gassosa?"

"No, thank you, Mr. DeLuca. I should just go right home. My mom and brother will be miffed if we have to eat late on my account."

Mr. DeLuca nodded as he stuck his thumb between his belt buckle and rotund stomach, well aware of the importance of a prompt supper.

Once outside, Beatrice took off down Chapel Street, slicing through the thick July humidity, her legs booster-charged by a surge of endorphins. She couldn't wait for night to come to read more about Beth and Laura after her mother had fallen asleep watching television.

She burst into the apartment, intent on stashing her ill-gotten treasure safely in her bedroom.

"Beatrice, hold your horses," her mother barked from the kitchen.

Beatrice skidded to a halt short of her bedroom door. Normally, she would pretend she hadn't heard her mother and continue into her room, but guilt arrested her.

Her mother peered around the refrigerator. "Why are you so late? Cooking dinner all week is your punishment, not some good deed you volunteered for."

"I'm sorry. I uh, I had to stay late at work. They're redesigning the children's section." She paused for a moment to marvel at her previously unknown talent for concocting elaborate pretenses on the draw.

"I don't know why you kill yourself for that boss of yours. You won't even be working there much longer."

Beatrice squirmed at the pressure of the book now stuffed in the waistband of her skirt. "Well, it's like you say, Mom, do unto others…"

Her mother nodded thoughtfully. "I'm glad to hear you do occasionally listen to me."

Beatrice's mouth twitched as her eyes fell short of making contact with her mother's.

"Now go on. Wash yourself up and get dinner going. Your brother and I are hungry."

In her room, Beatrice shook her head at the collection of sins she'd accumulated over the last two days. The corner of the concealed book scraped against her skin. Did adolescent sins carry less weight than grown-up sins? Or if you racked up sins as a kid, did you have to pay more penances later? She resolved to settle her account with God at a later date. Right now, this delicious, forbidden novel required her immediate attention. She lifted her pillow and tucked the book under it, pressing down and smoothing the floral bedspread over it.

"Bea," Quentin said, peeking into her room.

"What?" she said with a start, spinning around and sitting on her pillow.

"Jeez, what are you so jumpy about?"

"Nothing. Guilty about skipping church."

He looked at her quizzically. "Still?"

She rolled her eyes, anxious for Quentin to walk away. "You may not care about roasting in hell for all eternity, but I do."

"God's got commies to worry about," Quentin said. "He doesn't care about me ditching Sunday mass once in a while."

"I'll pray for your soul," she said dryly, touching her pillow for reassurance.

He screwed up his mouth. "What a pal. By the way, thanks for not squealing on me. You're an okay kid. Weird, but okay."

"What do you mean?" she snapped, her excitement over the novel still prickling her skin.

"You know, when that stoolie, Pritchett, called Mom."

Beatrice shrugged. "One hand washes the other. You can return the favor someday."

"Yeah, sure," he said, rolling his eyes. "Now would you start cooking? We're starving already."

She crossed her eyes and flipped him the bird. He wagged a playful finger at her before disappearing into the bathroom.

❖

Beatrice was still awake at two a.m., an hour after she'd finished reading the novel. Her mind swirled with the sordid tale of Beth and Laura's romance as she lay in bed, her sheet tangled around her legs. Her skin was damp from the mid-summer humidity that showed no mercy even at that late hour. Did that kind of thing really go on between college girls? She was starting college in less than two months. Could something like that happen to her? What would she do if it did? Butterflies bounced in her stomach as she allowed herself to imagine that she was Laura.

The fantasy of kissing some imaginary college girl took off on its own. Soon, however, she wasn't kissing a nameless, faceless girl—she was kissing Abby Gill, her much-older supervisor at the New Haven Public Library. Miss Gill was unlike any woman Beatrice had known in all her seventeen years, a petite, self-confident pill of a gal with rich olive skin and choppy brown hair that always seemed to need combing. She'd found herself drawn to Miss Gill since she started working with her, but now her intense, confusing feelings were finally starting to make sense.

In her visions, Miss Gill pecked at her lips, caressed her bare arms, pulled her closer, and kissed her harder. A warmth spread up her legs as sweat began to bead her forehead. She licked her lips as she imagined Miss Gill kissing them raw. Before she realized what was happening, her hand had crept under the thin bed sheet.

Her eyes sprang open as shame crawled over her. Where were those dirty thoughts coming from? It was the book, that smutty book. She sat up and fanned herself with a copy of *Modern Screen* on her nightstand, training her eyes on familiar objects in her room shadowed by the incoming light from the street. Her heart raced at the vividness of her fantasy.

She lay down again and flung aside the sheet to cool off, staring at the ceiling. She shouldn't be thinking those kinds of things about other girls. She used to be able to gently escort them from her mind as soon as they crept in, but now they were becoming too powerful to stop.

Not long after she began working at the library during her senior year in high school, she began entertaining her idle mind with carefree thoughts of spending time with Miss Gill outside of work, going to DeLuca's drugstore, window shopping Chapel Street, all the things she'd wished she could do with a best girlfriend. But of course, Miss Gill was a grown woman. Why would she want to spend her leisure time with a teenager? Still, it pleased Beatrice to imagine a close friendship with her supervisor, who'd always felt more like a friend than an authority figure. But lately, perverted thoughts were overtaking the innocent ones. Quietly she often stewed, chastising herself, making promises her maturing body couldn't keep. She didn't know what to do about it, but she certainly couldn't ask anyone for advice.

She exhaled. Maybe skipping Sunday mass to frolic at the shore hadn't been the brightest thing to do considering the turmoil going on inside her.

She eventually fell asleep, but not much before the clang of the alarm clock jolted her awake at seven a.m. She relished a stretch in the rays of sun pouring in from Franklin Street, until last night's incident disrupted her calm. She took a moment to expel the whole matter from her mind, confident in her promise to herself. After another long stretch, she leapt out of bed, swept up her hair in a ponytail, and splashed cold water at her eyes.

As she dug her spoon into a bowl of cornflakes, she was pleased with her new idea that the provocative scenes were a product of her fondness for Miss Gill, simple admiration for the sophisticated, independent woman that she had somehow blown out of proportion. Her face felt flush again, but she focused on the note next to her cereal bowl from her mother that reminded her of the long list of chores she needed to complete before she rushed off to work.

She slurped the last soggy spoonful of flakes, catching the milk drip in the corner of her mouth with the back of her hand. In another month, she'd be gone, a college freshman living in a dorm free from her domineering mother. Then who would she order around? Quentin? Not likely. He worked so hard at the bicycle repair shop every day. Why should he have to lift a finger when he got home? Beatrice might have had to wash his dishes and do his laundry, but she drew the line at picking up his skivvies.

❖

Beatrice had spent most of the day at the library arranging periodical displays, assisting patrons, and stealing glances at Miss Gill, her attention thoroughly scattered. Butterflies had mamboed in her stomach whenever she noticed Miss Gill flash a patron her dimpled grin.

As the day progressed, the unsettled feeling she awoke with and attributed to that strange novel reemerged. She'd found some relief in knowing other girls out there had those same thoughts. Suddenly, deep down, Beatrice realized that her desire for Miss Gill wasn't mere admiration. Her neck suddenly grew hot and tight. How would Miss Gill react if she ever knew of the secret things Beatrice had envisioned doing with her the night before?

Toward the end of her shift, Beatrice was helping an elderly woman locate *Peyton Place* in the fiction section. Once she spotted the title, she nudged the step stool aside with her foot and, using her long wingspan, snatched the copy off the top shelf.

"How convenient to be so tall," the old woman said.

"It's been an experience, all right," Beatrice said with a faint smile.

Suddenly, she caught Miss Gill in her periphery, approaching in a brisk walk, and her peanut-butter sandwich cartwheeled in her stomach. She braced herself against the stacks and absently fingered the novel's binding. As Miss Gill breezed past, she offered Beatrice a playful wink.

She inhaled the exotic wake of Evening in Paris that trailed Miss Gill as she headed toward the front desk, watching Miss Gill's curvaceous rear end each step of the way. Her heart raced as she anticipated the husk of that mature voice, the words that would invite Beatrice to stand close to her.

"Oh, Bea," she called quietly, at last. "Would you return these to nonfiction for me when you're free?"

"Oh, miss, can you also help me find..." the old woman said, but Beatrice had already sprinted to Miss Gill's side.

"Gee, too bad you're spending your last summer of freedom stuck in this musty old place," Miss Gill said. "Don't you ever just feel like taking off and getting out in the sun or having a swim at Lighthouse?"

"That didn't work out so well the last time I tried it," she said with a frown. "Besides, my mom would get in a tizzy if I missed a day of work."

"How would she know? I wouldn't tell."

"She'd notice it in my paycheck."

"I suppose she would." Miss Gill shook her head. "You know, Bea," she narrowed her eyes, "sometimes being bad feels pretty good. There's no crime in having a lark once in a while. And you're so young yet. Like the Romans say, Carpe diem."

Beatrice shrugged as she traced symmetrical patterns in the rug with the tip of her shoe. It was fun playing against type for once, even with the consequences, but as she zeroed in on Miss Gill's glistening lips, she couldn't imagine why on earth she'd want to be anywhere but right here.

"Well, here you go." Miss Gill seemed disheartened as she wheeled the book-return cart around for her. "When you're done, meet me in the reference room."

As Beatrice replaced each title to its rightful position within Mr. Dewey's decimal system, she cringed, thinking about disappointing her paramour. Would doing something rebellious impress her? Beatrice had always done what was expected of her in school and at home, especially when her father's death seven years earlier had fractured the family. Beatrice had so wanted to make him proud, and the best way to do that was to continue being his "good girl."

Later in the reference room, she shifted the heavy stack of encyclopedias in her arms and slouched in defeat. Despite her best effort, she couldn't suppress the urge to peek as Miss Gill stretched to reach the highest shelf, her breasts bulging against a peach sweater. As Miss Gill bit at her bottom lip while pushing two volumes into position, Beatrice practically salivated.

"You must be thrilled about leaving for college in a few weeks," Miss Gill said as she tugged at the bottom of her sweater.

"Yes, I suppose."

"What do you mean suppose?" Miss Gill glared down at her from her perch. "You were so excited in the spring when you learned you got a full scholarship. When we celebrated at DeLuca's you seemed out of your head with excitement, remember?"

How could Beatrice forget? They'd sat together at the drugstore counter sipping cream-soda floats while Miss Gill regaled her with such thrilling tales of sorority life. Beatrice's most cherished memory of the afternoon was when Miss Gill giggled so hard recalling a prank she and her sisters had pulled that she'd accidentally tumbled against Beatrice's arm in dramatic fashion.

"It's just that, well..." She fumbled for words. "Well, I'll miss working here and helping you."

"Aw." Miss Gill placed her hand on Beatrice's shoulder as she descended the stepladder. "I'll miss having your help," she added with a smile brighter than Marilyn Monroe's in the Lustre-Crème Shampoo ads.

"Will you?" Beatrice asked, surprised.

"Why sure," she replied with a gentle stroke across Beatrice's shoulder. "You've been great fun, especially this summer when libraries can be ghost towns."

Beatrice curled her lips to prevent her smile from leaping off her face.

"Are you blushing, Bea?" Miss Gill grinned.

Her cheeks flamed. "No," she whispered, looking down at her shoes.

"I think you are." Miss Gill then sang, "Beatrice is blushing, Beatrice is blushing."

"No, I'm not." She faked a scowl to hide the excitement charging through her.

Miss Gill chuckled. "Aw, don't be mad. You're adorable when you blush." She gently pinched Beatrice's belly.

Beatrice touched the part of her shirt where Miss Gill pinched her.

"Oh, I'm sorry. Did I hurt you?"

She watched Miss Gill's mouth form the words and then shook her head.

Their eyes locked for an awkward moment, Miss Gill's with an intensity Beatrice had never noticed before. God, what was she thinking? What would it really be like to kiss her?

"What do you say, kid? Time to blow this clambake," Miss Gill said.

Beatrice wrenched her lips into a smile and followed her to the break room. Punching out each day was like flipping to the next page of a riveting novel and realizing it was the last.

❖

The next morning, Beatrice surveyed her reflection in horror. Her eyes were puffy, the side of her face marred by sheet wrinkles from a fitful sleep. It was well after three by the time she'd fallen asleep, thanks to visions of Miss Gill and her in various scenarios of intimacy. Why couldn't she stop these thoughts?

She closed her eyes as she brushed her teeth and tried to imagine kissing her best friend, Robert Carlin. She wrinkled her forehead and scrunched her eyes tight as she forced the image in her mind's eye. Nothing remotely close to kissing Miss Gill—in fact, she accidentally poked her tonsil with her toothbrush and gagged into the sink.

As she walked to the library, she passed Robert on the street washing his father's '56 Ford Fairlane. She'd known Robert since he moved to the neighborhood in the fifth grade, earning his loyalty by tutoring him through eighth-grade Algebra, saving him his spot on the junior-varsity basketball team. Robert was a nice boy, cute and sort of shy around girls—that is until they got to know him. Beatrice didn't have many friends in high school, but she certainly counted Robert as her closest.

Toward the end of his graduation party in June, he'd tried to ask her out on a real date, but when she picked up on what he was spluttering about, she managed to change the subject before he could spit it out. And before she knew it, Maria Perillo came along, and Robert was happy just being friends again.

"Hiya, Bea," Robert said, shaking the soapsuds from his hands. "Off to work on this beautiful day? Sorry about that."

She nodded. "Gee, you sure wash your dad's car a lot."

"Say, what do you mean?" Robert said with a scowl. "This is my car. My dad gave it to me."

He was lying. "Well, it's a really keen car. I'm sure Maria enjoys tooling around in it."

"Sure she does. Maybe I can take you for a spin sometime," he said with a blushing smile.

She considered the offer. According to most of the stories from girls she knew who dated boys, accepting a ride in a boy's car meant you could expect to wind up at the top of East Rock steaming up the windows. She looked at Robert's expectant smile, the fine brown hair on his top lip gleaming with sweat. He was cute. Very cute. So why didn't she think about him the way she thought of Miss Gill? She closed her eyes and tried again to picture him kissing her, pantomiming as she forced the image.

"What's the matter, Bea? You got something from breakfast stuck in your teeth?"

She opened her eyes and smiled awkwardly. Nothing. No tingles, no butterflies, zilch.

"So how about that ride?"

"I'd like to, Robert, but my mother won't allow me in cars with boys until I'm eighteen."

"That's in October, isn't it?"

She nodded confidently, knowing she'd be safely nestled away on Salve Regina's Rhode Island campus by the time that day arrived.

"Okay, I'll see you then for that ride," he said with a grin.

She grinned back. "Not if I see you first."

He flung soapsuds at her as she trundled off down the street.

"That's okay," he called out after her. "Maria would probably get sore if you came with me anyway."

"You certainly wouldn't want that," Beatrice said over her shoulder with a satisfied grin.

At lunchtime in the break room, Beatrice peeled her tuna sandwich from its waxed-paper wrapping and poked it. Her suspicions were correct—mushy bread from a runny tomato slice. She sighed and sank it like a basketball into the garbage can. She wasn't hungry anyway. Waiting for Miss Gill to come in had her stomach in knots.

She absently picked at something crusty on the table's surface, making another attempt to rationalize her exuberance as admiration. After all, Miss Gill was thirty-one, never married, and a self-assured career girl, the kind of woman Beatrice had long aspired to be, not the apron-wearing, slotted-spoon-wielding homemaker all the girls in school seemed bent on becoming.

Finally, Miss Gill arrived in a huff. "Damn it. Now I barely have enough time to eat. I swear that Draper does this to me on purpose. 'And another thing, Miss Gill…'" After she mocked her, she looked directly at Beatrice. "What the hell is wrong with an Emily Dickinson display anyway?"

"Nothing," Beatrice replied timidly. She loved it when Miss Gill had her eyeglasses pushed up into her hair, little black strands poking out this way and that.

"Here," Miss Gill said, sending her Scooter Pie skittering across the table. "I won't have time to eat this."

Beatrice offered an innocent smile. "Want me to help fix the display after?"

"You're such a sweet kid," Miss Gill said with a wink.

Beatrice adored any kind of personal acknowledgement from Miss Gill except when she referred to her as a kid. She absolutely was not a kid. She was a young woman, almost eighteen, and practically a college girl.

Later, as Beatrice stood holding Nathaniel Hawthorne novels and story collections, Miss Gill repositioned the hardcovers around the small square table with each one she added. She stepped back and eyed the display. She then scooped up the books and shoved them at Beatrice.

"Draper may not want a Nineteenth-Century Great American Poets display, but she's getting a Great American Something display."

Beatrice smiled at her defiance.

"What are you grinning at, you little monkey?" Miss Gill said.

For some reason, Beatrice suddenly felt emboldened. "I'm wondering how long you're going to make me hold these books. Hawthorne's been dead a long time. He doesn't care how they're positioned."

"Well, aren't you fresh?" Miss Gill eyed her flirtatiously. "Good. I'm starting to rub off on you."

Beatrice grinned and launched *The House of Seven Gables* at her. "Here you go."

"I asked you to hold it," Miss Gill replied, launching it back.

They began to struggle playfully with the book, shoving it at each other, forcing the other one to hold on to it. During one of the frenzied exchanges, Beatrice's hand grazed the side of Miss Gill's breast, stirring an arousal in her much like what she'd been experiencing since reading *Odd Girl Out,* swapping images of Miss Gill and herself in the steamy scenes. Before Beatrice could process her feelings, Miss Gill one-upped her by tickling her in the stomach and on her sides. The pages of the novel flapped liked wings as it fell to the floor, and Beatrice backed away as the sensation surging through her grew more intense.

"Oh, I'm sorry, Bea," Miss Gill said as she bent to pick it up. "Did I pinch you or something?"

"Uh, no, no," Beatrice stammered. "Your uh, your hands are cold."

Miss Gill chuckled. "My hands aren't cold. In fact, they're too damn warm—feel." She pressed both palms against Beatrice's cheeks.

Beatrice's heart fluttered wildly as the ecstasy of the moment gave way to an awkward self-awareness.

"Miss Gill," Mrs. Draper barked from the end of the stacks, scaring her hands off Beatrice's face. "If you can spare Beatrice for a moment, her mother would like a word with her on the telephone."

"Of course, Mrs. Draper," Miss Gill said with an obedient smile. "You take all the time you need, Bea."

Beatrice shuffled to the phone at the front desk, trying to make sense of what had just happened, to rationalize why her body was now responding in such a shameful way whenever she was close to Miss Gill. They were friends, yet Beatrice was having more and more difficulty controlling her thoughts. How would Miss Gill feel if she ever knew? Repulsed? Definitely repulsed. She shuddered as she picked up the telephone receiver.

"Hello?"

"Bea, darling, I'm out of my pills. Would you stop by DeLuca's on your way home and pick up my new prescription?"

"I don't have any money on me, Mother."

"Have him put it on my account."

Beatrice huffed. She resented being her mother's pharmaceutical mule, especially when Mr. DeLuca gave her the hairy eyeball over their past-due account. "Can't Quentin stop and get them on his way home?"

"It's right on your way home, dear. I'd appreciate it if you didn't turn into Sarah Bernhardt over every little thing I ask you to do."

"All right, Mother. Good-bye." She replaced the receiver and was startled by Mrs. Draper, lingering behind the desk with a glare that could have surely penetrated Beatrice's skull and into her private thoughts. Beatrice offered her a solemn nod and decided to make herself scarce for the rest of the day, if only to allow her feet to return to earth.

CHAPTER TWO

After work, Beatrice enjoyed a leisurely walk to DeLuca's drugstore before heading home. An early evening breeze had kicked up along Chapel Street, and the coolness of the wind against her damp face and throat refreshed her. As she passed an elm tree, she plucked a lush leaf from a low branch and began tearing it into slices at the veins. Her mind wandered to the library and Miss Gill. She glanced down at her knuckles and ran her fingers over them as though she might be able to feel Miss Gill's breast again.

She entered the drugstore, and as she was approaching the counter, inspiration struck. She took a detour to the back of the store and the display of romance novels, eager to see what else she'd discover in the mix, fully prepared for the moral consequence of another pilfering job. She slowed when she noticed Mr. DeLuca waving his hand around in the florid face of the suit-and-tied pulp-fiction vendor. She moved closer to them and pretended to compare different brands of bubble bath.

"I don't care what your excuse is," Mr. DeLuca said. "You better check what you're stuffing my display racks with, or I'm gonna offer my business elsewhere."

"Jeez, I'm awful sorry, Mr. DeLuca," the young man said, scratching his buzzed hair. "I just figured they was all them romance novels, you know, the kind like all the housewives read?"

"Well, this isn't romance, Mr. Wentworth," Mr. DeLuca said, raising a book to the young man's nose. "This is filth, deviant filth, and I will not have it in my store. *Women Without Men*." He scoffed. "Families and kids and little old ladies shop here, for Pete's sake."

"I understand, sir, and I can assure you it will never happen again."

Beatrice exhaled as she tossed a package of bath soap between her hands. *Deviant.* The word hung in the air like a pungent odor as she absorbed its full meaning. She recalled hearing it used before and not in a very pleasant context. It was probably best she didn't grab another book anyway. What if this time she'd been caught stealing? What if she'd been discovered with it at home?

While Mr. DeLuca was still berating the book vendor, Beatrice hurried over to Sally at the cash register about her mother's Valium prescription. Sally, with her soft, wrinkly face that smelled of dusting powder, was too nice to care if her mother's account was past due.

Beatrice's pace walking home was slower than her stroll to the drugstore from work. For some reason, she didn't want to go home yet. Mr. DeLuca's disgust over the type of literature she found intriguing stuck in her throat. The feeling suddenly reminded her of the jeering faces of the girls from her senior-year gym class. She swallowed a lump as she recalled the incident in the girls' locker room in April that capped off an anxious year of whispers and innuendo.

Shelly Pinkerton sauntered over to the corner where Beatrice was tying her red PF-Flyers and planted her hip into the locker.

"Say, Bea, none of us gals can figure out why you won't go to the senior dance with Frank DeFelice when he's so dreamy."

Beatrice had been preparing for the ambush since she'd observed Shelly and Margaret Lowell hovering by the showers as she dressed.

"He's a nice fellow, just not my type," she replied coolly.

"Then who are you going with?" Shelly asked.

Beatrice shrugged.

"Didn't you say the same thing about Charlie Cole and Tom Gaffney?" A small flock of girls gathered as Margaret questioned her.

"What's the matter, Bea? Are you too good for the fellas at Cross?" Shelly's question was more of a statement.

Beatrice kept her head low, taking extra time to double knot her laces. She recalled the one family trip they'd taken years earlier to

Ocean Beach in New London. As they swam in the open waters of the Atlantic, she'd asked her father about sharks.

"Don't worry about them, Bea," he'd said. "As long as they don't smell blood, they'll leave you alone."

But at that moment, the sharks were drawn to the aroma of something.

"Maybe she's a cold fish," Margaret said, and the collective laughter was piercing in the acoustics of locker-room tile and steel.

"Are you a cold fish?" Jackie Milner asked, emerging from the mob to poke Beatrice in the arm. "Yep, cold and fishy." She screeched with laughter.

Several other girls joined in the poking. Beatrice stood up, but as hard as she tried, she couldn't keep her boiling blood from spreading into rosy blotches across her face and neck.

"Leave me alone," she shouted, but no one was listening.

Margaret taunted her. "Maybe our boys here aren't classy enough for a snob like Beatrice."

"No, they're not tall enough. A giraffe like Bea probably gets a crick in her neck looking down all the time," Shelly said, and the pack roared with laughter.

An anonymous voice assailed her from the crowd. "Maybe she doesn't like boys."

Beatrice's heart pounded even harder. "Of course I do."

"Maybe she's afraid because she's never been kissed," Shelly added.

Laughter erupted again, and then came the familiar chorus of chants.

"Beatrice, Beatrice, the only girl at Cross who's never been kissed."

On and on went the song with the exuberance of a spiritual at a revival meeting.

"Shut up," Beatrice yelled. "Just shut up, all of you." She shoved past them and ran out into the hall, resolved not to give them the satisfaction of tears.

The mob continued shouting their mantra until she could detect only a faint rumble of laughter still emanating from the locker room.

She shook the horrid image from her mind as she climbed the four flights of stairs to her family's apartment.

"Hello, dear," her mother said, pulling the drugstore bag from her hand. "Please wash up and set the table for dinner right now. Your brother will be home from work any minute."

❖

Beatrice absently arranged forks and knives beside the daisy-print stoneware, lost in another daydream about Miss Gill.

"Honestly, Bea," her mother said with a scowl. "I wish you'd wear something besides those pedal pushers and oxfords once in a while."

Beatrice glanced down at her outfit. "But they're comfy."

"How do you expect to land a decent fellow looking so dowdy all the time?"

"I'm going off to college in a few weeks, Mother, not a wedding chapel." She continued circling their steel-trimmed Formica table.

"You have several lovely dresses that I scrimped and saved to buy you hanging there in your closet. Aren't you ever going to wear them?"

Another shrug as she folded three paper napkins into triangles.

"Don't you want to look like a girl?" Her mother banged a metal soup spoon against the pot.

"I do look like a girl, just not one of those girls who look like they jumped out of a vat of cotton candy, all pink cheeks and fluffy hair." She shuddered. "Aren't I supposed to be taking care of dinner?"

"You're not paying attention, and I don't want this meat overcooked. I paid enough for it."

"I'm not paying attention because you're grilling me about boys."

"Don't take that tone with me, Beatrice," her mother said, undeterred. "Boys like femininity. That might explain why you've never had a date."

"I've had dates." She rolled her eyes behind her mother. Who cared about dates, anyway? She'd much rather spend time with Miss Gill.

"I blame your father for this, may he rest in peace." Her mother propped her hands on her hips, her fingers sinking into her doughy flesh. "He never treated you like a little girl."

Beatrice smiled to herself, remembering with delight the summertime ball tosses with her father before dinner.

"Throw me a pop-up, Daddy," ten-year-old Beatrice shouted.

Always happy to comply, her father hurled the ball into the sky, and after adjusting Quentin's over-sized cap and glove, she leapt through the air and aced the catch.

"Good girl, Bea." Her father cheered for her. "You could give Mickey Mantle a run for his money."

"You mean I could play for the Yankees someday, Daddy?" A smile spread across her dirt-streaked face.

"Sure, why not? You'd be the prettiest center fielder in baseball."

And then the call that always ended the game. "Beatrice, come in here and set the table."

"Go ahead, Sugar," her father said. "The Yanks won't mind waiting."

Relishing the memory of her father, Beatrice stood grinning, blocking her mother's path to the icebox.

"What's so amusing, young lady?" she asked, folding her arms across her apron.

Beatrice retracted her smile. "Nothing."

"Beatrice, dear, you must understand what's at stake." Her mother softened her approach. "If you don't meet a husband at college, you might end up marrying some shelf-stocker with an eighth-grade education. Then you'll really be stuck."

Beatrice looked at her mother's grave face and suddenly felt sad. I love the shelf-stocker you married, she wanted to say, but thought better of it.

"You're right, Mother. Maybe we can go shopping for a new dress that's more today's style." Her mother would never go for buying a new dress before the last stitch fell out of the old ones.

Mrs. Darby smiled with satisfaction, a move that used to infuriate Beatrice. But after years of hard-fought, seldom-won battles over why she should be more like other girls, Beatrice had recently discovered the neutralizing power of the words, "You're right, Mother."

"Hiya, Mom. Hey, booger," Quentin said as he bounded into the kitchen and plopped down at the table. "How's tricks in the exciting world of library books?" he drawled as he tore into a slice of Italian bread.

"What do you care?" She was weary of her brother's usual sardonic remarks.

Her mother whirled around wielding the pot of potatoes and cabbage. "What a thing to say. You're lucky to have a big brother who cares enough to ask. It's admirable how he's always looking out for you."

Where the hell had she been? Quentin's favorite pastime had always been trying to get a rise out of her in some form or another, and she was making him out to be Brother of the Year.

As their mother piled potatoes onto Quentin's plate, he studied Beatrice.

Her shoulders stiffened. "What are you staring at?"

He narrowed his eyes. "You know Bob Criscuolo at the bike shop?"

"No," she replied, swirling mushy cabbage leaves around her plate.

"Sure you do. I introduced you to him at the Savin Rock Festival last month."

Beatrice rolled her eyes. "What about him?"

"For some reason, he thinks you're pretty. Wanna double this Saturday night?"

"I'm busy," she snapped, filling her mouth with cabbage, hoping to end the conversation there.

"Busy doing what? Reading *Wuthering Heights* for the eighth time?"

"Bea, I think that's a terrific idea," her mother said, smiling as she chewed.

"I don't. He has hairy knuckles."

Quentin and her mother exchanged puzzled looks.

"That's the silliest thing I've ever heard," her mother said.

"No, it's not, Mother. I have to think of my future children. I don't want to give birth to little Neanderthals. Kids can be quite cruel when they discover you have an obvious difference."

"Oh, honey, someday you'll be grateful for your height. You're statuesque."

Quentin snorted into his glass of milk. "Come on, Bea. We'll get some burgers and catch a movie. I'll even tell Bob to shave his monkey hands for the occasion."

Beatrice squirmed in her seat. She hadn't stopped thinking about Miss Gill all day. She simply had no interest in spending an evening with Bob Something-or-other, but she was running out of excuses.

"Tell Bob she'd be delighted to join him Saturday night," her mother said to Quentin as she tapped Beatrice's hand and smiled.

Outnumbered, Beatrice pushed her plate away. Maybe Bob would be the boy who made her feel the same way as Miss Gill. She emptied her plate in the garbage and placed it in the sink.

"Sure, Quent. We'll have a swell time." She walked out of the kitchen.

❖

"Bea, you hardly touched your cheeseburger. Is it okay? I can order ya something else if it's lousy." Bob Criscuolo had the longest eyelashes on a guy that Beatrice had ever seen. They waved at her nervously from the driver's seat of his car.

"No thanks, Bob. It's fine. I guess I'm a little full from lunch still."

She gazed out the window at the girls skating around the parking lot balancing trays full of burgers, fries, soda pop, and frothy milkshakes. She couldn't wait to get to the drive-in to relieve the pressure of having to make polite conversation and seem interested in Bob's job in shipping and receiving at the bike shop. It was so strange. She could listen to Miss Gill talk for hours about things as meaningless as why ketchup is better than mustard on hotdogs, yet the longer the conversation with Bob lingered, the heavier her eyelids became.

"Don't worry about her, Bob," Quentin said from the backseat. "Just get her a box of Jujubes at the drive-in, and she'll be fine."

"Gee, I feel kinda bad. Maybe she don't feel good. You want me to take you home, Bea?" He self-consciously scratched his knuckles when he noticed Beatrice staring at them.

"Of course she doesn't," Quentin said. "Bea, tell the poor guy you're fine."

Why did this fellow have to be so nice? If he were a jerk, she could take the opportunity he was offering without remorse. But as it was…

"It's okay, Bob. I'll pep up once I get a box of Jujubes," she said, plastering a silly smile on her face.

Later, when Bob pulled the car in front of the apartment building, Beatrice's arm muscles ached from keeping them folded so tight across her chest all night. The sound of Quentin's lips smacking Dottie the Doormat Rubino's in the backseat unsettled her, as did Bob, drumming his furry fingers on the steering wheel. Holding Bob's hand during *An Affair to Remember* was okay, a little sweaty but nothing she couldn't handle, but she began to shake as she anticipated him getting the same idea as Quentin.

The situation called for swift action. "Well, thanks a lot, Bob." She swung open the passenger door and offered a handshake. "It was a hoot," she added before sprinting to the front stoop. She gently twisted the doorknob so as not to wake her mother from her Friday-night coma in front of the Philco.

Once in her room, she flopped down on her bed like a flounder on a fishing boat. Hugging her pillow beneath her, she cried into it. Was Miss Gill on a date somewhere with some creepy man pawing her in his backseat? If only they could double date. Then maybe she'd feel better about the whole thing. She continued sobbing, no longer aware of what had initially upset her. When she was finally cried out, she flipped the pillow over to the dry side and fell asleep in her clothes.

CHAPTER THREE

The next day at work Miss Gill slipped out on lunch break for a smoke, and, naturally, Beatrice tagged along. They leaned against the brick wall behind the library—Miss Gill puffing a long brown cigarette, Beatrice biting large chunks out of a crisp McIntosh apple. She watched Miss Gill's mouth make an O as it pushed out little ringlets of smoke that collapsed and evaporated in the August air.

"I tell ya, Bea, that Draper made up that cockamamie *no smoking* rule on purpose, just to honk me off," Miss Gill said as she snapped her chewing gum. "Early stages of emphysema, my eye. She has it in for me, that's all."

"She's just a nasty old woman in uncomfortable shoes. She's not that nice to me either."

"That's because you're always hanging around me. She's been scrutinizing my every move since she saw us laughing near the card catalogue last month."

Suddenly self-conscious that others were aware she was "always around" Miss Gill, she feigned nonchalance. "Why should that make her sore?"

Miss Gill looked at her a moment, and then dragged on her cigarette. "Kid, if there's a God in heaven, you won't have to find out."

"I'm not a kid," Beatrice said, slightly insulted.

Miss Gill smiled. "I'm sorry. I guess you're not. Eighteen soon, right?"

Beatrice smiled proudly and nodded. "Did you have a fight with Draper or something?"

"Yeah, you might say we had a fight. Suffice it to say, we both knew enough to stay out of each other's way—that is until you and I became pals."

"We're pals?" Beatrice asked, tossing her apple core toward a foraging squirrel.

"Sure we are." Miss Gill absently crushed out the filter with the toe of her ankle-high lace-up boots. "I gotta get out of here. This rinky-dink town's too small for me."

"But New Haven isn't a small town."

"It is for people like me."

"You mean because you're so sophisticated?"

Miss Gill smirked as she lit another cigarette. "Sophisticated? I never heard it put that way before, but sure. Why not?"

Beatrice smiled, unsure of the meaning in Miss Gill's tone but unwilling to reveal her naïveté.

Miss Gill eyed her intently for a moment. "So, Bea, how come you don't have a steady?"

Beatrice stopped peeling the waxed paper from her bologna sandwich and looked up. "I don't know," she replied, the suddenness of the question unnerving her.

"I don't either. You're such a pretty girl," Miss Gill said, and exhaled a stream of smoke.

She chewed a bite of the sandwich slowly, twitching as sweat broke out on her. "I don't think I'm that pretty."

"Oh, don't be absurd. Of course you are. You're very pretty. You have the nicest almond-shaped eyes. So blue."

"Thanks. I'm just very studious, I guess. I don't have time for that mushy gushy stuff other girls go in for. I never understood it. Seems like a waste of time."

"Bea, all girls your age go in for that sort of thing with boys. I mean most girls do, but not all of them."

Beatrice tossed the crust of her sandwich on the lawn. "What about the ones who don't? Something's wrong with them."

"What do you mean by wrong?"

"Well, maybe not wrong, but you know, unusual. They become spinsters. I don't want to be a spinster. They're strange and lonely women."

Miss Gill giggled. "What makes you think you're destined to be a spinster?"

Beatrice glanced from side to side to make sure they were still alone. "I don't know. I feel strange sometimes." She glanced at Miss Gill, bracing for a reaction.

"What do you mean by strange, hon?"

She peeked over both of her shoulders again and then whispered, "Because I've never really liked a boy."

Miss Gill smiled warmly. "Oh, that's nothing to feel strange about. You're probably just a late bloomer. You'll find a boy when you go off to college."

Beatrice whispered, "I don't think so."

"Well, sure you will," Miss Gill said with a chuckle.

Beatrice leaned against the wall and folded her arms across her chest, observing an ant lumbering along beneath a dead bug three times its size.

"Is something wrong, Bea? Something you want to talk about?"

"No," Beatrice said softly.

"Are you sure? 'Cause I'm a pretty good listener."

After a long pause, she finally said, "I have peculiar thoughts sometimes."

Miss Gill glanced around and lowered her voice. "What exactly do you mean by peculiar?"

Beatrice bit her lip, the answer lodged in her throat.

Miss Gill gave her a moment, then asked out the side of her mouth, "Do you think about girls, Bea? You can tell me if you do."

Although the grave look on her face frightened Beatrice, she nodded anyway.

Miss Gill's lips parted and closed several times before any words made it out. "This may sound, crazy, but having thoughts about girls really isn't so strange—at least not to some people."

"But that's queer."

Miss Gill groaned. "Yeah, to most people. Look, I know it feels like it sometimes, well, probably most times, but you're not alone."

"How do you know?"

"I just do. Trust me."

"But it's abnormal for girls to think about other girls—right?"

Miss Gill shrugged. "Depends on who you ask."

"I'm asking you."

Miss Gill took a long drag off her cigarette and gazed into the distance before responding.

"I say, if it's what you feel in your heart, then how could it be abnormal?" She gave Beatrice a comforting pat on the arm.

Something stirred in Beatrice, the familiar ache she'd felt only when reading that drugstore novel or imagining herself intimately with Miss Gill. But this time the object of her fascination wasn't tucked safely away in her mind—she was standing right in front of her, and before Beatrice realized what she was doing, her lips were touching Miss Gill's.

"Bea, honey, take it easy," Miss Gill said, gently pushing her away.

"I'm sorry," Beatrice stammered. "I'm so sorry, Miss Gill. I don't know why I did that. I'm so—"

"It's okay, Bea, it's okay." Miss Gill was flushed, her eyes darting around the parking lot behind them. "But you can't do things like that in public. You'll find yourself in big trouble if you do. And don't forget—I'm thirteen years older than you. I'll lose my job or even worse."

Beatrice's shoulders stooped.

"Listen, hon, don't take it so hard. When you get a little older you'll find there are places for gals like us. You'll see. And you won't have to feel like you need to look over your shoulder constantly either."

"What kind of places? Where?"

"There's a joint over on York Street that opens for us every Monday night."

"Right here in New Haven?"

"Beneath D'Addorio's restaurant."

Beatrice gasped. "Can I go with you this Monday?"

"I'm sorry, honey, but it's not a place for kids. Uh, I mean it's for people over eighteen."

Beatrice wasn't thinking about when she turned eighteen. All she could think about was the sweet sensation of Miss Gill's lips on hers and her hunger to feel it again.

"We better get back to work," Miss Gill said. "And keep your lips to yourself before you get us both canned." She gave her a playful wink.

They rounded the corner to the time clock in the break room. Noticing that Miss Gill stopped smiling as they passed Mrs. Draper, Beatrice took her cue and lowered her head in a posture suitable for church services, funerals, and tax audits. They both gave Mrs. Draper a reverent nod and then rushed to the clock where they stumbled over each other, giggling conspiratorially.

Mrs. Draper appeared around the corner, her square heels clicking on the tile floor. "You're four minutes late punching in, Miss Gill," she said, sounding like a crow. "And now Beatrice is, too, thanks to you."

"I'm sorry, Mrs. Draper," Miss Gill said solemnly. "Beatrice had a girl problem she wanted some advice about. It won't happen again."

Beatrice was surprised at the way Miss Gill shrank into herself, almost bowing in obedience to Mrs. Draper.

"I hope not. I don't think there's room in your personnel file for any more demerits." Mrs. Draper spun around on one heel and marched out.

"I'm sorry I got you in trouble with her," Beatrice said.

"Forget it. Getting out of bed in the morning gets me in hot water with that battle-ax. Look, do me a favor, huh? Help Mrs. Dugan in the children's section the rest of the day, okay?"

"Sure." Beatrice took the sword to her heart like a Spartan. The last thing she wanted to do was get Miss Gill fired.

After work, Beatrice retreated to the sanctuary of her bedroom. She dug out her flowery lavender diary stashed behind novels by Edith Wharton and the Brontë sisters, intending to channel her nervous, ecstatic energy into words. Dear Diary, she wrote, I am in love with Miss Gill…

It was exhilarating to actually express her feelings, to allow her desires to occupy a space outside her imagination. But after she saw the words in her neat cursive handwriting, her pencil refused to continue. There it was, in Dixon-Ticonderoga gray. She was in love with another girl.

She gazed out her bedroom window at a couple of sparrows flitting around in the courtyard dirt. As the little birds flapped their wings and nudged each other like they were in love, she imagined they were both females. If they were, who would object?

Quentin's sharp rap on her door jolted her from her speculation. She flipped the diary closed and stuffed it under her pillow.

"Come in," she mumbled.

"Bob said you didn't return his call. What's wrong? Didn't you like him?"

Beatrice scrambled for words, surprised by the inquiry. "Oh, sure, I liked him fine."

"Then why not go to dinner with him, just the two of you?"

"Quent, I'm leaving for college soon. I wouldn't want the poor guy to fall head over heels in love with me, and then I'll have to leave him." Confident in her quick response, she grinned.

He rolled his eyes. "I wouldn't worry about that."

"Gee, thanks," she fired back. "If I'm such a dog, why would you want to fix me up with your friend in the first place?"

"He's not that good a friend."

"Can you please leave my room? It's starting to smell funny in here."

"You've got a whole month of summer left. Can't you just go out with the guy? He's a poor, lonely schlub who, for some crazy reason, thinks you're a real beauty." He mimed a vomit face.

"I wouldn't trust his taste if he's friends with you."

"So can I tell him you'll go to dinner with him?"

Quentin's serious tone unnerved her. She thought for sure she'd evaded the topic. "I don't think so."

"You're passing up a free dinner with a nice guy. Sometimes I wonder about you, Bea."

Beatrice could feel the blood draining from her face. "What the hell is that supposed to mean?"

"Nothing," he said, flinging his hands up in surrender. "I figured since you're always moping around here, alone every weekend, you'd like to get out of the apartment and go on a date once in a while."

"I don't need you playing matchmaker for me, Quent. It's humiliating."

"Humiliating? You really are nuttier than squirrel turd."

"What's the big deal? I just don't want to go out with him again."

"Why not? Did he make a move on you or something?"

"No," Beatrice shouted, her cool finally slipping through her hot fingers. "If you must know, I didn't feel any magic with him, okay? A girl needs to feel that magic."

"All right, fine," he snapped. "Suit yourself. But I don't know what you're waiting for."

"I'll know when I find it."

After Quentin left, Beatrice crumpled onto her pillow, relieved to have survived the inquisition. But she couldn't help contemplating whether she should go out with Bob again as a cover. What if there was something about him she'd missed? She desperately wanted to believe in the possibility, until thoughts of Miss Gill snuck into what was becoming their permanent place in her mind.

Beatrice hadn't had a good weekend. The oppressive humidity made her lethargic, especially after doing the extra housework her mother couldn't do thanks to another nervous spell. She even declined a Saturday-afternoon trip to Savin Rock for ice cream with Robert Carlin and his girlfriend, Maria, who was always shooting her the stink eye whenever Robert's back was turned.

Monday at work was even worse. Miss Gill had called in sick, leaving Beatrice to suffer the day in sheer boredom completing tasks that required little or no thought. She was amazed at how exciting her library job had seemed until she had to work a day there without Miss Gill. By afternoon, her angst had given way to full-blown shame and guilt. What if Miss Gill had quit because of the kiss? What if Mrs. Draper had seen them and fired her?

During dinner, as she pushed her macaroni and beans around in her bowl, she made a brave decision.

"Beatrice, your brother is talking to you."

"What?"

"I said what did you do this weekend?" Quentin asked.

"Not much and you know that, Quent. You live here."

He shook his head in mock disappointment. "Another lonely summer weekend when you could've been out with Bob."

Beatrice ignored him and brooded into her supper dish.

"Oh, Quentin, leave your sister alone. If she doesn't like him, she doesn't like him."

Beatrice glanced up at her mother, surprised by the unusual show of solidarity.

Her mother clutched her hand. "She's no fool. She's got her heart set on a college boy, don't you, darling?"

Beatrice smirked at her brother. "Yeah, one not on the six-year plan."

Quentin flung a heel of Italian bread at her.

"Now that's enough, both of you," their mother said. "Bea, you know your brother has to work to put himself through school. Not everyone is lucky enough to get a full scholarship."

"Luck had nothing to do with my scholarship," Beatrice said, taking her dish to the sink. "I earned it."

"Oh, of course you did, dear," her mother replied absently. "Quentin got a raise. Did you know that? Five cents an hour."

"Well, bully for him. Let me know when you're both done, and I'll come back to do the dishes."

Beatrice shuffled down the hall to her bedroom, disappointment weighing her feet down like an anchor. If her father were still alive, he wouldn't have let the conversation jump to Quentin's pay raise so quickly. In fact, he'd still be bragging to his buddies at the bar about his daughter earning the scholarship for near-perfect honors and two essay-writing awards.

❖

By eight p.m., Beatrice had nearly worn a path in the throw rug in her bedroom working up the nerve to sneak out of the apartment and down to D'Addorio's restaurant. Quentin was at the bowling alley for the night with his summer league, and her mother would fall sound asleep on the couch before long. Still, scaling down the fire escape with the hopes of sneaking into a secret nightclub was a risky proposition for anyone, let alone the good little Catholic, Beatrice Darby.

As she pedaled Quentin's bicycle up Chapel Street heading to D'Addorio's, her mind raced with unsettling thoughts. What if someone witnessed her going in? What would she find once inside? Was Sister Madeline, her old catechism teacher, right? Was God really always watching? Suddenly, her mother's judgmental sneer flashed like the headlights of the DeSoto that nearly ran her into a sewer grate. What would her mother do if she found out where she was heading? She couldn't bear to think about it. After all, a family's dignity means everything.

"Did you hear me, Bea?" her mother's voice shrilled in her head. "A family's dignity means everything," she'd said as she tamed Beatrice's uncooperative hair with spit fingers and a fine-tooth comb last June.

Beatrice recalled wriggling in her dress on their building's stoop. "I don't understand why we have to go to Cousin Gretchen's wedding if we can't afford it."

"Oh, we can afford it," her mother replied. She then raked the comb through her own graying hair. "We'll eat beans every night for a year if we have to, but I'm not going to be shamed by having to decline the invitation. Shame is a terrible thing to bring to your family, Bea. I hope you never forget that." Her eyes flared with intensity. "And in a few years, you're going to marry a wealthy college boy, and it's going to be the biggest affair this family's ever seen. That'll show your snobby Darby aunts what's what."

Beatrice forced her mother's image from her head as she pedaled around the corner onto York Street, skidding worn rubber tires to a stop at the restaurant's basement entrance. She propped the bike against the wall and froze in a moment of panicked indecision. She had to make a move—whatever awaited her in the club couldn't possibly be any worse than what was in store if she was spotted outside. She bounded down the steps, feeling to make sure her chestnut locks were still neatly hanging over her shoulders. As she pushed open the heavy metal door, the throb of Elvis's "Heartbreak Hotel" thundered out in a wave of smoky heat.

"You lost, kid?" A woman's voice snarled, but the face from which it emanated looked like Beatrice's Uncle Eddie after a long shift at New Haven Clock Company.

"I'm meeting a friend," she said, shrunken by the bouncer's imposing figure.

The woman bore down on her with a look of suspicion. "Yeah? Who?"

"Miss Gi…I mean, Abby Gill."

The bouncer scrutinized her from head to toe. "How old are you?"

"Eighteen," Beatrice lied.

She slowly extended her arm and allowed Beatrice passage. More the size of a few storerooms crammed together than a nightclub, Pixie's, as it was known, was intimate, to say the least. Beatrice trudged through the sweaty crowd, bumping shoulders in the fog of cigarette smoke, swallowing from the sour odor of spilt beer on the sticky cement floor. Her heart pounded through her cousin's hand-me-down angora sweater as she observed the variety of female revelers talking, dancing, laughing—even kissing.

She stopped cold in the middle of the gyrating masses at the vision of Miss Gill blowing smoke ringlets at the corner of the bar, laughing with her friends. She started when a lanky woman draped in black, her hair pulled severely back, crashed into her as she forged her way through the congested dance floor.

"Hello, baby girl," the woman said.

Beatrice backed away from the woman's tart alcohol breath.

"Where ya running off to so soon, baby?" The woman held out her hand to Beatrice for a dance.

"No, no, I'm sorry," Beatrice said. "I'm here to see my—"

"Sorry. She's with us," Miss Gill said, and pulled Beatrice to safety.

"That's a real shame," the woman said with a lustful grin.

"Bea, what are you doing here?" Miss Gill asked as she led her by the arm toward the spot she occupied at the bar with her friends. "You gotta be eighteen to get in here, hon."

"I am. Well, I will be in two months."

Miss Gill chewed her lip as she scanned the club. "Bartender, how about a special brew for my friend here?"

The bartender slid an icy bottle of Coca-Cola down the bar into Beatrice's hand and regarded Miss Gill with a sharp head tilt toward the door.

She nodded knowingly and then addressed Beatrice. "Did you sneak out of your house to come here?"

Beatrice nodded and grinned.

"Well, here's to the rebel without a cause," said Miss Gill's friend, Donna, a Montgomery Clift look-alike with a pack of cigarettes rolled in her T-shirt sleeve and a pompadour slicked high with hair grease. "Drink up, kid," she said, surveying Beatrice from head to toe. "It'll take the edge off."

As Beatrice guzzled the cola, she saw Miss Gill glare at Donna. The bubbles tickled her nose, and she stifled a giant belch, praying Miss Gill didn't notice. Her eyes felt as big as bicycle wheels as she marveled at her surroundings. A movie poster of Kim Novak in *Picnic*, larger than anything she'd drooled over in *Modern Screen*, hung invitingly over the jukebox, and she tried not to gape at the dazzling spectacle of women in such intimate situations.

"I never imagined places like this existed," she said.

"It's not exactly like they can advertise," Miss Gill's friend Peggy said, adjusting her pointy cat-eye glasses that were sliding down her pointy nose. "And it's really bad for business when kids sneak in."

Miss Gill placed a protective hand on Beatrice's shoulder. "Don't worry, Peg. She's gonna leave right after she finishes her Coke. Right, Bea?"

Beatrice promised with a solemn nod.

"She's right, kid," Donna added. "You want to get this placed closed down?"

"Take it easy, Donna, and don't call her that," Miss Gill said softly. "I said she's only staying for this one drink."

"Make sure when you go, you're not seen coming out of here," Peggy said. "Nobody wants to end up like your gym teacher."

"Miss Helmond?" Beatrice asked. "What about her? She moved to Albuquerque to take care of her mother."

The trio of ladies chuckled, although none of them seemed amused.

"Yeah, sure," said Donna. "She moved to Albuquerque all right, after the principal hauled her into his office and threatened to publicly disgrace her and strip her of her pension if she didn't."

Beatrice crinkled her eyebrows as she tried to process the information. "Why? For being in here?"

"All you have to do is know the wrong cop, and pretty soon the whole world knows your business," Peggy said.

"Everyone loves the taste of a juicy rumor," Miss Gill said, "but take a look around, Bea. We're not the freaks of nature they say we are."

"My mother says homosexuality is a mental illness," Beatrice said. "That people shouldn't hate queers. They should feel sorry for them."

The ladies exchanged smirks.

Donna hiked up her jeans. "I think I speak for these three queers when I say even though it isn't easy living this lifestyle, I'd rather be who I am than marry some poor, unsuspecting bastard and make us both miserable."

Peggy and Donna clinked their drink glasses against Miss Gill's.

"Speaking of juicy rumors," Peggy said, "shouldn't we get this one out of here before someone blabs?"

Miss Gill nodded gravely and looked toward Donna and Beatrice.

Beatrice watched their eyes, desperate to stay in their company longer. "So is this the only place people like us can go to socialize?"

"People like us." Donna snorted. "You mean dykes? Lesbians? If you're gonna be one, you ought to at least be able to say the word."

Donna's laugh made Beatrice feel silly. Worse than that, the few times Beatrice had heard those words, they'd been spewed with mocking hatred.

"Pipe down, Don. She's an ingénue," Peggy drawled, patting the back of her head to verify her bun wasn't unraveling.

"This is our only place for now," Miss Gill said. "Until some group of uptight grannies or suits or bible thumpers nag the City Council to shut us down." She cupped her hand around the corner of her mouth. "We're lucky the mob runs D'Addorio's. They don't care what your lifestyle is as long as they get their cut of the booze profits."

Intrigued, Beatrice leaned closer. "But don't you get scared someone's going to hurt you, or start a scandal about you?" she asked, wearing her naïveté like a gaudy brooch.

"It's like this," Peggy began. "Ever read *Passing*, by Nella Larsen?" Beatrice shook her head.

"Well, you ought to." Peggy jiggled the ice in her screwdriver. "See, Clare Kendry is this mulatto woman who realizes she can escape poverty and discrimination by acting like she's white. A 'beat 'em at their own game' kind of thing. It's the same deal with us. As long as they don't know you're a lesbian, they can't hurt you or scandalize you. You just pass for straight. Make believe you're interested in boys but never let one catch you."

Beatrice frowned. "That seems like a lot of work."

"So is having to find a new job or apartment every time someone gets wind of your secret lifestyle."

"Betty Helmond found that out the hard way, poor toad." Miss Gill bowed her head as if observing a moment of silence for a fallen sister.

Beatrice grew pensive over this "passing" business. But it sure beat the alternative. "I've gotta go the ladies' room," she said as she drank the last sip of her cola.

Under the flickering light, she stared at her distorted image in the filmy mirror. How strange that she felt so safe within the walls of this strange new world, like none of the ugliness of the real world could touch her. She smoothed down her fuzzy sweater and ran a wet finger across her front teeth before walking out into the dark hallway, where she bumped into Miss Gill coming in.

"Oh, Bea," she said, obviously a bit tipsy from a collection of 7 and 7s. "It's getting late. You better vamoose now. I'll walk you out."

Smitten by Miss Gill's eyes, the color of maple leaves dying in autumn, glowing under the fire-exit sign, Beatrice kissed her familiar, succulent lips. This time Miss Gill didn't recoil. She kissed her back—gently at first, then with passion.

Peggy's and Donna's chorus of "Oooohs" from behind them jolted Miss Gill into backing off.

"Bea, you shouldn't do that," Miss Gill said, lacking all conviction. Her eyes sparkled as she licked the moisture from her lips.

"You only said I shouldn't do it at work," Beatrice said, almost in a childlike whine.

"Abby, you dirty devil," Donna said, elbowing her arm.

"It was only a peck, and frankly, you caught me by surprise," Miss Gill said.

Beatrice's eyes watered. "You think I'm some dumb kid, don't you?"

"No, Bea, of course I don't."

"Or that I'm ugly."

"No, no, honey. I mean, look at you. Gorgeous hair, contagious smile. You're a lovely girl, but you're still a girl."

Beatrice clenched her jaw in indignation. "I'm not a girl. I'm turning eighteen in October."

"She's turning eighteen, Abby. Knock her socks off," Donna said with a mischievous grin.

"She's jail bait," muttered Peggy.

Miss Gill took Beatrice's hand in hers. "Listen, doll, I'm thirty-one years old, and I'm sure not looking for any trouble."

Donna glanced down the deserted hall and egged her on. "Come on, Abby, who's gonna tell?"

Beatrice glanced between the women, settling her gaze on Miss Gill, willing her not to let go of her hand.

Donna shoved Miss Gill into Beatrice, and they kissed again. Beatrice's knees buckled from the sensation of her secret crush's hands sliding around her waist and sprawling across her fuzzy back.

Peggy admonished her, tugging at her arm. "Abby."

Miss Gill finally pushed Beatrice away. "Bea, we can't do this. You shouldn't even be in here. You're a minor." She avoided Beatrice's eyes as she scratched at her forehead.

Beatrice's heart plunged into her shoes. The last few days were the brightest she'd ever experienced in all of her high-school years. No, even long before that.

"Why are you doing this to me?"

"You're too young," Miss Gill said, seeming frustrated.

Beatrice glared at her and then shoved her way toward the exit. She hiked up the stairs into the thick night air, her eyes blurry with tears. She searched frantically for Quentin's bike, but apparently someone had helped themselves to it earlier in the evening.

Miss Gill huffed up the stairs after her. "Bea, I'm sorry."

"Leave me alone," she sobbed through hiccups.

"I didn't mean to mislead you." She touched a hand to Beatrice's cheek. "I'm very attracted to you, but I shouldn't be," she added through mournful eyes. "It just isn't right."

Beatrice flung Miss Gill's hand away and dashed off down the street.

"At least let me give you a ride," Miss Gill called out. "It's so late."

Beatrice ignored her and continued down the sidewalk, grumbling and kicking a crushed beer can out of her path.

A squad car rolled up, and the officer followed Beatrice for a moment.

"You're Charlie Darby's girl, aren't you?" he asked, sounding certain of the answer.

She nodded through her tears and kept walking.

"Why don't you get in the car, darlin'? You're too young to be out gallivanting alone in this city at this ungodly hour."

Beatrice exhaled, exhausted from the evening's denouement. She got in the car, tucked her chin to her chest, and swore that if one more person told her she was too young for anything, she'd clobber them.

"Now what kind of business does a teenage girl got at D'Addorio's?" the officer asked in his kindliest father-figure voice.

"It's a restaurant," she said softly, at the moment too heart-broken to realize the potential crisis.

"On Mondays it's a closed restaurant."

"I must've got my restaurants mixed up," she said, still sniffling.

The officer looked ahead as he drove, his fat, freckly hands gripping the wheel.

"Just so you know, they got nothing but riff-raff that hangs out there. You ought to steer clear of them places, an impressionable youngster like yourself. Next thing you know, they'll have you..." He tapped his fingertips on the steering wheel as he drove. "Don't know how they ever got a liquor license, to tell ya the truth, but I know darn well the community ain't too pleased having that kind of establishment around here. Them doors should be padlocked and all them loons sent straight to the asylum."

His sentiments seeped into her skin like poison. She wanted so badly to speak up and tell him he was wrong, but what could she say? Scream at the top of her lungs that the women in Pixie's weren't the deviants everyone thought they were? Who'd listen to her anyway? Besides, it was clear the die had been cast in this man's mind long ago.

"My point is you're a good girl, Bea. You don't want to be associatin' with the people in that kind of place."

As the officer rattled on for the rest of the ride home, Beatrice humored him with a few "yes sirs" until he stopped his cruiser at the curb in front of her apartment building.

"Are you going to tell my mother?"

"I'll make a deal with you in memory of my old friend Charlie," he said. "I don't catch you coming out of that joint anymore and your ma never has to be the wiser."

She smiled politely over the urge to tell the ignorant bastard to go to hell.

❖

Shortly after one a.m., Beatrice climbed the fire escape with the stealth of a cat burglar and straddled the sill of her bedroom window. She thought she'd made it, too, except for the blinding flashlight shining in her face. She shrieked like she'd witnessed the dead rising.

"Where ya been, Bea?" Quentin asked. The light of the full moon cast an ominous glow across his face. He stood in his baggy pajamas, waiting for an answer, his blond hair poking up on one side like a rooster's comb.

"What are you doing in here?" she asked as she stuffed herself through the window and tumbled to the floor.

"I asked you first."

She got to her feet and smoothed down the front of her clothes. "None of your beeswax."

"It is my beeswax when my little sister is out carousing with the lunatic fringe."

Though alarmed by the accusation, she played it cool. "What are you talking about?"

"You know what I'm talking about. The basement under D'Addorio's?"

She gulped air and tried not to look guilty as she kicked off her shoes. "What about it?"

"Okay, if that's how you want to play it. I noticed you borrowed my bike, too. You put it back?"

After a moment of his glare bearing down on her, she caved. "Someone stole it."

He shook his head. "You take my bike to some seedy dive you shouldn't be anywhere near and then get it stolen. That's rich, Bea."

He shone the flashlight directly into her eyes.

She walked past him toward her bookshelf. "You don't care about that stupid old bike, and you know it."

"Maybe so, but I do care about you disgracing our family name."

She ignored him as she began clawing at the books for her diary.

"Not even going to deny it?"

"Where is it, Quentin? Where the fuck is my diary?" Her heart pounded against her chest as she scanned the entire shelf.

"What language. Did you learn that from your librarian friend, too?"

"Quent, I'm not messing around with you. It's my property."

"You'll get it back. But I must say it was quite an interesting read. It's no wonder you wouldn't want it to slip into the wrong hands."

She stiffened as the gravity of the situation fully dawned on her. He'd read her diary. How was she going to explain its contents?

"You dirty louse," she said as indignation took over. "You have nothing better to do than rummage through my stuff?"

"Hey, it's not my fault. All I did was borrow the dictionary, and the thing practically fell into my hands. You should've done a better job hiding it, especially since it's nothing but smut."

"How dare you? That's an invasion of my privacy."

"The way I see it, it's my duty to protect this family and you, since you obviously don't know how to use the common sense God gave you."

"You're not my father, and I don't have to listen to you. Now get out of my room."

"I wouldn't be so smart with me if I were you. How do you think Mother would react to what you've been up to this summer at the library with Miss Gill?"

Beatrice licked her dry lips. "Quentin, you better not say anything to Mom. You don't even know what you read. It's just a silly little collection of miscellaneous ideas. You'll upset her over nothing. You know what a neurotic she is."

"What do you mean? That stuff you wrote isn't true?"

She said no out of desperation, but inside she ached at having to deny her feelings. Would it be so bad if she told her family the truth, let them know who she really was?

"It better not be," Quentin said as if on cue. "Because that's some sick shit you wrote, and if you think Mom's neurotic now, just let her take a gander at that."

"Okay, okay. Now give me my diary."

"What about that librarian? Is she really that way? I'm sure her boss would like to know about her friendships with teenagers."

"No, no, no, she's not like that." Beatrice stammered, trying to control her growing agitation. "Look, it was just some junk I was doodling for a story idea. That's all."

He eyed her with skepticism. "I always knew you were an oddball, but that story's awfully odd, even for you. I hope you're going to use a pen name if that's the kind of crap you plan to write."

"You just don't understand the avant-garde."

"The avant what?"

"Precisely."

"Then what were you doing sneaking out to that gin mill tonight?"

"Research." She grasped for a believable lie. "For my story."

"Listen to me, Bea." His tone was dead serious. "I'm telling you this for your own good. If anything's going on with you and that depraved cradle robber, you better end it."

"I told you there's nothing. Now quit badgering me."

"Don't you set foot in that joint again either. I mean, God, you know Mother hasn't been able to handle things since Daddy died. Do you really want to send her completely over the edge?"

"No, of course not."

"All right then. Now don't let me find out you did anything like this again, or I'll tell Mom."

"I said all right, Quent. You want me to swear it in blood?"

He pulled her diary from the waistband of his pajamas and held it out to her.

"Eww, disgusting." She grabbed it from his hand and slowly closed her bedroom door until she squeezed him out.

Clutching her diary across her chest, she collapsed onto her bed and stared at the ceiling, letting the tears streak down her temples.

❖

After another sleepless night of thinking and imagining, shuddering in the ecstasy of her desire for Miss Gill, and then writhing from the shame, Beatrice greeted the next morning with renewed hope. She was leaving for college in less than two weeks, leaving behind the reproving eyes of her nosy brother, mother, and old Officer Fatso to start life on her own as a grownup. Surely the real reason Miss Gill said she couldn't be with her was because she was afraid of losing her job. But Beatrice had a plan.

As the late-August sun rose into a golden hue, she strolled to the library, kicking pebbles and stepping over chewed stogies abandoned in the street by old Italians at the bocce court. She quickened her pace at the thought of Miss Gill and their future.

She approached the library's entrance just in time to meet Miss Gill walking out, carrying a small box of personal items.

"Miss Gill, what are you doing?"

"What's it look like I'm doing? I'm leaving. By the way, in light of recent circumstances, you can call me Abby."

Her demeanor rattled Beatrice. Abby was usually so unflappable, so carefree. Now her chiseled features were distorted with angst.

"Why?" Beatrice asked.

"Why don't you go ask that old biddy? I got the sack, Bea. Some hooey about insubordination."

"How could she do that? It's not even true."

"Oh, that was only an excuse," Abby said. She folded her arms. "But of course that isn't the real reason. She's always had her suspicions about me, but I'm betting some son of a bitch fink saw or heard something and went blabbing to Draper. I got her number. She's always had it in for me, but since you started, she's had a bug up her can."

"Me?" Beatrice blinked away Quentin's threat.

"It bugged her that we were always together, whispering or laughing, the jealous goat. Back in June, she accused me of being flirtatious with you. I had a good mind to tell her to blow it out her tailpipe, but did I? No, like an obedient little pissant, I just said, 'Why Mrs. Draper, I didn't mean anything improper. Guess I'm just too friendly. But I'll be sure to mind my Ps and Qs from now on.' Then I made up some bullshit about a date I had the night before with a handsome druggist. That shut her pie hole."

Beatrice grinned, remembering why she loved Abby. "Come with me to Newport," she said, her mood lightened with possibility.

"What?" Abby asked through a chuckle, her crinkled forehead relaxing.

"Come to Newport with me when I leave next week," Beatrice pleaded. "They have lots of places that would hire you. You could work in their library, or even give tours of the mansions. We could get an apartment together after I finish freshman year. Please, Abby." Beatrice gently touched Abby's hand as it supported the cardboard box. "Please."

Abby's eyes watered. "Oh, Bea, aren't you just the sweetest thing. But you know we can't."

"Why not?"

"Well, come on, let's be reasonable. I'm thirty-one, and you're not even eighteen yet."

"But I will be soon. I love you, Abby, and you wouldn't have kissed me if you didn't have feelings for me."

"Sure, I feel something for you, honey, but this is the wrong time and the wrong place, and it's time for me to get the hell out of Dodge."

"What do you mean? Where are you going?"

"Peggy and I have had it, that's what. We've been talking about moving down to the Village with Donna, and that's what we're going to do. It's the only place we can be free. You just worry about doing well in school, okay?"

"But it isn't fair," Beatrice said, her voice cracking.

"I know it isn't, but I'll find a job in the City. I'm not sweating it. Good luck, honey. It's been a kick knowing you."

Abby went in for a quick hug and started off, the heels of her flats clicking as she walked down the rest of the concrete steps.

"That's not what I meant," Beatrice said, wiping away tears.

Abby whirled around and approached her with a warm smile. "I'm sorry, Bea. You're going to fall in love some day with someone your own age. Just give it some time."

As Beatrice watched Abby's shape get smaller down the street, her breaths grew shorter until she collapsed on the step and sobbed into her knees.

❖

Beatrice had wandered through her workday in a fog, unable to eat or focus on anything except disappearing into one musty corner of the library or another whenever her emotions threatened to overwhelm her. When five o'clock finally arrived, she punched out and jogged all the way home, huffing and puffing in the humid city air. How foolish she'd been for laying her soul bare to Miss Gill and thinking they could ever be more than friends. Even worse than that, were dingy basement bars, leering eyes, secrets, and lies all that lay ahead for her? Could being in love with a girl be anything more than heart wrenching? She thought about her father and how much she missed him, how he had been the only person on earth who always made her feel she was perfect just the way she was. Maybe if she could meet a boy who would treat her as nicely as he had, the idea of marriage wouldn't seem so unappealing after all.

She stopped running when she reached her bedroom, which now seemed as oppressive as the air outside. Panting and beaded with sweat, she drew open her closet door, sat at the foot of the bed, and stared in earnest at the clutter of hanging dresses and frilly blouses her mother had bought her. She pulled her diary from under her mattress and began tearing it up, page by page, until her thoughts and dreams were a pile of confetti.

CHAPTER FOUR

A breeze off the Atlantic snuck onto Salve Regina's campus, tempering the Indian-summer sun that stung Beatrice's forearms as she read Emerson's "Self-Reliance" essay. After only six weeks of college life, she'd settled into a comfortable routine. She was making her own decisions, keeping up with her studies, and delighted to trade two irritating family members for one gum-smacking roommate. Sailing along on the ebb and flow of this new life, she found even the anguish associated with Abby Gill's memory had begun to wane. With no hope of running into Abby or temptation to contact her, Beatrice could focus on excelling as an undergrad.

On this particular afternoon, she focused on stemming the flow of chocolate ice cream dripping from her cone down her fingers as she studied on a bench. Every now and then she eyed the familiar blonde coed contending with math problems, a human outgrowth of the Quad's lush lawn. Lying on her belly, the girl nibbled her pencil's eraser as her feet dangled in the air.

"Hiya, Gwen," said a handsome letterman as he passed her. He was about the fourth one of his kind, and by then, Beatrice had grown tired of counting them.

As her attention drifted to Gwen's rear end curving up like a firm nectarine, Beatrice licked the remaining blob of ice cream so hard it toppled from the cone into the crevice of her literature book.

"Damn it," she muttered. With no napkin, she used her thumb to clean the mess, but the more she wiped the ice cream, the longer and wider the smear grew. She casually glanced up and noticed the blonde approaching.

"Hanky?" Gwen offered, poised like a Roman goddess from Beatrice's Art History textbook.

"Oh, thank you," Beatrice said as her grimace melted into a smile. She took the hanky from Gwen's fingers, lingering on her eyes, as round and brown as Milk Duds. "I'm such a clod."

"Don't be silly. You should've seen me eating my tuna sandwich earlier. I think you're in my Art History class. I'm Gwen Ridgeway." She extended her hand.

Beatrice recognized Gwen as the girl from across the lecture hall she'd been sneaking peeks at since the first week of classes. She gushed as she shook Gwen's hand with her sticky one. "Nice to meet you. And I'm sure you look lovely eating a Sloppy Joe."

"Eating who?"

Beatrice giggled in embarrassment. "It's not a who; it's a what. Ground beef in spicy tomato sauce on a bun?"

Gwen still looked puzzled.

"Never mind. I guess I'm just a hopeless case."

"Are you kidding? Why, with that bone structure and your height, you could be a fashion model."

Beatrice looked down at her white sneakers, her cheeks stinging with self-consciousness. "Oh, I don't think so. I'm just plain old Beatrice."

Gwen studied her for a moment. "Well, plain old Beatrice, I'm convinced there's a beautiful girl being held hostage behind that headband and those…" Gwen eyed her outfit disapprovingly. "So anyway, how about we free her sometime? I loved playing dress-up as a kid. Guess I haven't outgrown it yet."

"Sure." Beatrice flashed a toothy grin.

"Say, have you started the ancient-Greece project yet?" Gwen said, sitting down next to her on the bench.

Beatrice squinted in the high afternoon sun. "Oh, yes. I got a jump on it as soon as I heard the assignment."

"You don't say. What are you doing it on?"

"Women's impact on ancient architecture."

"Really? Wow, that's amazing. I didn't know women were allowed to do anything back then besides serve men."

"Well, it didn't happen too often, and it isn't easy to find documentation. That's why I'm still not finished. I'm almost sorry I picked that subject."

"Oh, don't be sorry. That's a great idea."

Beatrice smiled. Gwen's dark, dreamy eyes, creamy complexion, and rosy cheeks reminded her of an undisturbed gallon of Neapolitan ice cream.

"I'm planning to spend the entire day at the library this Saturday," Gwen said. "Maybe we can meet up and do our research together and then get a bite for lunch."

Beatrice chose to dismiss the flutter in her stomach as the excitement of having made a new friend. Although her studies had been keeping her busy, she couldn't help feeling wistful whenever she heard the other girls in her dormitory clamor down the halls giggling about the silliest things. She could hardly deny that even the most independent woman would enjoy someone to share meals with occasionally in the cafeteria. She was sort of friendly with her roommate, Ruth, the gum-smacker, but when Beatrice realized she was a nympho, she determined they weren't likely to become bosom buddies.

"Sure, that would be great." The stained literature book collapsed through Beatrice's knees into the grass between her feet.

Gwen flashed an angelic smile. "Okay, then, Beatrice Darby. See you Saturday morning."

Beatrice watched Gwen's swan-like form until it disappeared around a corner. She suddenly longed to tell Abby about her new friend, to talk to her about what she was feeling, to see her face. How could she have walked away without so much as a forwarding address? With a long sigh, she closed her book, stood, and inhaled a breath of light ocean air. She'd deal with Emerson later.

In the reference room surrounded by encyclopedias, Beatrice sat at a table fidgeting as she scribbled facts on a notepad, her mind more engrossed in the stream of people entering the room. She tapped her pencil's eraser against the pad with the rapid flutter of a drum roll until the boy a few seats away gave her an irritated glance. Staring at the meaningless arrangement of letters on the page, she drifted off into a reverie of her lunch with Gwen later that day. Would they dine in the campus café or hopefully walk to a nearby luncheonette crowded with people who would see her with her new, beautiful friend? When her elbow slipped off the edge of the encyclopedia and landed hard on the desk, she winced and tried to refocus on her research.

"Hey there, Darby," Gwen said in a loud whisper. "I'm sorry I'm late. I must've rolled over after I hit the alarm. What a goof."

"Oh, that's all right. I'd lost all track of time anyway," she lied, slapping the shiny encyclopedia page for emphasis.

Gwen skidded into the chair next to Beatrice, her large open purse spewing its contents on the table. Lipstick tubes, chewed pencils, loose change, and elastics for her honey-blond hair landed on Beatrice's notepad.

"Oh, sorry about that." Gwen cupped her delicate hands to scoop up her things.

"That's okay. Here you go." As she handed Gwen some nickels and dimes, her whole arm tingled when Gwen swept the change from her hand.

"Let me go get my books, and then I'll tell you what I'm up to next weekend." Gwen got up and disappeared into the World History section.

Beatrice shivered at the suggestion. Next weekend? What did Gwen mean by that? She probably just wanted to tell Beatrice about the social escapades she had planned—a date or maybe a party at a sorority house. She couldn't possibly intend to include Beatrice. Could she?

After a few minutes, Gwen returned to the table buried behind a pile of books.

"I envy you for having the gumption to get yourself started early on these kinds of things." She let the books cascade through her arms onto the table. "Now I've really got to scramble."

Beatrice smiled to herself. Gwen envied her? All her life she'd dreamed of having what Gwen had—that easy, effervescent personality everyone loved to be around. Instead, she was aloof, bedeviled by a persistent need to keep up her guard.

"I can help you if you need me to," Beatrice said. "I'm pretty good at writing."

"You're a peach. I might have to take you up on that."

The warmth and sincerity in Gwen's smile radiated through Beatrice. Before long, they settled into a focused research session, with pencil lead etching words and scribbles on page after page of legal pads. Beatrice made herself ever more helpful to Gwen as she struggled for the appropriate words and phrases for her term paper.

Beatrice found herself staring at Gwen during moments of thought, careful to hide her glances before being caught—most of the time.

"Do I have something on my face?" Gwen finally asked.

"Uh, no, no," Beatrice stammered. "I was just, uh, trying to figure out what famous actress you look like."

"Jayne Mansfield," Gwen said without hesitation. "I've gotten that before. Must be the blonde hair and brown eyes 'cause it's certainly not the boobs."

She smiled at her joke, but Beatrice was too preoccupied fighting the urge to survey her boobs to appreciate it.

"Maybe the lips, too," Beatrice added, fascinated by the lusciousness of Gwen's plump bottom lip.

"Screen-siren lips? That's a new one," Gwen said with a smile, "but I'll take it."

"You must have a lot of boyfriends," Beatrice said, dreamily.

"No more than the average girl. You must have a bunch, too."

"Nah." Beatrice gazed fiercely into her book, fearing she was on the verge of revealing too much.

"Come on, you don't date at all?"

"No, I do. I mean I did. I had lots of boyfriends in high school, but of course, I couldn't take them with me." She forced a grin, hating that she was such a convincing liar.

"Fret not, my friend. Mixer season is upon us," Gwen said, pointing an index finger in the air. "We'll have to start ourselves a new collection."

"Super," Beatrice drawled.

❖

It was nearly four p.m. by the time they remembered they'd made plans to have lunch together. They settled for the relaxing atmosphere of an off-campus luncheonette that catered strictly to a college clientele.

"Boy, I realize how much of a math person I am every time I try to write one of those papers," Gwen said, stretching her arms across the Formica restaurant table. "Please, let me buy your sandwich as a thank you." She aimed her straw at Beatrice's chest like a blowgun and, in one hard puff, launched the wrapper at her.

Beatrice clutched the paper spear and rolled it into a little ball, too distracted by the implication of Gwen's offer to appreciate her playful gesture. "Oh, no, Gwen. That's really not necessary. I didn't mind at all."

"I know you didn't mind. It's a little thing I'd like to do."

Beatrice worried that Gwen somehow knew that the only way she was at Salve was thanks to her scholarship. "I mean if you think I can't afford to pay—"

"What? No, please don't view it that way."

Beatrice looked away, embarrassed by her defensiveness. "I can afford it, you know," she said softly.

"Sure you can. I just want to thank you," Gwen said, seeming confused. "Bea, have I offended you?"

Maybe she didn't know after all.

"No, no, I just, I'm just not used to people offering to buy me lunch."

Gwen smiled in relief. "Oh, well, if that's all, then you put that change purse away. Your money's no good here."

"If you insist," Beatrice said, smiling and relaxing into the red vinyl booth.

After a moment of awkward silence, Gwen asked, "So, what type of boy do you go for?"

"Uh, I don't really have a type. Cute and nice, I guess."

"Everyone has a type. Do you like the James Dean type or the Troy Donahue type? Roughneck or clean-cut?"

Beatrice's palms started sweating from Gwen's persistence on a subject in which she had no interest. "Right now, I'd rather focus on my schoolwork."

"Well, sure, but you don't want to spend every Saturday night doing homework, do you?"

"No," she replied sheepishly. "Is that why you mentioned next weekend earlier?"

"Boys? Oh, no. I'm rushing Delta Lambda next Saturday night. Thought it'd be a hoot." She shrugged with what seemed moderate interest. "Say, since I know you won't be busy, how about rushing with me? I'm a legacy so I'm all but guaranteed. I can put in a good word for you."

Beatrice squirmed. Her shyness made it so difficult for her in large groups. And a large group of girls she'd never met? She shuddered as she flashed to the horror show her gym class had been earlier that year—all those girls ganging up on her, trying to expose her, laughing while doing so.

"Ah, I don't know, Gwen. I don't think I'm sorority material."

"That's ridiculous," Gwen said. "What is sorority material anyway?"

Beatrice's knees started knocking wildly under the table. "I'm not really that outgoing, and even though I've had plenty of dates, I'm kind of shy around boys."

"Then joining a sorority is the perfect remedy. You'll learn how to be outgoing, and there'll be plenty of boys to help you break out of your shell." Gwen chuckled. "If there's one good thing about sororities, there's never a shortage of boys to choose from. Now what do you say?"

Gwen's dazzling smile was too much for Beatrice. How could she possibly refuse?

The harvest moon shone big and orange as they approached the steps to the Delta Lambda house, a white, two-story clapboard with pink cornice and shutters. Beatrice stopped for the third time to scratch her calves, which had broken out in unbearable hives.

"Are you nervous or something?" Gwen finally asked.

"Aren't you?"

"Nah. What's to be nervous about? My mom pledged in '34, so I'm not sweating it. They'll probably accept me, but if they don't, it's no skin off my apple."

Beatrice ambled over to the steps and sat. "If it's all the same, I'll wait here for you."

"It's not all the same. Now don't be a party pooper. I even did your hair and makeup all nice and snazzy for the occasion."

"I know, Gwen, but I just don't feel like I'll fit in. You go ahead." Beatrice looked away to hide her pooling eyes.

Gwen sat down next to her. "Why don't you at least meet the girls before you abandon the idea?"

Beatrice tapped her shoe on the step.

"Come on, Bea." Gwen nudged her playfully. "You don't want to be unpoopular, do you? You don't want to pop out at parties."

Beatrice tried to resist a grin as she recognized the lines from her favorite *I Love Lucy* episode. "The answer to all your problems is in this bittle lottle."

"Atta girl." Gwen hoisted Beatrice to her feet by her armpit. "Come on. Let's go face the firing squad."

"Couldn't you have phrased that some other way?"

Gwen giggled and threw her arm around Beatrice as they went inside.

Beatrice spent most of the hour-long ceremony cowering on a lopsided tweed sofa in the Delta Lambda sitting room. She'd watched Gwen win acceptance without much ado but grew increasingly uncomfortable as she witnessed each subsequent candidate get grilled. A few pledges fell victim to the randomness of the black ball, while others were summarily rejected for not possessing the right look or pedigree. As the night went on, she realized she would end up being the last to face the panel of girls with folded arms and menacing glares, a small favor for which she was immensely grateful.

When Shirley Dandridge was called forth to face the inquisitionist, she approached and tripped on her own heels, eliciting roaring cackles from the rest of the girls. Her kinky red hair and crooked eyeglasses were equivalent to wearing a giant bull's eye on her chest.

"Miss Dandridge," Claire Billingsley, Delta's president, began. "What prompted you to attempt to join our illustrious sorority?"

Shirley cleared her throat and began speaking slowly and deliberately. "Well, I want to spend my time here at Salve with an organization dedicated to doing good deeds for the community and making a difference in the world."

To everyone's surprise, the panel burst into laughter, evidently a private joke.

"That's very commendable, Miss Dandridge," Claire said, pacing in front of her like Perry Mason. "But first we must ask you a series of questions to ensure your character measures up to the high standards set decades ago by our foremothers. Are you ready?"

Shirley fidgeted in the hard wooden dining-room chair and nodded.

"If you're accepted as a Delta Lambda, would you lay down your own life to save the life of one of your sisters?"

"Of course," Shirley said, sounding considerably less sure than her words proclaimed.

Claire dispatched a look to the other girls on the panel and smirked as one girl elbowed another, who giggled aloud. Beatrice crossed and uncrossed her legs, sensing this wouldn't turn out well for Shirley.

"Do you know who your father is, Shirley?"

Shirley glanced around, seeming confused. "Sure, I do. William Dandridge."

"How can you be sure?" Claire asked.

"Well, 'cause I'm sure," Shirley said, her voice quavering. "My mom always says I have his smile."

Claire stared at her for what seemed like an hour with eyes sparkling full of mock sympathy. "Shirley, we've done some investigating, and I'm sorry to say that we've determined that Mr. William Dandridge is not your real father."

A snicker came from the panel as several of the girls in the room gasped. Even Beatrice was drawn in.

"What are you talking about?" Shirley asked.

"Is it not true that the identity of your real father, given the color of your hair and your speckled complexion, is, in fact—Howdy Doody?"

The room erupted into laughter, all except for Gwen and Beatrice, who watched in suspense and surprise. Shirley sat silently, paralyzed by the mocking laughter.

"Which leads us to believe then that your natural mother can be none other than—Clarabell the Clown."

Laughter erupted again, this time with girls doubling over and falling to the floor. Someone hurled a bucketful of wet, mushy beans into Shirley's lap as another girl approached her and tried to place a red clown's nose on her face. When the inquisition panel began chanting "Howdy Doody, Howdy Doody" in demonic unison, Shirley couldn't take any more and ran, skirt sodden with beans, out of the room and out the door.

Claire signaled with her hands for the girls to calm down. "Unfortunately, ladies, sometimes it isn't pretty weeding out the undesirables, but as you know, this process is a necessary evil. Shirley Dandridge is clearly not of Delta Lambda ilk."

Beatrice whispered in Gwen's ear. "That was awful. I can't do this."

"It'll be okay. They'll go easy on you. They know you're with me."

"Last but not least, Beatrice Darby. Please approach the panel, Miss Darby."

She rose from the couch, mildly reassured by Gwen's words. After flicking a bean off the chair, she sank into the hot seat and looked Claire directly in the eyes with a polite smile. She remembered her father telling her to look people in the eyes whenever they talked to her, man or woman. He said it would make her appear confident even if she wasn't.

Claire stood before Beatrice with a phony smile, scrutinizing her from head to toe. Beatrice didn't know which was worse—being laughed at or being on the receiving end of Claire's silent scorn. She cleared her throat though nothing was obstructing it.

Claire finally broke the awful silence. "I have ESP. Did you know that, Beatrice?"

"You have what?" She glanced over at Gwen.

"Extra…Sensory…Perception," she drawled like Beatrice was half deaf. "I can tell things about people just by looking at them—things they'd never want anyone else to know—their deepest, darkest secrets."

Beatrice's stomach plummeted. What the hell was Claire talking about? ESP wasn't real. Claire's eyes bore into hers without even blinking. Or was it? Could someone actually be capable of detecting the feelings for Gwen she'd been careful to conceal since their friendship began? Did they know what she imagined doing with Gwen, the things that made her feel dirty, images she fought so hard until she couldn't fight them anymore?

"I don't believe in that," she said, her mouth lined with cotton.

"Oh, don't you? You mean to tell this panel, this entire room that you have absolutely nothing to hide? No secret you're guarding from the rest of us?"

Beatrice tucked her trembling hands under her rear end. She suddenly felt trapped, panicked that she was about to be exposed. She glanced at Gwen, who offered her a supportive nod, but what did she know about the desperation of hidden truths?

"I know your secret, Beatrice," Claire said, leaning in close to her ear. "And in a moment so will everyone else."

Beatrice sprang from the chair, about to rush out of the room.

"Bea, don't," Gwen said. "She's bluffing."

Claire swung around to Gwen. "You may be a legacy, Miss Ridgeway, but you're still nothing more than a lowly freshman pledge."

Beatrice sat down and white-knuckled the armrests.

"Now we'll see who's bluffing. Why don't you tell everyone how you're a student here, Miss Darby?"

"How?" Beatrice repeated, momentarily relieved by the question. "I applied and got accepted."

"No, how is your tuition paid?"

"Scholarship," Beatrice replied, confidently.

"Full scholarship?"

Beatrice nodded.

"Well done. And without that scholarship, could your parents afford to keep you here?"

Beatrice swallowed hard and looked around the room. After a moment, she shook her head. A low, collective groan filled the air.

"I'm sorry, I didn't hear you," Claire said, cupping her hand around her ear.

"No," Beatrice whispered.

"We can't hear you, Miss Darby." Claire's voice rocked the room. "Are you too poor to attend this college without your scholarship?"

Beatrice fixed her eyes on Gwen, whose helpless, sympathetic expression humiliated her even more. Gwen Ridgeway came from old Boston money. How could Beatrice face her now that the truth was out and everyone knew?

"Does your family own the house you live in?"

She paused and sucked in a deep breath. "No. It's not a house either. It's an apartment."

Another gasp from the crowd.

"You're not serious," Claire said.

Beatrice nodded as she wiped her damp palms on her pants. "I am serious."

Claire chuckled. "Delta Lambda is the most prestigious sorority at this school, with a long lineage of women of breeding and refinement. You have your nerve coming in here and taking up our valuable time—"

"Claire, I asked her to pledge. She's my friend," Gwen said, standing in protest.

"You're not ashamed to admit that?" Claire asked.

"I'm proud to. Beatrice is a great girl, and this organization would greatly benefit—"

"We've heard enough from you tonight, Miss Ridgeway," Claire said.

"But you're being very narrow-minded," Gwen said.

As Gwen continued to argue her case, Beatrice skulked out the door, thoroughly humiliated. She trotted to the stone wall surrounding the property, choking back her tears, refusing to allow herself to cry over those vicious girls. Why did she need to be part of that business anyway? She'd gotten along fine on her own all her life. Why should now be any different? She thought of Shirley Dandridge and wondered if she was okay.

Lifting herself up on the stone wall, she gazed up at the starry sky. She should have known from the moment she set eyes on Gwen Ridgeway that she could never have had a real friendship with her, a girl of wealth straight from the social register, so pretty and self-assured. What would she ever have to gain from a friendship with a girl like Beatrice?

"Well, that was interesting, wasn't it?"

Gwen's voice floated over her shoulder. She climbed up on the wall and sat next to Beatrice.

"What are you doing out here?"

"Joining the rest of the castoffs."

"What do you mean? They accepted you."

"I thought that was a good thing until I saw what they did to that poor Shirley, and then you. I'm glad you got out of there before they could take it further."

"I'm sorry I let you down."

"You didn't let me down. Oh, Bea, I'm the one who should be sorry."

"For what?"

"For dragging you into that hornets' nest. Who needs them?"

"What did you do, tell them you changed your mind?"

"No, actually, I never got the chance. When I called Claire a Nazi sympathizer with a fat ass, she revoked my acceptance."

Beatrice laughed. "I hope I didn't ruin everything for you."

"Aw, you didn't ruin anything. Truth is I know these kinds of girls. They're insufferable—pretentious and catty. Just because they're from privileged families and in private schools, they think the world owes them something. They call themselves a sisterhood, yet they wouldn't hesitate to climb over one another to get somewhere, especially with guys. I can't stand it."

Beatrice nodded. "My mother expects me to jump right into the fray. She doesn't get the part about breeding. She thinks it'll be so easy for some rich boy to fall in love with me and want to marry me."

"I meant what I said in there. You're a great girl. If some boy lets you go simply because you don't come from a family with a name, it'll be his loss." Gwen gazed up at the stars. "You're the genuine article, Bea. I'm glad we met."

Beatrice smiled shyly, bumping the heels of her shoes against the stone wall. "Me too."

"My mother's going to go ape when she finds out about this," Gwen said, shaking her head.

"It looks like we're both going to need a huge supply of bananas," Beatrice said, sober as a priest.

Gwen erupted into giggles as they started walking away. "Let's hit the soda fountain. Sundaes are on me."

"Make it banana splits," Beatrice said with a grin.

By the end of freshman year, Beatrice found herself increasingly burdened by her attachment to Gwen, an emotional bond amplified by the fact that Gwen stirred in her all the same shameful physical feelings she thought she'd left behind with Abby Gill. As friends, they were inseparable—evenings studying at the coffee shop, a malted at the drugstore on East Bowery, tandem beauty regimens. Whatever the activity, Gwen and Beatrice gravitated toward it together.

The most unpleasant part for Beatrice was bearing witness when Gwen would go all to mush over a boy she met at some social event arranged by the college and then having to pretend that she felt the same way about the occasional fix-up by Gwen. It was becoming exhausting.

"Oh, Bea, he's so wonderful," Gwen would gush, and Beatrice would force a smile and attempt to detour the conversation to something less provocative. Luckily, though, Tom or Reggie or Desmond would fade away with autumn's crimson, winter's icy white, and spring's soggy green. Since, according to Beatrice's mother, women only went to college to meet husbands, Beatrice often stopped by the chapel to send up a quick prayer that Gwen wouldn't fall into the clutches of some fresh-faced fraternity boy who'd sweep her off her feet and far away from her.

Recently, however, Beatrice had stopped by the chapel for a different reason.

"What is your sin, my child?" the priest said through the confessional grate.

Beatrice hated the smell of the confessional, the tight air reeking of old wood and the strong breath of the Father assigned to return each wayward sheep to the flock. This one's musty Halls Mentho-Lyptus breath prompted her to bury her nose in her shirt collar.

"I, uh, I think I'm having impure thoughts."

"You think? Well, what is the nature of these thoughts?"

She tried to identify the Father through the grate but could only make out obscured facial features. "I can't say. They're too impure."

"I'm sure what you have to say is no more shocking than that of anyone else who's dropped by."

"I wouldn't be so sure," she said and squirmed on the hard bench.

"Do you feel that you're inclined to act on them?"

"Oh, I certainly hope not."

"Are these thoughts of a sexual nature—about a young man you're dating?"

Beatrice remained tight-lipped.

"Are they about a man you're not dating? A married man perhaps?"

"No," Beatrice said softly. "I'd never date a married man. They're not about a man at all."

"I'm sorry. Would you repeat that last part?"

Beatrice leaned to the side in an attempt to shield her identity from him. "This is very hard for me to say, Father."

"I imagine it is, but you can tell me. That's why I'm here—so you can unburden yourself."

Unburden herself. She liked the sound of that. She loosened her balled fists. "Okay, here it goes. I'm, um, I'm having impure thoughts about a girl." She felt sour hearing the words in her own voice. What must he be thinking?

"My, well, this is rather serious," the priest said, and then seemed to remember himself. "But it isn't the end of the world. You're not the first young person who's come to me with this dilemma."

Her revelation sparked panic in her as she looked closely into the partition. "Do you see my face? Can I get thrown out of school for this?"

"Relax, child. No one can read your mind. But I must impress upon you the direness if your thoughts turn into action. That would result in immediate expulsion—not to mention what it would do to your soul."

"I don't know what to do, Father. I've tried to stop myself from thinking these thoughts, but I just can't."

"Prayer, child. When we don't have the strength to fight the demons on our own, we must call upon God. Pray for His strength to help you fight those unnatural feelings every time they occur."

"But I have been praying, since last fall. Nothing's changed."

"Clearly, you haven't been praying hard enough. You've got to dedicate yourself morning, noon, and night to eradicating those evil thoughts. If you don't, a lifetime of self-loathing and dissatisfaction awaits you. Not to mention the fate that awaits your soul in the afterlife."

Beatrice sighed, familiar with the fire-and-brimstone bit, having heard it enough from her mother whenever she was spending a lot of time with Robert. Then she could dismiss it because she wasn't doing anything wrong with him. This was different. All these awful words: demons, unnatural, evil.

"What should I do?"

"You're going to start by saying ten Hail Marys as soon as you leave here. Then go right home and read Leviticus Eighteen, so you can see with your own eyes how God feels about that sort of thing. And then, most importantly, we must begin your education in resisting temptation. Start with Hebrews Chapter Two and Four and Matthew Chapter Four. Come back next week, and we'll go on from there."

"Is that going to do it?"

"It's a step in the right direction."

"Okay, Father, thank you."

"Go with God, my child."

Beatrice was about to leave but stopped. "Father?"

"Yes?"

"Why would something so unnatural feel so natural to me in the first place? Why would God do that to me?"

"Oh, this isn't the work of God, my dear," he said gravely.

"If it's not God then—oh, you don't mean…" Beatrice's mouth hung open in disbelief.

"I'm afraid so," he added. "If you allow yourself to believe those kinds of feelings are natural, then your struggle to conquer them and the evil that is trying to overtake you is going to be much greater than you ever anticipated."

"How did I get on his list? I'm not a bad person."

"Lucifer doesn't discriminate. We're all at risk, child. It's what we do with his influence that matters. You can give in to his temptation because it feels good, or you can fight it and win God's glory in the afterlife. The choice is yours."

Beatrice frowned. "Okay, Father, I'll do my best to resist."

"Very good. And remember this, child, 'Resist the devil, and he will flee from you,' James Four, Verse Seven."

"Right, 'James Four, Verse Seven.'"

Just what she needed—having to fight off the devil while trying to maintain a grade point average. She left the confessional feeling worse than when she went in. Although she understood society's view that it was wrong and as convincing as the old priest was, she simply couldn't accept that her feelings for Abby Gill and Gwen were the work of Satan. Still, she would do her reading like a good Catholic, and hopefully, when she completed it, she would have those feelings under control and everything would be all right.

CHAPTER FIVE

Midway through sophomore year, Beatrice had lost her enthusiasm for prayer. It simply hadn't worked. She met with the Father in the confessional several times after her initial soul-purge, but his words and scriptures did little to stop what dwelled in her heart and body. God, it seemed, had forsaken her, so the best she could do was to keep her feelings locked away and hope she'd outgrow them in time.

"Hey, Darby." Gwen knocked on Beatrice's dorm door and barged in at the same time.

Lying on her bed, her long legs crossed at the ankles, Beatrice glanced up from *The Sun Also Rises* at Gwen standing in front of her with an enormous, expectant grin.

"Guess what we're doing tonight."

"Studying and then going for a burger and shake," Beatrice said.

"Bor-ring," Gwen replied. "It's high time we mix up our dull routine, my friend."

Dull? Beatrice loved Saturday nights studying and eating burgers and fries with Gwen. She daydreamed about it all week. "What do you have in mind?" she asked, eyeing Gwen with suspicion.

"We're going on a double date." Gwen bounced around as she replied, landing on the bed next to Beatrice.

"Oh, Christ, a double date? With who?"

"Aaron Douglas and his friend, Phil."

"Should I know these people?"

"Aaron Douglas, the boy I met at the Christmas mixer with Brown. If you'd gone with me like I asked, you would've remembered."

"You know I wasn't feeling well," Beatrice said, trying to ignore the prickly heat on her neck.

"You always seem to come down with something whenever I try to set you up. You must be allergic to boys." Gwen giggled.

"No, I'm not. What a thing to say," Beatrice said.

"I'm joking. Gosh, lighten up."

Beatrice wanted to kick herself for getting so defensive.

"What kind of a best friend are you anyway?" Gwen continued. "I've only been talking about Aaron for weeks."

Beatrice knew very well who Aaron Douglas was—a thorn in her side since the moment Gwen grabbed her by the shoulders in December, proclaiming she had the last dance with the dreamiest man the heavens ever created. She was sick of hearing his name, sick of seeing Gwen's eyes bloom luminous whenever she talked about how brilliant he was and how he'd captivate everyone in his pre-law classes with his brilliant observations.

"Why do I have to go? Can't you go out with him alone?"

"Sure, I can, and I will after tonight, but Phil sounds like a nice fella, so who knows? Maybe we'll both finally have the men of our dreams." She snatched one of Beatrice's hands and examined the chipped fingernail polish.

Beatrice's eyelids grew heavy, savoring the touch of Gwen's delicate fingers.

"Look at these nails," Gwen said. "Are you a part-time bricklayer or something?"

Beatrice swatted Gwen's thigh with the pliant novel. "I bite my nails when I get nervous. I can't help it. Maybe you can fix them for me."

Gwen rose from the bed and stretched. "I'm going to have to. I wouldn't be caught dead with you waving those cheese graters around tonight."

Beatrice shuddered. The feel of the emery board scraping across her nails, the pressure of not chipping Gwen's pristine polish work. But if Gwen wanted to dress her in a blouse made of porcupine needles, Beatrice would gladly consent.

"What time should I be ready for this fiasco?" Beatrice asked through a yawn.

"Be at my room at six thirty, sharp. The boys will be here at seven sharp. Oh, I'm so excited, Bea."

Beatrice whirled her finger around with a hyperbolic lack of interest until Gwen landed on the side of her bed, grabbed her around the shoulders, and hugged her tightly. She loved the sweet torture of Gwen's silky cheek and soft breasts crushing against her. That alone was worth the discomfort she would most likely have to endure on their double date.

❖

Hearing about Gwen's dates was one thing, but seeing her with Aaron was another beast entirely. Beatrice remained calm when he placed a territorial hand on Gwen's back as he followed her into the restaurant overlooking Newport harbor. She managed very well through dinner, even though he ordered for Gwen, tied her bib for her, and cracked her lobster for her. Up until this moment, Beatrice had Gwen on a pedestal—the epitome of beauty and grace, never a false move, never a sentence anything less than sheer eloquence, but now, her phony laughter at Aaron's corny jokes grated on her nerves.

For his part, Phil was the perfect date—completely uninterested in her. He nodded politely when Beatrice spoke and even swiped a fork off another table when she dropped hers. So when he knocked his water glass into her lap after a pretty waitress bent over to pick up a napkin in front of him, Beatrice was nothing less than a sport about it.

"Oh gee, I'm sorry, Bea," Phil said, blotting her lap awkwardly with his napkin. "I don't know how that happened."

Beatrice smiled sincerely. "Yes, I wonder. Don't worry about my slacks, Phil. It's only water. I'll pop on over to the ladies' room."

"You're an all-right girl, Bea. Most girls would've clocked me for that."

Beatrice smiled again and patted his shoulder for reassurance before leaving the table. Gwen followed her into the ladies' room, sailing on a breeze.

"What do you think, Darby, huh? Phil's pretty cute. Love his duck's ass." She giggled as she teased the top of her hair with her fingers.

"He's all right." Beatrice refused to make eye contact as she blotted her slacks with a wad of paper towels.

"What do you think of Aaron? He's really something, isn't he? Just like I knew he would be. Such manners and refinement. Oh, Bea," she said, swinging around to face her. "I think he could be the one."

Beatrice grimaced as she studied her complexion in the mirror—her face florid, her forehead wrinkled from the agitation of sitting across from Aaron and watching him do with Gwen everything she wished she could.

"You said that about the last guy you dated."

"Who? Christopher? No, no. He definitely was not the one. Aaron is just a dream."

"A regular Adonis," Beatrice mumbled as she blotted a streak of mascara under her eye.

"Why's your neck all red?" Gwen asked, trying to get a closer look. "Are you allergic to shellfish or something?"

Beatrice cursed her sensitive skin for betraying her jealousy. She shooed Gwen's hand away. "I don't know. Let's go back before they call in a search party."

Gwen nodded, and as they headed to the table Beatrice slowed her pace, annoyed that her mood had grown increasingly solemn as the night progressed, and Gwen hadn't even noticed.

"We took the liberty of ordering a round of cheesecakes while you gals were in the powder room," Aaron said, all smiles.

"Naturally," Beatrice said, and then mumbled, "I hate cheesecake."

Finally, Gwen noticed Beatrice's disposition, acknowledging it with a kick to her shin under the table.

"Was that really necessary?" Beatrice asked quietly, rubbing her leg.

Gwen scolded Beatrice with her eyes. "I'm sorry, pal. I was crossing my legs and misjudged the distance between us."

Beatrice settled down and decided to focus on the cluster of sailboats swaying in the harbor, out of commission for the winter. What she wouldn't give to deposit Aaron on one of them right now, unmoor it, and let it blow away in the February wind. Suddenly, she curled the fingers on her right hand into a fist as Aaron's weaved through the ends of Gwen's champagne hair. By the time their desserts arrived, what little appetite she had left was gone. When Gwen began feeding Aaron some of her cheesecake with her spoon, giggling like Barbie would have if her head wasn't made of plastic, Beatrice imploded with rage.

"Excuse me."

She shoved her way out of the booth and ran to the bathroom. She was rinsing her face with cool water at the sink when Gwen finally came in.

"Are you all right?"

"I'm better now." She blotted the excess water with a paper towel.

"You look terrible, so pale. Did you get sick?"

Beatrice pressed two fingers to her lips. "Just a little nauseated."

"Why didn't you tell me you weren't feeling well? We could've asked the guys to take you home."

Gwen's choice of you instead of us sparked a jealousy Beatrice had had no prior experience with. "Well, I certainly didn't want to ruin your date with your precious Aaron. God knows it's all you seem to care about."

"Bea, that's not true," Gwen said softly. Her wounded eyes fed Beatrice full of satisfaction.

"That's sure what it feels like lately."

"I'm sorry, but I couldn't help being excited. I've liked him for such a long while."

"I know, but you don't have to push your best friend aside." Beatrice was spiraling. She sensed she was bordering on cruelty with Gwen but couldn't stop herself.

"Gee, I guess I didn't realize I was doing that."

"Gee, I guess that's what you do when you like a boy." Beatrice mocked her. "I'm sorry I'm getting in the way." She glided past her in dramatic fashion, hoping Gwen would stop her.

"Beatrice, would you wait a minute." Gwen latched onto her arm. "I said I was sorry. I didn't mean to make you feel bad."

"If you don't have time for me anymore, I wish you'd just come out with it. I'll understand."

Gwen looked genuinely confused. "You're my best friend. If I don't have time for you, then I don't have time for anyone. Look, Aaron's just a guy. He's not worth ruining a friendship over."

"I don't want it ruined either." Beatrice faced the mirror, monitoring Gwen's reaction in her periphery. "On the other hand, I don't want to be a nuisance to you."

Gwen smiled warmly. "A nuisance? That's crazy. I love you, Darby." She threw her arms around Beatrice's shoulders.

Beatrice hugged her tightly, pressing her close. "I love you, too." A tear rolled off her cheek onto Gwen's hair. Usually the first to disengage from hugs in defense of her secret, this time she held onto Gwen for as long as Gwen would allow.

"Cripes, Darby, is it that time of the month or what?" Gwen wiped away Beatrice's tears with her thumbs.

Beatrice chuckled, relieved to have an excuse. "Yes, it must be."

"Are you okay, or do you want the boys to take us home?"

There it was, the us Beatrice wanted to keep forever. Her shoulders relaxed in gratification—she hadn't lost Gwen to Aaron after all.

She smiled. "No, I'm all right now."

❖

As they dropped Beatrice off after the movie, she wasted no time jumping out of the car. Exhausted, she fumbled for the key to get into her dormitory and tiptoed into the darkened room so she wouldn't wake her roommate, Ruth. But when she started to undress in the blackness, she heard strange moans, almost nightmarish whimpers coming from Ruth's bed. She flipped on the light to wake Ruth, only to find her already awake.

"Beatrice, what the hell?" Ruth uttered breathlessly.

She examined the bed and noticed a large lump under the covers midway down Ruth and a pair of hairy calves jutting out at the foot of the bed.

"What on earth," Beatrice said, squinting to decipher what was happening.

"Do you think you could come back in about half an hour?" Ruth asked. "And turn off the light on your way out."

"Yeah, uh, okay," Beatrice said, creeping out of the room.

As she sat on the brick wall surrounding a dead rose garden, watching her breath stream out in the frigid night, she realized Ruth had to go. The gum-smacking and the borrowing of her clothes without permission were bad enough, but thanks to visits from Rudy, the custodian, Beatrice was about ready to build herself an igloo outside their dorm and move in. It was such a clear, beautiful night she decided to take a walk to Gwen's to kill some time until Ruth was done receiving her weekly janitorial service. She trod across campus, crunching the hardened snow beneath her shoes.

Gwen was a captive audience sitting on her bed Indian-style, as Beatrice explained the situation with her roommate.

"I can't stand her anymore, and it's not only 'cause of her visits from the jolly janitor. We're simply not compatible and haven't been from the start."

After a chuckle, Gwen yanked a sticky pair of Twizzlers from the package and nibbled pensively. "So, my roommate is transferring schools at the end of the year and yours is a nymphomaniac. Sounds like the perfect opportunity for us to become roomies. What do you think?"

Beatrice scratched through her ponytail, making sure she heard Gwen right. "Roomies?"

"Sure," Gwen said. "One of us is always over at the other's dorm anyway. Why not? We already know we get along famously—unless you think it's a bad idea. You know, familiarity breeding contempt and all."

"No, no, I think it's a great idea."

"Yeah? Great. I'll contact the Residence Life office tomorrow and see about making arrangements. Say, how about a cup of cocoa to celebrate?"

"Sure."

Beatrice smiled to herself. Living with Gwen—waking to her every morning and seeing her every night before she went to bed—they would become closer than ever. Finally, one of her dreams was coming true.

"Can you toss me my nightie over here?" Gwen asked. "It's behind the door."

Beatrice reached for the flowery flannel nightgown hanging behind the closet door and handed it to Gwen, who was standing stripped to her bra and panties. After taking in an eyeful, Beatrice stared at her shoes, panicked that Gwen had noticed her looking at her body.

"Thanks," Gwen said, raising the nightgown over her head.

Beatrice's heart pounded as she sneaked another quick glance at her slender torso, beautifully elongated as Gwen struggled into the nightgown from the top down. She then cringed as her face flamed with shame.

Still staring at the floor, Beatrice stuttered, "Uh, do you want me to go get the water down the hall?"

"Oh, sure. Stop at Margaret's room on the way back. She has marshmallows."

Beatrice took the teapot and walked toward the door, still unable to face Gwen. Once outside in the hall, she leaned against the wall and closed her eyes. Was she about to make a horrible mistake moving in with Gwen? Suppose Gwen made a habit of changing clothes in front of her? Suppose next time she didn't look away fast enough, and Gwen caught her leering? Or she did more than just steal a glance? Beatrice shuddered.

She was still shaking as she sucked in a deep breath. "Pull yourself together, Darby," she mumbled, and started for the bathroom. "You're an intelligent woman with a strong moral center. Even if Gwen pulls a Gypsy Rose Lee every night, you can certainly control yourself."

After she completed her water-and-marshmallow mission, she returned to Gwen's room only slightly less agitated than when she left.

"Here you go. I think I'm gonna pass on the cocoa. It's getting late."

"Bea, it's almost two in the morning. Sleep here. Melanie won't be here all weekend."

Sudden images of kissing Gwen's shoulders began taunting Beatrice. She ached for Gwen with alarming intensity.

"No, no, I really have to go," she said, backing toward the door.

"Are you still feeling sick?" Gwen asked, following her.

"Well, no, but I just, well, now that you mention it, my stomach does feel a little funny," she said and banged the back of her head on the door.

"You're looking awfully flush," Gwen said, trapping her against the door. "Do you have a fever?" She cupped her hands on Beatrice's cheeks.

"Gwen, don't." Beatrice wrested Gwen's wrists, terrified she was about to do something she'd undoubtedly regret.

"Okay, okay," Gwen said. "Gosh, you're a cranky patient."

Beatrice released Gwen's arms and forced a smile. "Yeah, yeah, I've always been. I'm sorry."

Gwen nodded with understanding. "Go then if you insist, but be careful. It's late. And watch out for creeps."

"Yes, Mother."

"If we're going to be roomies, you'd better get used to that. I can't help mothering people I care about."

Beatrice looked away, afraid her eyes would betray her. She'd heard people say the eyes were the windows to the soul. Did that include the heart, too? If Gwen knew the things Beatrice thought about her, the romantic feelings she harbored, she'd never consent to being her roommate and would undoubtedly end the friendship. But for the moment, the euphoria of it all calmed the tempest of anxiety.

She descended the front steps of Gwen's dorm without her feet ever touching cement. Clouds had rolled in off the Atlantic, covering the moon, and she could taste the smoke of wood-burning stoves as she ran home, a blur of adrenaline streaking across campus. She never slackened her pace, not even for a breath.

CHAPTER SIX

Beatrice had never once wished for a summer to end. Freezing her knees off and sloshing through mounds of snow and slush left much to be desired. But in 1959, as August faded in New Haven, it couldn't have departed fast enough. She and Gwen were going to be roommates for the rest of their time at Salve, which only made the pettiness of living with her mother and Quentin for the last three months all the more insufferable.

"Quentin, I'm sick of telling Theresa you're not home," she yelled from the kitchen. "Why are you torturing that poor fool?" She glanced at her mother for support as she replaced the telephone receiver on the wall.

"I don't blame him one bit for ignoring her," their mother said, wiping her hands on her apron. "What kind of girl calls a young man?"

Quentin sauntered in, took a swig from a glass milk bottle, and placed it on the counter.

Mrs. Darby put it in the refrigerator as though it were her duty. "Quent, drink from a glass, for heaven's sake."

"Yeah, who wants your germs? God knows where those lips have been."

"Beatrice," her mother said. "What an awful thing to say. Is that what you're learning at that fancy college?"

"Jealous?" Quentin said.

"Why don't you be a man and take Theresa's phone calls? Or better yet, stop treating girls like your personal playthings."

"Beatrice, what are you saying?" her mother asked.

"He's a regular lothario, a two-timer."

"I already told Theresa I didn't want to see her anymore," Quentin said casually as he bit at a hangnail on his thumb. "It's not my fault if she's a sucker for punishment. She's looking for a husband, and frankly, I'm not getting hooked up with her wop family."

"I can't believe you're saying that about her. You dated her for months."

"Darling, your brother isn't going to marry just anyone. He can do better than Theresa Santoro."

Beatrice rolled her eyes at them and retreated to her bedroom. She couldn't remember when their family had broken into factions—her mother and Quentin versus her father and her—but it felt like it had been forever. Since her dad had passed away years ago, her family was a lonely place. It didn't matter anymore. In a few more days, she'd be going home to her real family, Gwen.

Beatrice stood at the open door of Gwen's dorm room as Robert placed the last of the cardboard boxes stuffed with Beatrice's clothing and belongings at the foot of her bed. She watched him look around her room as he absently rubbed the muscles in his tanned arms.

"Thanks for giving me a lift and helping with all this, Rob."

"No sweat," Robert said. "I enjoyed the ride. I always enjoy talking with you." He blinked his unassuming eyes at her and blotted the sweat from his forehead with a hanky.

His boyish charm always made Beatrice smile. She'd been friends with him forever, it seemed, and a few times she'd seriously considered dating him, but something in her always hindered her. Maybe now that they were both twenty years old and no longer kids, she could start viewing him as boyfriend material.

"I suppose you want your pizza now," she said with a grin.

"That was the deal." He smiled as he adjusted the belt slipping down his narrow waist.

"Well, I'm no welsher. We'll go to Atlantic Pizza."

She nodded matter-of-factly and licked her fingers to smooth the wisps of hair that had escaped her ponytail.

"Is it any good?"

"We grew up on Pepe's pizza," she said. "Of course it isn't any good. But it's all we got, unless you want cafeteria food."

"Atlantic Pizza it is."

Outside on a picnic table at the pizzeria, Beatrice managed to snatch two slices of pepperoni and onion off the tray before Robert devoured the rest of it, along with three root beers. She watched in awe as his last piece disappeared in two bites.

"I'd love to see how much pizza you can actually eat in one sitting, but I don't have money for another pie."

"'At's okay," he said, stifling an enormous belch. "I'm full anyways." He wiped the corners of his mouth with the frayed napkin he'd used all through the meal. "So, do you have a lot of hoity-toity boyfriends here or what?"

"I was wondering when you'd get around to asking me. Did my mother put you up to that?"

"No, I was just curious. I've kinda had the feeling I'm gonna lose you to some preppie with a lot of daddy-o's dough."

Beatrice chuckled. "Lose me? You never had me to lose."

"Sure, rub salt in my wounds."

She tapped the top of his hand like a grandmother would. "Maria was a fool to let you go, Rob. She'll regret it one day."

He tugged at the napkin until it was little more than a pile of cottony bits. "Will you ever regret saying no to me all the time?" He looked up with eyes full of disappointment.

He was quite appealing at that moment, vulnerable and innocent, imbued with a gentleness she hadn't known to exist in young men. She felt a slight urge to lean across the table and kiss his tanned, fuzzy cheek—just not enough to actually do it. So why not? It took every ounce of self-control she could muster not to give in to her urges around Gwen. And how could she ever forget kissing Abby Gill that summer of '57?

"Rob, we're friends, good friends," she said. "I wouldn't want to mess it all up by dating you. What if it didn't work out?"

She paused, feeling awful about lying to him. Friendship wasn't the issue. If Gwen ever wanted to become romantically involved, she wouldn't hesitate to take the risk.

"What makes you think it wouldn't?" Rob asked, appearing slightly offended.

"Sometimes these things just don't."

"Bea, we were best friends as kids," he said. "But we're adults now. Men and women can't be friends. It doesn't happen like that once you grow up."

She scoffed. "Who says it can't?"

"Come on. Get real. When you get married, how's it gonna look if you're hanging around another man? Same thing goes for me when I get married. Now if we married each other…"

"Oh, Rob, this whole conversation is silly. Let's get going. I have just enough money left for some ice-cream cones."

She was about to rise from the table when he took her wrist and pulled her down on the bench.

"Think about it, Bea. We've always had a swell time together. You've never had a boyfriend, and I can't seem to keep a girlfriend. Why do you suppose that is?"

She gazed at him quizzically. "I'm too busy with my studies, and you're a goof."

He let go of her wrist. "Fine, Beatrice Darby. But just so you know, I won't be waiting around for you forever. One of these days, I'm gonna meet a girl who's gonna jump at the chance to marry a guy like me. Then you'll be sorry."

She swung her leg over the picnic table bench with a smile. "Well, I promise to let you be the first to tell me 'I told you so.' I'll deserve it."

❖

After ice-cream cones and a walk along the windy pier, Robert was finally ready to hit the road home to Connecticut. He walked her up to her dorm and leaned the side of his body against the door expectantly.

She eyed him. "Rob, what are you doing?"

"Look, since that was the one and only date we're ever gonna have, I figured maybe you wouldn't mind kissing me good night."

"If that were a date, you would've bought the pizza and ice cream."

He shook his head playfully. "I may never see you again, Bea, especially if one of these Richie Riches comes along and sweeps you off your feet."

His corny smile was adorable. How could she say no to a little kiss good night?

"Suit yourself," she said, closing her eyes and puckering her lips tightly.

She expected a wet lip smack, quick and sloppy, but before his lips even made contact, the fingers on his left hand laced through hers as he glided the others under her chin and along her jawbone. It was very sweet and, dare she even say, romantic. So why hadn't she felt the way she did when she was with Gwen—the stirring, the yearning, the desire to go beyond what was happening at the moment?

Her head began throbbing as she rehashed that tired idea. Should she give it a go with Robert? Maybe those feelings would come after they were together awhile. It happened in arranged marriages. Those people weren't in love when they married—they fell in love after they'd been together and got used to each other.

"See you 'round, Beatrice," Robert said, wiping the moisture from her bottom lip with his thumb.

"Good-bye, Rob." The words fell from her lips without effort.

She watched him shuffle to the end of the hallway and wave in his sweet, good-natured way before descending the staircase. Maybe she needed to try harder. In truth, she really hadn't made much of an effort not to think about Gwen that way.

She remembered how her dad had helped her get over her stage fright in the fourth grade. She was a finalist in the New Haven County School District spelling bee and was terrified about having to stand up in front of everyone under the glaring stage lights.

"Come on, Bea, you can do this," he'd said as he arranged her stuffed animals like an audience on her bed.

"I can't, Daddy. My knees are shaking so hard," she replied, almost in tears.

"It's okay that you're nervous. Everyone up there will be nervous, but that doesn't mean you can't do it. You're the best speller in New Haven, darling. All you have to do is get up there and do what you do best."

"But everyone's gonna be staring at me, Daddy. I don't want them to."

"Then pretend they're not. Look down at me in the front row, and you won't even notice anyone else." He took hold of her little hand. *"I know you can do it, Bea. You're just about the toughest girl I know."*

Things would be so much easier if her dad were still here. After pausing a moment to gather herself, she pushed open the door to her new dorm room.

"Darby," Gwen shouted, and ambushed her with a hug. "Long time, no see."

Beatrice's arms wound naturally around Gwen's upper torso. "Did you have a nice summer?"

"Oh, sure. Sunning, boating, lobster bakes, the usual." Gwen released Beatrice from her hold. "I do wish you'd come to Newport for a visit when I called in July."

"I couldn't get the time off from work," she said.

"Are you sure you weren't trying to elude meeting my snobby family?" Gwen said with a wink.

Beatrice grinned. "Are you kidding? I love snobs. I was born to be a snob."

Gwen giggled and threw her arms around Beatrice again. "It's so good to see you. I missed you like crazy."

She allowed herself the luxury of melting into Gwen's familiar softness, the flowery smell of her skin.

"I've missed you, too," she whispered, her lips grazing Gwen's ear and cheek as Gwen pulled away.

In all the confusion that was Beatrice Darby's life, at least one thing was clear—this was how she wanted to feel forever.

The November wind blew off the Atlantic so hard outside the dormitory it caused their drapes to waltz against the window. Gwen and Beatrice lay feet to feet on Gwen's bed, huddled under her electric blanket as they prepared their discussion of George Bernard Shaw's *Saint Joan* for Monday's literature class surveying classic tragedies.

"It stinks that the only way to get canonized is to suffer and die a martyr first," Gwen said.

"Were you hoping to be canonized some day?"

Gwen giggled. "Well, I hadn't ruled it out."

Beatrice smiled, burrowed her big toe into Gwen's armpit, and gave it a wiggle.

"Knock it off, stretch." Gwen grabbed Beatrice's toes and bent them.

"Ouch," she shouted, trying to wriggle free. "No fair, let me go."

"Do you promise to keep your big feet to yourself?"

"I promise no such thing," Beatrice said gravely.

Gwen stared her down, unflinching. "Then I'm sorry. I can't let you go."

Beatrice paused for a moment to let the ecstasy of hearing Gwen say 'I can't let you go' wash over her.

"Unhand me," she then demanded.

"Nope."

Beatrice reached under the blanket and tickled the back of Gwen's knees. At that, Gwen leaped up and surprised Beatrice with a flurry of tickling on the sides of her stomach and under her arms. She tried to restrain Gwen's hands but couldn't grab them for their lightning speed. Her only defense was to shove Gwen down on her back and use her own size to subdue her. Once she had Gwen's arms pinned to the pillow, their snorting laughter faded to panting as they wrestled for position. Gwen was flushed, her milk-chocolate eyes gazing up at Beatrice for mercy. Her blond hair fanned across the pillow, framing her face like daisy petals.

Beatrice's pulse pounded in her ears as she slowly descended toward Gwen's mouth. She closed her eyes, licked her lips, and prepared for the exquisite landing.

"You're hurting my wrists," Gwen said casually.

"Oh, oh, I'm sorry." She released her grip and rolled off Gwen. The sides of their bodies wedged against each other. Too ashamed to face her, she lay frozen, staring at the ceiling, waiting for Gwen to bolt from the bed to the other side of the room—then demand to know what the hell she was doing.

Gwen folded her arms across her chest and got quiet for a moment. "Bea, I want to talk to you about something."

Beatrice clutched at the bedspread as her throat closed in a panic. Here it comes. How was she going to explain to Gwen what she just did or had almost done?

"Did you hear me?" Gwen kicked her in the leg with her ankle.

"What?"

"I have to ask you something."

"I don't know what you're talking about."

Gwen looked at her quizzically. "I haven't asked you anything yet."

Beatrice sprang up and swallowed the bile that had risen in her throat. "What?" she asked, avoiding eye contact.

"Have you decided if you're going home for Thanksgiving or staying here?"

"Huh?"

"You heard me."

That was it? She wanted to know about Thanksgiving? Beatrice relaxed her stiff shoulders and reclined against the pillows again.

"I have to go home. My mom's all alone this year. My brother's working."

Gwen propped herself up on an elbow and flashed an angelic smile. "Mind if I tag along?"

"You can't be serious."

Surprised by the request, she beamed, greedy to spend any extra moment with Gwen. On the inside, though, she was apprehensive. What would Gwen think of their working-class neighborhood, the lace tablecloth full of holes, or the dull, blotchy wood flooring?

"No, dummy. I asked you for my health."

"You're really willing to trade a gourmet Thanksgiving feast prepared by a private chef in Newport for dry turkey and canned cranberry sauce in New Haven?"

"I'd just like to have one holiday dinner where I don't have to listen to my mother say how disappointed she is I didn't get accepted into Vassar, the Ridgeway Alma mater." Gwen's face grew somber. "It's exhausting always hearing 'Ridgeways have a standard to uphold.'" She mocked her mother. "Funny thing is, she didn't get accepted either. That's why I'm a legacy here."

Beatrice nodded in sympathy. "You haven't heard anything till you've heard Eloise Darby's patented, 'You need to marry a college boy, or you'll end up with some bum who'll have you living in a tenement' speech."

She leapt up and pretended to feel faint as she imitated her mother for Gwen's amusement.

"'Your father was a no-account who had me squeezing nickels till Jefferson farted.'" She collapsed dramatically on her bed and then popped her head up, reveling in Gwen's uncontrollable giggles. "'You'll be forced to make your kids sell pencils on the street corner to feed them,'" she added, showing no mercy as Gwen clutched her stomach.

"Oh, Bea, you're such a card." She gasped for breath.

"Our mothers make a fine pair, don't they?"

"God, yes," Gwen said as she caught her breath.

Beatrice suddenly grew dreamy watching Gwen twirl the ends of her shiny blond hair. She and Gwen made a fine pair, too.

"Penny for your thoughts," Gwen said as she sat up.

She shook away her daydream. "Having you over for Thanksgiving dinner is a swell idea. Maybe your presence will keep my mother out of my hair all weekend."

"It's official. We'll be each other's mother-repellant this holiday season," Gwen said, and they both broke into raucous laughter.

Beatrice sat with her hands folded at the edge of the kitchen table watching in amazement as her mother fawned over Gwen. One would think it were President and Mamie Eisenhower joining them for Thanksgiving dinner. Like her daughter, Mrs. Darby was drawn to Gwen but with an entirely different agenda.

"I understand your father owns his own business in Boston, Gwen," Mrs. Darby said. It was like watching Bela Lugosi lure Renfield into his clutches in *Dracula*.

"Yes, ma'am. Ridgeway Enterprises. My great-grandfather started it over seventy years ago."

"What type of business?"

"Exporting."

Mrs. Darby's eyes sparkled. "Oh, now isn't that interesting."

Old money. This topic should keep her mother off her back for the rest of the day. "When are we going to cut the turkey, Mom?"

"Very soon, dear. I have a surprise for us."

Beatrice and Gwen looked at each other.

"What kind of surprise?" Beatrice asked.

Mrs. Darby glanced up at the kitchen clock. "Oh, you'll see. Any minute now." She whipped her head toward Gwen. "Now do you live in Boston?"

"Yes," Gwen said, looking modest.

"In the city?"

"The Beacon Hill section."

"Oh, I read that's where all the millionaires live."

"Mom, maybe we can stop grilling Gwen and start slicing some turkey."

"Beatrice, I taught you better table manners than that. I'm trying to get to know your friend." Back to Gwen. "Beatrice mentioned something about living in Newport?"

Gwen's eyes darted self-consciously between Beatrice and Mrs. Darby. "Well, sort of. My family summers and sometimes takes holidays in Newport."

"How lovely," Mrs. Darby said. "We summer here in New Haven—summer, fall, winter, and spring," she added with a laugh lousy with affectation.

Beatrice rolled her eyes. This was going to be a long dinner.

"Happy Turkey Day." Quentin's voice boomed from the hallway. He blew into the kitchen, his sport jacket slung over his shoulder in a Tab Hunter sort of way, grinning at everyone like he could sell flood insurance in the Sahara.

"Surprise," Mrs. Darby exclaimed, lightly clapping her hands.

Beatrice gaped at him like she was witnessing an avalanche.

"We've been waiting, darling. What kept you?"

"Lots of traffic. Guess everyone's going over the river and through the woods today," he said, oozing charm.

"Well, better late than never," Mrs. Darby said.

Beatrice's jaw nearly fell into her butternut squash when she observed Gwen's eyes following Quentin's every move, every gesture. What in the hell was he doing here?

Quentin kissed his mother's cheek, winked at Beatrice, and grinned at Gwen as he began to carve the bird. "So, Bea," he said as the blade sliced through the browned turkey breast, "when did you start getting chummy with beautiful girls?" His velvet blue eyes shimmered in the glow from the hanging light fixture.

"This is Gwen," she mumbled flatly. "We're dorm mates…and friends."

"Best friends." Gwen corrected her with a flirtatious lilt in her voice.

"What a pleasure it is to meet you, Gwen." Quentin winked as he placed several thin slices of white meat on Gwen's plate.

Beatrice was furious. This son of a bitch was supposed to be lost on the road somewhere in Pennsylvania peddling bicycle parts first thing in the morning for the big-deal sales job he boasted about. If he had to show up today, why couldn't it be with one of those curvy bubbleheads that seemed to stick to him like gum on a sneaker.

Sensing the threat of competition, Beatrice suddenly lost her appetite. Girls got all stupid when they were around Quentin. All that dirty-blond hair that waved across his head like a lush wheat field, those crystal-blue eyes, his strong jaw and cleft chin made girls lose all sense of reason. Sure, Quentin was Mr. Charm at first glance, but Beatrice had witnessed too many young ladies cast out like the day's eggshells and apple cores, weeping at their front stoop while Quentin ducked out the back. But why was she working herself into a froth now? Gwen wasn't like other girls. She was intelligent enough to recognize a fraud when she saw one.

Mrs. Darby handed Quentin her plate. "Gwen was just telling us that her father owns Ridgeway Enterprises." She winked at Gwen as though they were part of the same secret society. "Quentin has aspirations to be a business executive someday, too."

"Ridgeway Enterprises," he said. "They're one of Boston's biggest exporters."

Gwen leaned toward him with dreamy eyes. "Oh, you've heard."

What was happening here? How the hell did Quentin know about Ridgeway Enterprises? Beatrice didn't believe for a second that the company was mentioned in his crummy community-college business class. She looked at her mother, who winked conspiratorially at her.

"Are you girls here for the whole weekend?" he asked.

"Yes," Beatrice said. "I'm taking Gwen on a tour of the city tomorrow."

"Do you like pizza, Gwen?" Quentin asked.

"Sure, who doesn't?"

"Well, you haven't tasted pizza until you've had a pie from Frank Pepe's. What's say I treat you gals to dinner tomorrow night after your tour?"

Before Beatrice could voice her objection, Gwen replied, "Oh, that would be lovely."

Beatrice glanced at her mother, who was watching the sparks fire between Quentin and Gwen with a knowing grin. So that was why Quentin had ended up home when he was supposed to be on the road until Saturday. Beatrice seethed at her mother for choosing Quentin's best interests over hers. Gwen was her friend. What right did her mother have interfering with her friendship so she could play Cupid for Quentin? He never seemed to have any difficulty finding girls on his own.

As the evening went on, she began to wonder if she was still in the room. The flirtatious banter between Gwen and Quentin was nauseating, almost as nauseating as her mother trying to nose her way into their conversation like they were the Three Musketeers. Tired of picking at the turkey and trimmings on her plate, she emptied them into the garbage can.

By the end of the holiday weekend, Beatrice was hard-pressed to decide whom she found more annoying, her brother or her best friend for making her feel like a third wheel on what was supposed to be quality girlfriend time for two. As they boarded the Greyhound in the New Haven terminal Sunday evening, she entertained visions of pouring her bottle of Foxon Park white birch beer over Gwen's head—anything to wipe that irritating smile off her face.

After they settled into their seats, Gwen closed her eyes with the dreamiest of smiles. "What a lovely weekend."

Beatrice played it cagey. "It would've been better if my dopey brother hadn't wormed his way into everything we did. Sorry about that."

"Oh, I didn't find him dopey at all. He's so handsome and rugged."

Beatrice scoffed. "Rugged? Did I ever tell you about the time he got stung by a yellow jacket and ran into the house screaming for my mom while I had to finish whacking down their nest under our porch?"

"Oh, you were kids then."

"He was fifteen, and I was only eleven."

Gwen grinned. "Well, you're lucky you've always been a strong, self-sufficient woman."

"Yeah, and maybe in a few more years Quentin will be one, too."

Gwen elbowed her playfully. "You're so fresh. I've never met a girl so competitive with her own brother."

"He's the one that's fresh. I wouldn't get your hopes up that he'll call you. He takes lots of girls' numbers."

"Is he a womanizer?"

Beatrice exaggerated a grave expression. "Is he? Oh, boy."

She looked out the bus window to hide a mischievous grin, allowing ample time for her words to take root.

Gwen relaxed into her seat. "I'm glad you told me. Sometimes those kinds of guys are so good at making a great impression."

Beatrice took out the latest copy of *Modern Screen* and relaxed, too, pausing for a moment to decide if she shouldn't be feeling even the slightest bit guilty for what she'd just done…Nah.

CHAPTER SEVEN

Beatrice had learned an invaluable lesson over the last year: she was a survivor. Even after she secretly bombarded Gwen and Quentin with a barrage of Italian curses learned from her downstairs neighbor, Mrs. Rispoli, they still fell deeply in love with no signs of reversal in sight. Beatrice knew this because she'd searched for them like an archeologist digging for pottery from lost cultures. It was small consolation that she hadn't slithered into a hole and died, as she'd initially believed she would.

As a light snow fell in New Haven, Beatrice lay on the couch in the parlor watching television, her eyelids heavy as her mother rattled pots and pans in the kitchen. As long as she heard the rattling, she was safe. This had been a long Christmas break.

Her eyes opened when the rattling stopped.

"Beatrice, what are you doing?" her mother called from the kitchen.

She burrowed the side of her face into a sofa pillow. "Research for a paper."

Like a storm cloud, her mother drifted overhead. "You are not. You're watching Popeye cartoons."

"My research paper explores how Olive Oyl gets exploited in the struggle for male dominance between Popeye and Brutus."

Her mother narrowed her eyes. One of Beatrice's favorite guilty pleasures was the look of bewilderment on her mother's face whenever she decided to use her education for spite.

"Aren't you going to tell me what was in that package you received from New York?"

Beatrice sat up and straightened out her ponytail. "Information from New York University."

"What about?"

"I'm thinking of enrolling there in the fall for my master's degree."

"What do you need that for? You probably won't even end up using the degree you're getting in May once you get married and settle into family life."

Settle. The word invaded Beatrice's chest like a virus, halting her breath. Long ago she had interpreted from her mother's less-than-subtle insinuations that she herself had settled for less than she deserved. Why in the world would she wish the same fate for her daughter? She studied the wrinkles on her mother's forehead and tried to imagine what kind of woman she might have been if she'd taken the road less traveled.

"Have you earned another scholarship?" her mother asked.

"I'm looking into getting a loan."

Her mother chuckled derisively. "Who's going to give a twenty-one-year-old girl a loan?"

"No need to concern yourself, Mother. My academic advisor is helping me with all that."

"Once you get this master's degree, what do you plan to do with it?"

"I've told you before. I'm going to be a college professor. Gwen and I are both going to be professors."

"She's not going to be a professor. She's going to marry your brother."

Beatrice's stomach plummeted. "How do you know? Has Quent said anything to you?"

"Well, no, but I know my son. He's smitten with this girl."

Beatrice gritted her teeth to restrain a crest of jealousy. "I'm sure you're just reading what you want to happen into things. He's not ready for that."

Her mother smiled slyly. "I know my son."

"Even if you're right, which I'm sure you're not, why can't she do both? Marry him and be a professor?"

Her mother shook her head. "Oh, Beatrice, you and these pipe dreams."

"It's not a pipe dream, not for me anyway. You'll see."

"I don't know why I even bother trying to talk sense into you. You're only going to do what you want anyway. But why must you always insist on leaving the state to pursue these dreams? It's almost as if you're deliberately trying to stay away from me."

As tempted as she was, she let that one go. "NYU has an outstanding English-studies department."

Her mother propped her hands on her hips and scoffed. "Men don't like it when women flaunt their intelligence. You're going to educate yourself right into spinsterhood."

Beatrice stood up and stretched her long torso. "I have to go over to the McDonalds' now. They have tickets for the Shubert."

"Oh, that's good. Babysitting their little ones is exactly what you need. Something has to jump-start your mothering instinct."

"How do you know I even have one? I don't mind babysitting their kids, but I don't think I want any of my own." She grimaced as though forcing down a spoonful of Castor oil.

A cautious grin formed on her mother's lips. "You say these things just to get me going, don't you?"

Beatrice smiled and gave her mother an obligatory kiss on the cheek as she headed toward the door. "Have a nice evening, Mother. Don't wait up for me."

"Beatrice." Her mother stared at her with the most adoring of smiles. "You'll make such a good mother once you get past this selfish stage."

Beatrice gave her a mocking thumbs-up and shut the door. As she descended the stairs one leisurely step at a time, her mother's suggestion irked her. Was she really being selfish? In all her twenty-one years, all she'd ever considered was setting and achieving goals for herself. Was she wrong for desiring to accomplish things and pursue a career outside the home? If she wasn't, why weren't more girls her age doing it?

❖

This past year had been difficult, to say the least. Since Quentin and Gwen became an item during last year's Christmas break, Beatrice's stomach was in a perpetual state of knots. She'd lost ten pounds and found herself bickering with Gwen over the silliest things. She'd fooled herself into believing her change in disposition came from a fear of losing Gwen's friendship. It was simply more convenient to believe that than deal with the reality that she desperately ached for Gwen.

Beatrice had returned to campus a week before winter break was over to get a jump on her senior honors thesis, due a month before graduation. But if the truth be known, she couldn't suffer another moment of her mother's blathering about Quentin and Gwen. "Quentin and Gwen are such a beautiful couple, like two peas in a pod, inseparable, made for each other, two crazy kids in love, what attractive children they'll make." Blah, blah, blah.

With an Emily Dickinson biography open, facedown on her chest, Beatrice lay in her bed in a dreamy twilight sleep. It was Christmas Eve all over again, and Gwen unwrapped the sweater Beatrice had given her, but instead of a thank-you hug, Gwen kissed her gently on the cheek and then kept pecking her until her lips were kissing Beatrice's, slowly and sensually. Beatrice traced the contour of Gwen's waist with her hands until the thud against the door and the giggling in the hall startled her awake. She leapt to the door and opened it in time to observe Gwen and Quentin locked in a passionate embrace.

"Oh, hello, Bea," Gwen said with a bashful grin as she pushed Quentin away.

"Hey, booger," Quentin said playfully.

She glared at him. "I'm a senior in college. Don't you think it's about time you stopped calling me that?" She walked to her bed and muttered "asshole" loud enough for both of them to hear.

"Good-bye, honey bear," Gwen whispered to Quentin. "Call me the second you get back to New Haven."

"Sure thing, baby doll," Quentin replied. "See you later, Miss Personality," he called out to Beatrice as he left.

Beatrice scowled in his direction as she picked up her book and pretended to read.

"So did you have a nice break, Bea?" Gwen asked, hanging up her coat.

"It was okay," Beatrice said, not looking up from the pages. "After Christmas it was kind of boring. I thought you and I were supposed to do something fun after New Year's."

"I know. I'm sorry, but between my family and your brother, I was so busy. I promise I'll make it up to you, a special girls' day in New York City. Cross my heart."

She hovered over Beatrice looking like she knew the answer to the sixty-four-thousand-dollar question.

Beatrice finally graced her with her attention. "What are you doing?"

Gwen took that as an invitation to plop down next to her on the bed. Her eyes were wide, almost maniacal. "Oh, Bea, you're never ever going to believe what happened tonight."

"Let me guess—my brother saved your life stopping a speeding train with his bare hands while simultaneously catching a bullet in his teeth?"

Gwen giggled. "You're so goofy. No, nothing like that but just as thrilling." She slowly uncurled her fingers and waved a shiny, square-cut diamond engagement ring under Beatrice's nose. "He proposed," she said, beaming. "We're getting married in July."

Beatrice's breath seized as though she'd taken a punch to the throat. She stared at the ring encircling Gwen's dainty pink finger. Regardless of its obvious inevitability, she still couldn't grasp that it was happening. It couldn't be happening.

"Bea," Gwen said, pausing nervously. "Aren't you going to say anything?"

She tried to speak but simply couldn't find the air to propel her words.

"Beatrice," Gwen said tersely.

"What? Oh, yeah. I'm so happy for you." She brandished a smile that wouldn't even convince a child.

"And of course, you're going to be my maid of honor."

Beatrice grinned awkwardly as she slowly regained her breath.

Gwen stood up and crossed her arms over her chest. "You don't seem very happy. What the heck's the matter?"

"Nothing." She tried her hardest to muster some semblance of sincerity. "I am happy for you, honest."

"But you don't even seem the least bit excited. Why aren't you jumping around with me like a crazy person?"

"You know I'm not a 'jumping around like a crazy person' kind of girl."

"That's true, but I would think this occasion would be an exception." Gwen became suspicious. "This isn't some peculiar possessive sister thing, is it? I mean, you do think I'm good enough for him, right?"

Beatrice guffawed. "Of course you're good enough for him."

"Then tell me why you're acting so strange."

Beatrice stood and faced Gwen. "All right, you want to know the truth? My brother's not good enough for you. You can do much better."

Gwen's lips parted in surprise. "How could you say that?"

"I just know my brother."

"Bea, I know what you've said about him, but he's been treating me like gold. He sends me flowers, calls me constantly, remembers our anniversary every month. He's the most thoughtful young man I've ever known."

Beatrice pursed her lips to stop them from quivering, but she couldn't do a thing to prevent her eyes from pooling.

"He's gonna hurt you."

"You don't know what you're saying."

"I've seen it. I've seen the way he's treated his other girlfriends. He's broken hearts all over New Haven County, and you're going to be next."

"Oh, now, don't you think you're being a little dramatic. So he sowed some wild oats when he was younger. All boys do that. But he's twenty-five now. He's been nothing but a gentleman with me."

Beatrice glared at her. "You're being very naive."

Gwen glared back, her usual lighthearted air dissipated. "You know, Bea, I'd hate to think this is just a rotten case of jealousy."

She laughed in disbelief. "Jealousy?"

"Sure. You haven't been able to find a decent guy the whole time we've been here, and you don't want me to have a fiancé if you can't have one. I thought you were a better friend than that."

"Are you loony?" she shouted, feeling her grip slipping. "I can't believe you could think such a thing. I'm your best friend, Gwen. I only have your best interests at heart."

"You could've fooled me. I can look out for myself, Bea. I'm a big girl now, and quite frankly, I'm tired of you playing my keeper all the time."

"Oh, is that right?"

"Yes, that's right. I'm perfectly capable of knowing who's right for me and who isn't. Maybe if you spent more time worrying about your own personal life instead of mine, you'd actually have someone."

"You're a fucking ingrate," Beatrice said, poking Gwen in the shoulder. "You're with my brother because of me. I didn't have to take you home for Thanksgiving dinner last year when you felt like slumming it."

"Slumming it?" Gwen's wounded eyes flared. "How dare you make such a horrible accusation? And don't you point at me either. I'm not your property—I don't belong to you."

"What the hell is that supposed to mean?"

"It means that just because we're friends, I don't have to check in with you about every decision I make."

By this time, Beatrice's face was on fire. She made fists to stop her hands from shaking. "Okay, fine. You fucking know everything." She stalked to the door and flung it open. "When he hurts you, don't come crying to me."

She slammed the door shut and darted down the hall out into the frigid night, walking—walking, walking, hearing nothing but the moan of a dying heart thrumming in her ears.

After what felt like hours but was little more than thirty minutes, she'd calmed enough to assess the damage from her outburst. What had come over her? How did she let herself get so out of control, saying those awful things to Gwen? She'd ruined her best friend's happiest moment. Her ears burned with numbness from the wind as she walked. She pressed her hands against her cheeks stinging with cold, praying she could find a way to diffuse this.

She made her way to the dorm and stood outside looking up at the light on in their room. What was Gwen doing up there? Crying? Packing? Tearing up photos and mementos of their friendship? Waiting for Quentin to come and pick her up and take her with him home to New Haven?

Beatrice was disgusted with herself for feeling what she felt for Gwen and, even more, for allowing it to jeopardize their friendship. She sat shivering on the icy wooden steps and wept into her arms folded over her knees.

"There you are," Gwen said softly as she approached holding Beatrice's coat. "You're going to freeze to death."

Beatrice swept her sleeve across her face to dry it off. "I deserve to freeze to death."

Gwen smiled wryly, hugging Beatrice's coat to her chest. "Finally, something we agree on. But if you do, then I'll be out a maid of honor." She tossed Beatrice her coat. "That is, if you want to be my maid of honor."

"I do," Beatrice said, full of remorse.

"Hey, that's my line."

Beatrice got up from the porch and hugged Gwen tightly, inhaling the pine scent of her shampoo. "I'm sorry, Gwen. I guess I got scared our friendship would change even more."

"Oh, Bea. I said I was sorry for not getting together over break. I really will make it up to you."

Beatrice frowned, milking Gwen's sympathy for all she could. "I mean after we graduate."

Gwen squeezed her hand. "Sure, it's going to change a little. We're going to have our own lives, but we'll always be the best of friends. That's for certain."

"I only want you to be happy. That's all I ever wanted."

Gwen pushed her away gently and held Beatrice's face in her hands. "I am happy."

She looked into Gwen's starry eyes and knew it was true.

"I'm so happy that I'm going to be part of your family now, Darby," Gwen added.

"My family? Have you met my mother?"

Gwen chuckled. "Let's go inside before your face falls off from frostbite. That would ruin the wedding photos."

Beatrice smiled as Gwen pulled her by the arm up the stairs.

❖

The next morning Beatrice awoke thankful for the first time about Gwen's early morning class. She needed time to think. Her reaction to the engagement and her lingering depression about it left her uneasy. She buried her face in her blankets, wishing she had someone to whom she could express all her feelings, someone who might possibly convince her she hadn't lost her mind completely. Robert had always been a confidant, but about simple things. How could she talk about this with him or anyone else? How she wished Abby were still in her life. She was the only one who could empathize with this whirl of confusion, isolation, and despair. It was time for another visit with Father Sheridan, the first clergyman with whom she'd ever felt safe. Since he had replaced that crusty old chaplain who seemed to take great pleasure in threatening the student body with eternal hellfire, religious counsel felt a little less like voluntarily facing a firing squad.

After dragging herself out of bed and bundling up, she trudged across campus to the chapel, crunching hard ground and blinking away snow flurries blowing in her eyes. She hesitated at the entrance of the chapel, staring at its stone façade, watching her breath float upward. Maybe Father Sheridan was still sleeping or too busy to see her. Maybe she was making too much of the engagement and simply needed to let the idea sink in. She entered the church, stopping to light a candle for her father.

Padding down the aisle, she shrank with guilt for not lighting candles for him more often and for the trail of wet footsteps she left on the carpet. At least she was in the appropriate place for it. She slipped into a pew, knelt, and prayed that her father was still watching over her. Did he know about the way she was, the thoughts that would creep into her mind, and the feelings of love and lust she harbored for Gwen? Would he still love her knowing who she truly was? Was he ashamed of her now—as ashamed as she was of herself sometimes?

She blotted her watery eyes with the thumbs of her knit gloves and whispered the Lord's Prayer.

"Beatrice?" the gentle voice called out.

She looked up at Father Sheridan waving her over from the side of the altar. She got up and followed him into the rectory, plunking down in a chair in front of his desk.

"You must be very troubled today." He folded his hands on the desk blotter.

"Wow. It's amazing how your powers tell you these things before anyone even opens their mouths."

He smiled easily, his young, rugged face a contrast to his cleric's collar. "It's not divine intervention. I just know kids don't come in here this early in the morning unless something is weighing heavily on their minds."

"I'm still having those feelings for my best friend, Father. Last night when she told me my brother proposed to her, and she said 'yes,' I cried and cried until I ran out of tears. I really thought I'd have a nervous breakdown."

"How have you been doing with your prayers?"

She sighed heavily. "To be honest, not very good. I mean I do pray, but nothing ever changes, so then I'll say to myself, 'what's the use' and go days, weeks even, without praying or thinking of God."

She bowed her head, waiting for the judgmental tone she had been conditioned to expect in confessional with other clergy. But Father Sheridan only exhaled lightly through his nose.

"I can imagine how frustrating this must be for you."

She looked up from her lap. "You can?"

"Of course. It's the dilemma of many a good Catholic. You pray and pray in earnest for something you need to happen, and when it doesn't, it's very tempting to want to give up."

"I feel like God doesn't care about me."

"I can understand that, too, but He does, that much I know. Faith requires patience, Beatrice. You may not have gotten the results you want from prayer, but right now God is doing for you what you need, not what you want."

"Is He going to make these feelings go away?"

He reclined his chair and lightly drummed his fingers on the armrest. "I don't know."

"You don't know?" His response agitated Beatrice. "But that other priest I talked to a few times in confession said He would if I prayed hard enough. I've prayed as hard as I know how to, and I'm still this way." Suddenly, she broke into tears. "What's wrong with me?"

Father Sheridan let her cry for a moment. "Beatrice, have you ever thought that if this is the way you are, it's the way God made you?"

"Huh?" she asked through sniffles.

"You're not a mistake. I don't know why God makes people homosexual, but the fact remains that He does." He paused and lowered his voice. "Look, I may sound like a heretic, but that's my belief. I also believe some homosexuals can live happy lives."

"How?"

"They find others like themselves, and if they're lucky enough to find that special someone, I suppose they can be content."

Beatrice tilted her head to the side. "Are you saying it's okay to be queer?"

"No, I'm not saying that. I'm saying that God has His reasons for everything, reasons we can never understand here in the physical world."

"Father, I don't mean to tell you your business, but aren't you contradicting the Bible?"

He folded his hands over his stomach. "I know what it says in the Bible about homosexuality. I also know it says it was okay to sell your daughter for livestock. My point is, in the modern world it's unrealistic to expect even the most faithful to follow the scripture down to the letter."

She paused for a moment to digest Father Sheridan's suggestion.

"I don't want to be queer. I don't want to be different from everyone else. What if everyone rejects me because I disgust or embarrass them? I just want to be normal." She glanced out into the gray morning, sucking in her cheeks against her tears.

"I'm going to give you the name of an analyst I think you should talk to."

Beatrice picked her head up. "Analyst? You mean a shrink?"

"Psychiatrist. Some people find analysis very beneficial, especially in cases like yours."

Fantastic. She'd gone from sinner to insane in a matter of ten minutes talking with Father Sheridan.

"Do you think I'm crazy?"

"No, Beatrice, I don't think you're crazy. I think you're upset and confused, and if prayer alone isn't working for you, perhaps speaking with a psychiatric professional will help you put things in perspective. Some people in situations like yours have even been known to change the way they think after several sessions with a good doctor."

"So then you're saying I should change?"

Father Sheridan smiled patiently. "I'm saying you should get another point of view."

As he scribbled down a name and phone number from his Rolodex, Beatrice gazed out at the gray formless sky, contemplating the implications of her latest counsel with Father Sheridan. Maybe she was crazy. She'd certainly reacted like a madwoman toward Gwen last night. Perhaps a visit to a shrink could help. After all, Freud thought everyone's problems stemmed from toilet training and ids and egos. Maybe all she needed was a doctor to help identify the damage caused sometime in her childhood. Then she would be able to change. A small sense of relief welled in her heart. How freeing it would be not to feel the constant pressure to keep such a dark secret hidden from the world.

Father Sheridan stood and handed her a folded slip of paper. "Give Doctor Stenquist a call, and then let me know how you make out."

"Thank you, Father," she said, and reached for the door.

"Beatrice."

She stopped and turned to him.

"God didn't give up on you. Promise me you won't give up on Him."

"I won't," she said with a meek smile.

She folded the paper even smaller and stuffed it in her coat pocket as she left the chapel. When she opened the door, the blast of cold air refreshed her senses for the psychology class to which she was about to be late.

❖

For the first half of the lecture on treatments for various debilitating psychiatric disorders and the criminally insane, Beatrice's mind floated through myriads of abstractions about life, faith, God, and love. In the end, the only idea that made any sense was the way she felt about Gwen, and Abby, years earlier. But like it or not, she had to accept the fact that her brother was going to marry Gwen.

As Professor Hawley droned about what drove homicidal maniacs like Leopold and Loeb to murder for no apparent reason, Beatrice entertained possible scenarios that would involve Quentin's mysterious disappearance. Of course, she didn't want any harm to come to her brother—just something simple like waking up in Amish country with a nasty case of amnesia that would last about twenty years.

She emerged from her fantasy when Hawley flipped off the lights and started the reel-to-reel projector to show a documentary about electroshock therapy. She slunk down in her seat watching the ghastly images as the narrator spoke in a calm, clinical tone. After the female patient's wrists, head, and ankles were secured to the gurney with thick leather straps and a bit wedged into her mouth, her eyes darted wildly at the cluster of white-coated bodies surrounding her.

Beatrice squirmed at the woman's helplessness and how her treatment appeared more like a medieval punishment for being sick than a remedy. Her hands trembled as she pictured herself in the film strapped to the table after months of sessions with the good Dr. Stenquist had yielded no change in her thoughts. When the patient on the screen convulsed in a wave of electrical current, Beatrice closed her eyes tightly, peeking out of her left one once the awful buzzing noise subsided.

"Often several administrations of electricity in separate intervals are required to produce the desired effect in the patient," the narrator said as another jolt rippled through a different wretched woman.

Beatrice lifted her three-ring binder in front of her face.

"Put that down, Bea," her classmate, Bobby, whispered. "You're gonna miss the best part: lobotomies."

"What's that?" she whispered from behind the notebook.

"It's when they go in through your eye socket and drill holes in the front of your brain," he said excitedly. "It's way out."

"Why on earth would they have to do that?"

"It's for the real nut cases when even the shock treatments fail."

"That's horrible," Beatrice said. "Does it help? What happens to the people after?"

"They usually end up locked away in an institution anyway."

"Oh God," she muttered, wiping perspiration from her forehead. "I don't think I can watch anymore of this."

Bobby shook his head. "This is exactly why girls should never be doctors."

"You mean executioners. Save me the notes, huh?"

She gathered her things and made her escape out the back of the lecture hall.

❖

Later that evening, Beatrice surprised Gwen with a culinary treat even more intriguing than the Sloppy Joe. Visions of a future sporting a snug-fitting white jacket in a padded room gave her a sharper perspective on her situation than even Dr. Freud himself could have.

"Wow, what's all this?" Gwen asked as she came in from an early evening trig class.

"It's a combination celebration and apology dinner." Beatrice smiled brightly as she presented two steaming, foiled-covered trays from their electric hot plate. "Fried chicken, mashed potatoes, and corn. Hope you're hungry."

"I'm starved," Gwen said as she sat on her bed in front of a television tray. "Is this one of those TV dinners?"

Beatrice nodded proudly. "A revolution in fine dining without ever having to leave the comfort of your own home. It would be even better if we had a TV instead of a radio."

"It's perfect just like this," Gwen said as she tore at the foil. "Bea, you didn't have to go to all this trouble."

"It's no trouble, and yes, I did. I still feel terrible about the mood I was in last night."

Gwen smiled. "Well, this wasn't necessary, but I sure appreciate it."

Beatrice sat on her bed and removed the foil from her meal. "My pleasure, *sis*."

"Sis," Gwen exclaimed. "Oh, I love it."

Beatrice smiled and bit into her fried chicken breast, concluding that the flutter of butterflies in her stomach Gwen still gave her was a lot easier to handle than a thousand watts of electricity zapping her cranium.

CHAPTER EIGHT

Two months after graduating summa cum laude from Salve Regina, things weren't exactly going according to Beatrice's meticulously drafted life plan. She tugged at her tight, scratchy chiffon maid-of-honor's dress with one hand while blotting the sweat in her cleavage with a balled-up tissue. She wobbled over the grass in a pair of misogynistic heels to the shade of one of several tents set up at the Ridgeways' summer home—a sprawling Newport estate on which Fitzgerald could have easily set *The Great Gatsby*.

She guzzled another glass of Dom Perignon as her dearest friend and her brother gently smeared blobs of French truffle wedding cake across each other's lips, laughing in the July sun. By this stage in the day, Beatrice had seen enough. She was light-headed, and her jaw ached from grinding her teeth nearly to dust every time they touched.

"Another glass of champagne, Bea?" her mother asked. "Maybe if you'd eaten your filet mignon you wouldn't look so green." She handed her a cocktail dish heaped with liver pâté and Melba toast.

"Thanks, Mother, but I can assure you, it's not the bubbly making me sick."

"Look around, Bea," her mother said, clueless to her daughter's agony. She devoured the opulence with famished eyes and quickly glanced in her purse to check on the lobster-puff pastry wrapped in a napkin. "Such a shame you didn't meet a nice young man at college, too. If you'd put forth more of an effort, perhaps we could've all been gathered in a place like this today for you instead of Gwen."

"I'm sure this is just a minor detail, but Quentin didn't even finish college. Shouldn't Gwen's parents be sobbing into their golden goblets right now?"

Mrs. Darby was ready on the draw. "Quentin is an exception. He's so brilliant and such a dedicated company man, he'll be an excellent provider for Gwen."

"Gwen doesn't need a provider. She's got a bachelor's degree."

"That's all well and good, but unless it's in homemaking and child-rearing, I'm afraid it won't be very useful."

"You and your Puritanical notions," Beatrice said, shaking her head. "Women can actually do other things besides raise kids and bake pies."

"Well, of course they can. I know that. I'm not from the Stone Age. Once her kids are off to college, Gwen can do anything she wants with that degree."

Beatrice rolled her eyes. "You act like it's the law that a woman has to get married and have kids."

"It's the natural law. Who's going to do it if women don't?"

"Then I guess it's a darn good thing New York University accepted me into their master's program so I can continue the great husband hunt."

"I hope you'll take this a little more seriously on your next go-round. You're almost twenty-two, dear. You're going to blink your eyes one day and be thirty years old and still without a husband. Then what will become of you? I'm not getting any younger. I can't take care of you forever."

"I don't need you or a man to take care of me. I'll be able to provide for myself."

Her mother pursed her lips and peeked in at the pastry again. "Now I know you've been in the sun too long."

"I don't think this is the time or place to be arguing about this."

Her mother adjusted the drooping lily over Beatrice's ear. "Oh, Beatrice, I don't want to argue at all. You look so lovely today. Maybe if you could keep yourself this feminine all the time you could attract a decent man."

"What do you suggest? I parade around in a maid-of-honor's dress every day?"

"Honestly, Bea."

Her mother scoffed and wandered off to mingle among the upper crust who on any other day would have mistaken her for the help.

As the sun hovered high over the estate, Beatrice stood in the shady refuge of a beech tree watching well-coiffed women and overdressed men move under the wedding-reception tents. Never mind that they were all cutouts of a social culture she would never be part of—nor cared to—but nearly everyone in attendance was paired off with someone of the opposite sex. Nearly everyone had a date, except for her and the children who were in the wedding party. She half-smiled as the frisky little ring-bearer chased the flower girl who wailed for him to let her alone.

"Stand your ground, Sally," Beatrice muttered as she licked pâté off a cracker, grimaced, and spit it on the grass.

Quentin approached her from behind. "Why are you all the way over here by yourself?"

She fixed her gaze on the blinding reflection off the Atlantic. "I needed to cool off. It's too hot over there."

"How about joining the party? My best man needs someone else to dance with."

"I wasn't aware I was on call. A dime a dance? No, thanks."

"Jeez, Bea, lighten up, will you? We're supposed to be dancing and having fun. This is a wedding reception, not an execution walk."

"Cousin Nancy will be happy to dance with him, I'm sure."

Quentin raised his eyebrows. "Maybe after she's completed all her shock treatments."

"You're terrible," she said casually.

"Hey, when someone goes out of their way to be an oddball, they shouldn't be surprised when people notice. Come on. You can't be having any fun by yourself."

"I'm a writer. We like to lurk in the shadows and observe."

Quentin shook his head. "You writers are weird. But I have to say, you look beautiful today, like a girl for a change."

She tossed the cracker away like a Frisbee. "Thanks."

"No, I mean it. You look very nice, feminine."

Beatrice crossed her arms and watched waves foam as they crashed into shore.

"Does this mean you're out of that phase?" he asked sincerely.

She broke her gaze on the ocean for a moment to look him square in the eye. "What phase is that, Quent?"

"Never mind. Let's go."

He tried to pull her by the arm, but she jerked it to her side.

"Look, what's your problem, Bea? If you're not happy for your own brother, can't you at least be happy for your best friend?"

"I know how you are with girls, Quentin. Happy isn't exactly the word I'd use to describe how I feel about Gwen marrying you."

"So I played the field a little in my younger days. Big deal. I love Gwen. I'll be a good husband. I know how to resist temptation, unlike some people I know."

She wheeled around to face him. "If you hurt her, Quentin, I will kill you."

He studied her like an abstract painting. "What, do you have a thing for her or something?"

She looked away, refusing to give him the satisfaction of reading the answer in her eyes.

"That's it, isn't it? Boy, that explains everything."

"As usual, you have no idea what you're talking about, so fuck off, all right?"

"Queer and has the mouth of a truck driver. You're doing the Darby name proud."

"I'm not queer. Now could you please leave me alone?"

He softened his tone. "All right, come on, Bea. Don't be a sore loser. Gwen's my wife now, so you'll just have to get used to it. I'd like to think we can all get along as a family."

Beatrice sighed in resignation. "I'll be there in a minute."

As Quentin walked back to the reception, Beatrice couldn't hold in her tears any longer. A warm stream of them flowed down her cheeks as she watched Gwen and Quentin kiss under the main tent.

❖

Beatrice stood by the stone wall watching the moon spread its light in a triangle where the ocean met the horizon. She was still reeling from the humiliation of getting jostled in the crowd of girls clamoring to snatch Gwen's bouquet and be the next bride. By ten p.m., she was sweaty and exhausted with a headache to beat the band. After pulling each petal from the white rose she'd plucked from the head table's centerpiece, she let the stem drop into the rocky surf below.

"Beatrice," Gwen called out, traipsing down the grassy incline. She had never looked more beautiful. Even if she hadn't been wearing a five-thousand-dollar Oleg Casini original gown, she'd still have had the countenance of a princess.

Beatrice smiled warmly and set her gaze back to the ocean.

"Incredible, isn't it?" Gwen said.

"Yep," she replied quietly.

"Well, this is it. I'm off to start my new life as Mrs. Quentin Darby. I'm so thrilled," she said, clutching Beatrice's hands in hers. "We have to get to the airport soon. The honeymoon suite awaits. God, I'm so nervous."

Beatrice knew if she spoke, she'd collapse into Gwen's arms. All she could do was smile through the fog of tears blurring her vision.

"Oh, Bea," Gwen said. "I know how you feel. I'm so happy I keep crying, too. Don't worry. We're still going to see each other at holidays and things, and then when you're done with your master's—"

"Remember how we said we were going to take the summer after we graduated and travel through Europe together?" Beatrice said wistfully.

"I remember, and it was a fun idea, but I assumed we'd do it only if we were both single. Didn't you?"

Beatrice shrugged.

"I fell in love with Quentin," Gwen said, a twinge of guilt in her voice. "I'm his wife now, and soon, I'll be the mother of his children."

"Instead of being college professors."

"I knew something was bothering you. I was afraid it was because I was getting married and you weren't."

Beatrice glared at her. "Really?"

Gwen grinned. "Yeah, that is kind of absurd, isn't it?"

"Yeah, kind of."

She brushed Beatrice's arm with her fingers. "Oh, Bea, we were kids when we said all those things. We're adults now. Look on the bright side—you'll be married, too, one day and having lots of babies. Won't it be such fun raising our kids together?"

Beatrice's gut boiled. The thought of Gwen intimate with Quentin, the touching and the nakedness, the sharing of laughter and secrets as a bond formed in their marriage bed—and then when the babies came. It was all too much. Her head was spinning from the champagne, the heat, and the utter despair that had been slowly eroding her heart since learning of their engagement. She dashed over to a blue hydrangea and showered it with champagne vomit.

"Oh dear." Gwen went after her and placed a hand on her shoulder. "Darby, are you okay?"

"Mother was right," she said, pulling herself upright. "I should've eaten my filet mignon."

❖

Beatrice had moped around for the rest of the summer, visiting Gwen only when Quentin was at work. She simply could not stomach the sight of them together, and when Gwen would mention that she and Quentin were already trying for a baby, it took Beatrice at least a day to purge the awful image of them "trying" from her head.

One August afternoon when Quentin was at work, she and Gwen lounged in white Adirondack chairs, enjoying glasses of fresh-squeezed lemonade in the shade of an oak tree. Beatrice surveyed their small yard with its tiny vegetable garden and miniature rose bushes that dotted a picket fence surrounding their modest, powder-blue cape. A picture postcard of the American Dream. The only things missing were little Susie and her pipe curls and Skippy and his propeller beanie. Beatrice's nostrils flared with revulsion.

"How can you stand going from mansions and servants to this?" she asked, fingering the condensation on her lemonade glass. "Your parents must be beside themselves."

Gwen smirked as she dangled a sandal off her toes. "I doubt it. My father, the big business tycoon, can't tell the difference between my sister and me half the time—and we're not even twins. As for my mother, well, she's been beside her miserable self from the minute she learned I was marrying beneath me, as she likes to put it. Serves her right, the snob."

"I'll never understand how you turned out so wonderfully down-to-earth."

"I told you before—my wonderfully down-to-earth Nanny Rose, of course," Gwen replied with a goofy smile. If Gwen only knew what that smile did to Beatrice. "Money and material things don't mean anything without love, Bea. Your mother is a dear, but I don't think she realizes that."

"She doesn't. My loving, yet under-employed father could've told you that. He gave her everything he could afford, yet she never missed an opportunity to point out all the things we couldn't afford."

"You still miss him, don't you?"

Beatrice nodded pensively. "He was a great dad, so positive about anything I wanted to do. He's the only person who ever got me."

Gwen playfully kicked Beatrice's foot, knocking off her sandal. "Ahem…"

"Oh, present company excluded," she said with a smile.

"Quent said your dad favored you."

"It wasn't so much that he favored me as he was sticking up for me. My mother's always had very specific expectations for me, and as you know, I've yet to meet any of them."

Gwen nodded. "She was complaining to me about how you haven't spent that much time with her all summer."

"It's for her own safety. If I hear her say how I'm doomed to a life of spinsterhood if I don't snag myself a rich college boy one more time, I'm gonna ring her goddamn neck."

Gwen laughed and pressed a hand into her chest, assuming her best snooty New England accent. "My goodness, Beatrice, such language."

"I'm being kind. She's truly insufferable."

"Let's face it," Gwen said. "Our parents are from the old generation. They'll never see things our way, so all we can do is grin and bear it."

Beatrice arched an eyebrow. "Is marrying a guy outside your social class and then moving a hundred and fifty miles away from home your idea of grinning and bearing it?"

"You know what I mean. At some point we've got to decide who we're going to live our lives for."

Beatrice shooed away a persistent horsefly as she pondered Gwen's sage words. If she was going to live life for herself, she couldn't stick around here.

"My mother's whole problem is she cares too much about what others think. Apparently, life is just some big competition for money and social status. I'm afraid she's been irreversibly brainwashed by Joan Crawford movies."

"What's that they say, the grass is always greener?"

"I don't understand why anyone should care how others live, especially if they aren't hurting anyone. It makes me crazy."

"That's why I'm so glad I met you and Quentin. We may not have everything, but he loves me, and I love him so much." Gwen gently squeezed Beatrice's forearm. "We're all a family now."

Beatrice forced a smile, then looked down and jiggled the melting ice cubes in her cup. Low, steady breaths. It was the only way to control herself whenever she felt like she was about to explode and deluge Gwen with tearful I love yous.

"I need to put the roast in the oven and start dinner. Quent will be home in about an hour. Please stay and join us."

Beatrice stood and gathered her glass and a bowl of barren grape branches.

"Thanks, but I'm not hungry. I have some reading I want to catch up on anyhow."

Gwen looked crestfallen. "But you're leaving for New York in a couple of weeks. Don't you want to spend as much time with us as you can until then? At least it'll save you from dinner with your mother," she added with a wink.

Beatrice despised how Gwen's "me" was now "us." Why did couples have to do that? It irked her that when women married, they traded in their individual identity to become half of an "us" or a Mrs. Somebody or so-and-so's mother. You were Gwen before you ever became Quentin's wife, she wanted to scream.

"Are you okay, Bea? Your face is all red."

Beatrice shook it off. "Oh, I'm fine. Think maybe the heat is getting to me."

"Come inside then. I've got the fans on."

Beatrice followed Gwen into the scorching kitchen, unable to fathom why she would even consider making a roast in this appalling heat.

Gwen stacked the cups and dishes in the sink and then faced Beatrice.

"You promise you'll come for dinner before you leave?" Suddenly, Gwen's eyes pooled with sadness.

Beatrice had to catch her breath. Gwen looked more beautiful every time she saw her. As much as she hated to admit it, marriage suited her, lending a maturity and grace to her flawless image.

"I promise." She offered a bright smile, but the ache in her heart threatened to overcome her. This was never going to work.

They studied each other's eyes for a moment as if they were both trying to solve a riddle. Beatrice kissed Gwen on her warm cheek. Slowly, her lips glided onto Gwen's, the sweat under their noses mingling as their kiss lingered. She stood motionless, lost in the sensation of kissing Gwen the way she'd imagined hundreds of times.

When she pressed her chest against Gwen's and draped her arms around her, Gwen nudged her back.

"Bea," she whispered, looking away as she smoothed down her blouse.

Beatrice trembled as she averted her eyes. She couldn't decide which felt worse, her humiliation at losing control or the look of discomfort on Gwen's face.

"I'm sorry." Her words were more of a spontaneous reaction than an earnest apology. Honestly, she wasn't sorry at all. That kiss had been four years in the making, and it was utterly spectacular.

"Why did you do that?"

Honesty was out of the question. She searched absently for her purse as she continued mumbling apologies. "I'm sorry. I have to go get the bus. I'm…"

As Beatrice headed for the screen door, Gwen grasped her arm. "Bea, answer me. Why did you do that?"

"I don't know," Beatrice lied. "I guess I got confused. I mean, I don't know. It's just that I'm going to miss our friendship, you know, the way things used to be."

She studied Beatrice for a moment. "Bea, Quentin isn't right about you, is he?"

A wave of heat swept over Beatrice's face that had nothing to do with the weather.

"What are you talking about?"

"Quent told me something on our honeymoon," she said pensively, "and I just couldn't believe it."

Beatrice's heart pounded at the walls of her ribcage. "What did he tell you?"

"That you're…" Gwen's eyes drifted toward the ceiling as she spoke softly. "That you're—oh, I don't know why he even said it."

Beatrice grinned awkwardly as she formulated a denial, one that would sound authentic and not like a random collection of desperate words.

"He's not right, is he?" Gwen's pleading tone cut deeper than the accusation. "He's mistaken, Bea, isn't he?"

Beatrice gritted her teeth to contain her tears, but her eyes pooled anyway. Although she couldn't bring herself to admit it, Gwen was the one person in the world to whom she couldn't sell herself out by making an outright denial.

"I'm gonna miss my bus," she said, and lunged down the porch steps two at a time, striding briskly toward the sidewalk.

"Bea, what the heck is going on with you?" Gwen called from the porch.

Beatrice waved without turning around, her heart still pounding. She finally noticed the patter of Gwen's sandals on the sidewalk as she trotted behind her.

Gwen grabbed at the tail of Beatrice's shirt. "Bea, will you talk to me?"

She stopped and whirled around to Gwen. "About what, whether or not I'm queer? What do you think? "

"You kissed me."

"You kissed me back."

"I know." Gwen said, stuffing her shaking hand into her pocket. "Look, I don't know why I did, but I do know you're my best friend, and I'm going to miss the way things were with us, too." She scanned their surroundings. "We probably shouldn't be talking about this stuff out here for the whole neighborhood to hear."

"So suddenly you do care what the Joneses think." Beatrice shook her head. "There's nothing to talk about."

Gwen stood, confounded into silence.

Beatrice wiped her cheek with the side of her hand.

"None of this matters anyway. I won't be here to talk about it with anyone."

"But for only two years, right?"

"That depends."

"On what?"

"How I feel once I figure out who I'm living my life for."

Beatrice rushed off toward the bus stop, panting in the oppressive heat, unable to look at Gwen even as the fading sound of Gwen's voice called after her. Why did she have to be queer and in love with her best friend? Why couldn't she just be normal like everyone else? Her whole childhood she'd wished for a friend like Gwen, and when she finally got one, she had to ruin everything.

As she boarded the train in New Haven two weeks later, Beatrice still felt guilty for not taking Gwen's phone call in the days after their visit. The curiosity of what Gwen was going to say nagged her, but she simply couldn't bear anymore heart-wrenching exchanges that would only end with the same result. She could barely handle seeing the initial disappointment and fear in Gwen's eyes. Beatrice couldn't face her, especially to say good-bye.

CHAPTER NINE

Beatrice's first year at NYU sailed by without much ado. She appreciated the low-key existence, eluding the disaster of her emotions by immersing herself in her studies: Victorian literature and a minor in the poetry of Emily Dickinson. She'd also taken a job waitressing at a Greenwich Village bistro that allowed her the small pleasure of living a vicarious social life through the conversations of eclectic patrons.

At the start of her second year, however, she brought new meaning to the phrase "giving it the old college try" with one of her professors. Paul Wainwright was thin and lanky with a baby face and shock of blond curly hair. He smoked profusely, wore elbow patches on his corduroy blazers, and, above all, he knew his Dickinson. By his third request to see her privately in his office, it was evident that he was interested in more than just her educational aspirations.

On their first date, she'd discovered Professor Wainwright was unlike any of the boys, few as they were, she'd dated. Paul was a man—confident, worldly, and intelligent. He took her to Ma Rainey's, a soul-food restaurant in Harlem where the smell of fresh corn bread and sounds of Ellington and Holiday enveloped the small space packed tightly with patrons of all backgrounds and an array of African art and architecture.

"This place is fantastic," Beatrice said as she gazed around at the collection of faces both living and artificial.

"Nothing keeps the creative juices flowing like surrounding yourself with culture: people, places, music, and food. They all inspire in their own fascinating ways." He smiled and took a sip of his martini. "Frankly, I've never understood how Dickinson was able to be so prolific while being a shut-in."

"I don't know how she was that prolific at all. I've tried to write like her a million times and failed miserably every time."

"That's your problem right there, Bea. You should be writing like Darby, not Dickinson. You think she tried to be like anyone else?"

Beatrice shrugged and sipped her 7 and 7, an ode to Abby Gill.

"Think of Dickinson's style," he went on. "The dashes, the seemingly random capitalizations—today's critics would eat her alive for that, but those are the most recognizable aspects of her writing."

"She's just marvelous. How anyone could write such a beautiful poem about wind blowing into her room, I'll never know. I keep trying to write poetry, but I'm just not any good at it."

He engaged her with piercing blue eyes as the weight of his full attention fell on her. "All you need to do is discover where your own writing strengths lie. It's in there, Bea. Don't be shy about letting it out."

"I was always good at essays and even short stories, but that was in high school." She hesitated. "I think I'm afraid my writing won't be mature enough now."

"Have you written anything recently?"

"Sort of." She hedged. "It's a really rough draft."

"Why don't you let me read it? I've had several pieces of fiction published. I'd be glad to give you some feedback."

She shrank in her seat. "Oh, I don't think I could. I wouldn't feel comfortable."

He offered an endearing smile and placed his hand on hers.

"I'm an English professor, your professor. If not me, who can you feel comfortable with?"

Beatrice raised an eyebrow. Was he still talking about writing? "It's a work in progress. I'm not ready to share it with anyone yet."

"Well, when you are, you know where to find me."

She took another sip of her drink to mask her awkwardness.

"If I may be so bold, Beatrice, you have the most enchanting eyes. They're blue as a crisp, clear January sky. I find myself getting lost in them every time we speak."

"Thank you," she said softly, grateful for the waitress's timing in bringing their dinners to the table.

"A beautiful, charming intellectual—my, but you are a rare breed." He casually folded his napkin across his lap and raised his martini to her. "I'm honored to share your company."

Beatrice couldn't help but smile.

Later that night, after the date, Beatrice plopped down on her couch, reflecting on how her time with Paul had been the most enjoyable she'd ever spent with a man. Not only did he know everything there was to know about Dickinson, but he actually wanted to hear her ideas about the poet and treated her like a contemporary in their discussions, not merely a student. The pièce de résistance: he bowed and kissed her hand, thanking her for her company after walking her to the door of her apartment building without trying to paw his way in. Was there anything more romantic than that?

After leaving New Haven so unceremoniously the year before, she was optimistic about the idea of moving forward with a mature, sophisticated academic. What would help clear the wreckage she'd left behind better than returning home on the arm of a man like Professor Wainwright? What a relief it would be not to have her mother constantly in her hair about landing a man. She still hadn't warmed to the idea of marriage, but the reprieve this would buy her was priceless—not to mention how far it would take her in restoring her friendship with Gwen since the unfortunate kitchen incident.

Five months into the relationship, Paul was already talking engagement, a conversation Beatrice was quite adept at averting each time it arose. However, it was the conversation that opened the door to a phone call to Gwen.

"Oh, that's so exciting," Gwen said from the other end of the line. Her tone was pleasant enough, but something seemed missing in her delivery. "Have you set a date?"

"No, not yet. I'm still so busy with school," Beatrice said grandly, relishing her first foray into normal girl chitchat. "Of course, you know that's not something one should rush into."

"Well, I'm really happy for you, Bea."

Although their conversation was amiable, bits of uncomfortable silence were the third party. It was Beatrice's turn to speak, but she'd lost herself in Gwen's velvety voice.

"When are you bringing him home so we can meet him?" Gwen asked. "You both have to come to dinner, and I won't take no for an answer."

"I think over spring break."

"Good, good. So how have you been?"

"Very well. I love my classes, and I'm working as a waitress in the cutest little bistro in Greenwich Village. I'm on my feet like crazy, but I do meet lots of interesting characters. How are you?"

"I'll be fine once the morning sickness passes."

The news was a one-two punch and a sucker one at that.

"Morning sickness?"

Gwen hesitated. "Yes, I'm going to have a baby."

"When were you going to tell me?"

"Oh, I was planning to," she said, "and I wanted to, but to be honest, I felt sort of funny about calling you."

"Gwen, I apologized for what happened in your kitchen. I would've hoped that by now, we could let bygones be bygones."

"That's not why I felt funny, Bea. You left here two summers ago acting like you wanted to disown the entire family. I phoned you several times before you went to New York, but you never called me back."

"Twice. You phoned twice."

"What difference does it make if it was twice or a hundred times? You didn't return any of them."

"Given the circumstances, can you blame me?"

Gwen exhaled into the receiver. "I suppose not. Well, anyway, that's all ancient history now. You've got a fiancé so Quentin doesn't have to—" She cut herself short.

"Quentin doesn't what?"

"Never mind, Bea, I'm just babbling. You know how I do that sometimes."

"Mmm. I also know how terrible you are at contrivances. Why don't you spit it out, Gwen?"

She attempted to laugh off Beatrice's suspicion. "This is silly, Bea. It doesn't matter. Let's move forward, not rehash the past."

"That's what I'm trying to do, Gwen, but as we both learned a while ago, keeping secrets in a friendship doesn't work. They only end up coming out in the end—usually badly."

"I don't see any point in going into it, but since you won't let it alone, I think Quentin will be very pleased that you're engaged. He was a little uneasy about us having such a close friendship when he thought—"

"Did you tell him about the kiss?"

"Oh, God, no," Gwen said. "I suppose I should have been honest with him, but oh, it would've only created a problem where there isn't one."

Beatrice let the phone rest on her shoulder for a moment. "I see. So you ignored me and four years of friendship simply because of your idiot husband's prejudices. That's great, Gwen."

"You ignored me first, Bea. I simply took the hint. And please don't call my husband an idiot."

"Oh, my apologies, Mrs. Darby. Tell me, did you bother to stick up for me like that when my idiot brother was filling your head with garbage about me?"

"You're a fine one to be throwing stones."

Beatrice curled the phone cord around her fingers, trying to keep her composure. "This is exactly what I was afraid of—I knew you weren't over what happened."

Gwen breathed quietly into the receiver. "What do you want from me, Bea? I have to consider my husband's feelings about things and respect his wishes. We wouldn't even be in this predicament if you hadn't kissed me."

Shame crawled up from Beatrice's core as she recalled that pivotal moment during that sticky, airless afternoon in Gwen's kitchen.

"Congratulations on the baby, Gwen. Please let me know when it's born."

Beatrice hung up the phone, disheartened. That was the phone call that was supposed to patch things up between them, but the truths they confronted only deepened the chasm.

When Paul arrived at her apartment later that evening, her despair still lingered. She'd contemplated cancelling with him, but he sounded particularly excited about their date on the phone, so she trudged on like a trooper.

"I have a surprise for you, my love," he said, and whipped out a bouquet of roses from behind his back.

"They're beautiful, Paul," she said, mustering a store of enthusiasm. "Thank you."

She wandered over to the sink in her tiny kitchenette and began arranging them in a large pitcher.

"Don't fuss with those now. We have to get to the theater."

"The theater?"

"Sure, doll, that's the surprise—orchestra seats for *How to Succeed in Business without Really Trying.*"

That brought a smile to her face, her first real Broadway show. "Oh, Paul."

"Well, don't I even get a kiss?" He held his arms open for her, and she walked into them. "Are you excited?"

"Oh, yes." She nodded against his shoulder. Locked in his embrace, she let thoughts of Gwen flutter through her mind but quickly ushered them away with a squeeze of her boyfriend's arms.

❖

After the play, Paul walked Beatrice to her apartment door, whistling the tune from "Happy to Keep His Dinner Warm."

She jerked his arm off her shoulder. "That's an awful song."

He grinned. "What's so awful about it?"

"If I spent all afternoon cooking dinner for someone, I wouldn't be happy if he showed up late for it. I'd be furious."

He laughed. "I'll make damn sure that when you do cook for me, I won't be late." He eyed her curiously. "By the way, do you even know how to cook?"

"Sure I do. I just don't particularly enjoy doing it."

"Then we'll have to give you a break a few times a week and have the maid cook."

He smiled and settled against the door, making it difficult for her to make her usual Houdini-like escape into the apartment.

Paul had recently begun making regular allusions to their future married life together, and each one wound her up tighter than a chorus boy's trousers. She'd never said yes to him and began to resent his cavalier attitude and presumption that their marriage was inevitable.

"I had a swell time, Paul. Thank you so much." She tossed her house key up and down in her hand for him to notice.

"I did, too," he said, snatching the key in mid-air. "I wish this night didn't have to end. I mean, it's still early."

"It's eleven thirty." She eyed the key ring, now a hostage in his hand.

"But it's Saturday night. Don't tell me you're tired again."

"Work and school keep me very busy."

"You need to start taking vitamins." A hint of frustration seasoned his voice.

"Well, maybe you can come in for a cup of tea."

A crooked smile brightened his face. "I'd love one," he said as he quickly unlocked her door.

"I have to get up and get started on a paper early tomorrow morning," she said as she headed toward the kitchen. "I have to work at the bistro in the afternoon."

"Oh, well, if it's a paper for my class, I think I can give you an extension," he said playfully.

She rolled her eyes as she listened to the hiss of the gas burner warming the teakettle. "It's not," she said flatly. "And Millhouse isn't the kind of professor who seems too keen on doing favors."

"Very true, but you know, I have solid relationships with all my colleagues. I'd be glad to put in a good word for you with old Millhouse if necessary."

The suggestion bugged her. "I'm sure it won't be necessary, Paul," she shouted over the whistling teakettle. "I'm capable of meeting all my obligations in a timely manner."

"Oh, of course. I didn't mean to imply…"

She carried both cups of steeping tea over to her sofa where Paul had already made himself at home. He took them from her and placed them on the coffee table, barely giving her rear end time to make a safe landing on the cushions before he began kissing her, passionately, as if knowing his big chance was now or never. He began caressing her arm and side, slowly making his way up to her breast, where she arrested his fingers after they gave her a squeeze.

"Come on, Bea. Don't you think it's time you let me touch you?" he whispered.

"It's too soon," she said. "I know what you'll think of me if I let you."

"I'll think you feel the same way for me I feel for you. I love you, Bea."

"I love you, too, Paul, but I'm not ready."

"How much longer do you think you can use that excuse? You're not a child," he said, kissing her neck. "You're a woman, a beautiful, sensual woman, and you drive me absolutely wild."

"If I give in, you'll lose respect for me."

"Nonsense. That's nothing more than an antiquated convention."

"What do you mean?"

"The notion that a woman who desires sex is unworthy of respect. I'd like to think that the woman I'm making love to is enjoying the physical sensation as much as I am."

"But girls with self-respect wait till they're married."

"Look, Bea, forget the propaganda your mother taught you," he said, marking her forehead and cheeks with kisses. "We're both adults, we're in love, and we're going to be married one day. That's all that matters. I promise I'll still respect you in the morning."

Beatrice tensed even more as images of Gwen flashed in her mind. As Paul kissed her lips, neck, and shoulders, she recalled her fleeting kiss with Gwen in the kitchen and how exquisite it had felt. Paul was handsome and gentle, yet kissing him didn't feel the same.

"Let's go get in your bed, baby," he whispered.

She wondered if Gwen was making love with Quentin at that same moment and was overcome with deep sadness.

"No, right here," she said, holding on to him loosely.

She tried to relax as his excitement imposed on her pelvis and his hands slipped under her blouse. With her eyes scrunched shut, she allowed his hands free range of her body but closed her legs as his fingers hovered toward her underpants. As he began working the waistband down, tears dripped from the corner of her eye and down her temples.

"You have to relax, baby. You're too rigid," he said after she whimpered in discomfort.

"It hurts," she whispered.

"It'll be a little uncomfortable, but I'll go easy, I promise."

As much as Paul did his best to go easy, Beatrice lay shaking for a long while after it was over. How could anyone consider that making love? It was more than a little uncomfortable physically, but the whole experience left her feeling dirtier than when she fantasized about girls. Thankfully, Paul was happy to lie there and hold her until she calmed down.

"We should've given you a few cocktails first," he whispered after a while.

"Now you think of it," she said.

"We better get up and clean off your couch before it stains," he said. "Looks like there's a little spot of blood."

"I have to go to the bathroom," she said, too queasy to examine the evidence.

After locking the door, she started the shower, covered her face with a hand towel, and let her sobs flow.

Saturday night at the Bleecker Street Bistro a few weeks later, Beatrice was occupied managing her busy section of hungry patrons. Her tactic of taking on all the weekend shifts she could scrounge to avoid being alone with Paul had backfired in grand fashion. There he sat at his corner table in Beatrice's section, on his third cup of espresso, grading a ruffled stack of student papers while waiting for her shift to end so he could escort her home.

Biting her lip to contain her frustration, she tightened her ponytail and went over to refill his water glass.

"Paul, there's no need for you to hang out here all night. Wouldn't you be much more comfortable doing that at home?"

"Nonsense. Chivalry is not dead, my dear," he said with a smile.

She felt a pang of guilt. Why was everything he said and did chafing her nerves? All he wanted was to ensure she got home safely from work. Oh, that's right, and to get under her skirt.

She huffed without meaning to. "I appreciate that, but I won't be alone. Ricky lives right around the corner, and we get off at the same time."

Paul raised an eyebrow playfully. "I can't risk losing you to Ricky, the lecherous dishwasher."

She grimaced detecting a note of condescension. "He's a nice boy and my friend."

"Nice boys and beautiful girls are a dangerous combination. I ought to know—I'm a nice boy, too." He winked as he reached for the last paper in the stack.

Beatrice shook her head and went into the kitchen to pick up an order. On her way out, the woman sitting alone in her section stopped her.

"Hey, honey, I'm getting lonely over here. And dry." She smirked and tapped an empty water glass.

"Be right there," Beatrice said.

"That's what you said twenty minutes ago," the woman said in a teasing manner.

Beatrice returned with a water pitcher, her mood suddenly brighter. "I might have to start charging you rent at this table."

"They charge enough for their fettuccini," the woman said, adding with a flirtatious grin, "but I do happen to like the help."

Beatrice blushed. "Another highball?"

"Yes, please." The woman raised her eyebrows. "You don't recognize me, do you?"

As soon as the woman said it, she realized this gruff yet likable character was familiar. Her hair was longer and darker, but the resemblance struck her.

"Donna."

"That's right. Nice to see you again, Beatrice."

Beatrice nodded, glancing toward Paul, dying to ask about Abby. "You, too."

Donna flicked her head in Paul's direction. "That your boyfriend?"

She nodded again, peering down at her shoes in defeat.

"Cute," Donna said, still studying him. "A little manly for my taste, but I suppose you could do worse. How'd you end up working here? It's quite a commute from New Haven."

"I'm getting my MA at NYU."

"That's an impressive bunch of initials. What are you studying?"

"English literature. So how is Abby?" Beatrice replied, surprising them both with the suddenness of the question.

Donna smiled knowingly. "Abby's good. She's head librarian up at Columbia University. You ever get up that way?"

"No," Beatrice said softly as she glanced toward Paul and the kitchen. "Uh, my boyfriend lives a few blocks away, but I use NYU's library."

"Well, I'm sure you have to get back to work, but if you ever have time for a cup of joe, I'd love to hear about how you ended up with a boyfriend."

Beatrice cringed, familiar with being the butt of someone's joke, but no longer the shrinking violet, she stared Donna down. "I don't think that's funny."

"It wasn't meant to be." Donna glanced at her check as she pulled crisp bills from her wallet and looked up with sincerity. "If you ever want to talk, I'm around."

Beatrice smiled as she smoothed down her bunched-up uniform. "When you see Abby, please tell her I said hello."

Donna nodded. "I will."

Her encounter with Donna left her nerves feeling more like live wires. Smiles blossomed randomly at the thought of Abby joining Donna the next time she came into the bistro and the warm embrace they might exchange. Had Abby thought of her over the years the way she had, occasionally yet always by surprise prompted by a familiar song, a scent, or a subway ad in which a carefree, long-fingered woman smiled broadly holding her tasty cigarette. Probably not. Abby was Beatrice's first love, so it was natural that she would. A girl never forgets her first love. But had Beatrice meant anything at all to

Abby? Recalling that unforgettable night in Pixie's when they kissed, she indulged the hope that for at least one moment in time she had.

"Hey, Bea, can I get another glass of Chablis?" Paul asked, engrossed in Ellison's *Invisible Man*.

Beatrice nodded as she strode past him, annoyed that his presence had so impolitely intruded on her daydream. She also resented his recent habit of not even looking at her when making his requests at the restaurant. When she brought him a new glass, her hand shook at the temptation to empty it in his lap.

"Thank you, my love." His innocuous smile made her dislike herself.

"I'm going to help with inventory tonight," she said. "I could use the extra money."

"That's okay. I don't mind waiting. Ellison is fascinating."

"It could take hours after my shift, Paul," she said in a huff. "I don't want you waiting here all that time."

He looked up in surprise. "As I've said before, I don't want you walking home alone."

"I won't be alone. I'll either get a cab or walk home with Ricky."

"Very well. Tell me what time, and I'll come back for you."

She groaned at his insistence. Who was he to order her around like that? He wasn't her father or her husband.

"No, Paul, I don't want to argue about this anymore. I can take care of myself."

She hurried into the kitchen, exhilarated by her immergence of backbone.

"What's going on out there?" Ricky asked. "You look like you just witnessed the Hindenburg disaster."

Ricky always made her smile with his kooky comments.

"I kind of feel like I did."

"Hang in there. It's almost closing time."

He aimed the hanging nozzle at her and shot her with a spritz of cold water. She screeched happily as she grabbed a tray of desserts.

After serving a young couple a strawberry cheesecake that they fed each other, she rolled her eyes as she scurried off. How corny. Weren't they a little old for such public exhibitions? She then noticed

Paul was gone. Under the stem of his wineglass, she found her tip and a note scrawled on a folded piece of loose-leaf paper.

Forgive my infringement on your independence, my love. Call me in the morning.
Yours, Paul.

Even his understanding nature got under her skin. Why couldn't he have the decency to be a bastard about it so she wouldn't have to feel so guilty?

At the end of her shift, Beatrice went into the kitchen, ready to help with inventory.

"Say, Bea, Mr. Francois is postponing inventory until Monday. How about coming out with me for a drink?"

She regarded Ricky with surprise. He was about four inches shorter than her and, worst of all, Puerto Rican, not that his ethnicity mattered at all to her. She was merely anticipating her mother's massive stroke at her bringing home some dishwasher—and a brown one at that.

"Ricky, I have a boyfriend."

"I know that," he whispered. "With any luck, soon I'll have one, too."

She could feel her eyebrows shoot to the ceiling.

"You're not surprised, are you?"

Beatrice smiled. "I suppose I shouldn't be." She'd always felt an affinity for Ricky. Now she knew why. "Where are you going for that drink?"

"Dandy's over on Christopher Street. Care to join me?"

"Is that a homosexual bar?" she asked in a scarcely audible whisper.

"Hmm," he said with a sneer. "It used to be mostly boys until the lesbos started infesting the place. But we all play nice for the most part. What do you say?"

She blinked away the kaleidoscope of faces—Paul's, Donna's, Abby's—swirling in her mind. The night had been a conflagration of emotion, and by that hour she was simply tired of thinking and feeling.

"Okay, I'll go," she said with tempered enthusiasm. "But I'm not a lesbo."

He studied her for a moment. "You're not afraid, are you?"

"Afraid? Of course not."

He nodded knowingly. "No one's going think you're a dyke. You're too girly."

The word was familiar. "Dyke?"

"You know, a butch," he said, then added for clarification, "a female homosexual that looks like a boy."

Beatrice eagerly absorbed the lesson. "So lesbians are the ones that don't look like boys?"

Ricky glanced over his shoulder as their coworkers filed in to start punching out their time cards.

"I don't know. I guess. Why don't you ask one at the bar?" He gave her a playful grin.

❖

Beatrice stopped on the sidewalk outside Dandy's, tugging Ricky's jacket sleeve. "I don't know about this. What if someone sees me in here?" She shifted her body toward the building away from the leering faces going by in taxis and on foot.

"Honey, there's sort of a code of ethics in these places. Once you're on the inside, if you don't recognize them, they won't recognize you."

She looked at him skeptically.

"Come on, Bea. You're safe inside. It's loitering out front like this that puts a target on your forehead."

He dragged open the door with one arm and yanked her after him with the other.

Beatrice glanced over her shoulders and all around the neighborhood bar packed with people milling in a haze of smoke. Although she'd witnessed women huddled so intimately before at Pixie's, it still felt as though she'd stepped through the looking glass. She stumbled into Ricky when she saw two men slow dancing.

"What the hell, Bea?" he shouted at her.

"I'm sorry, but look at those men cuddling. That one playing the girl looks like a longshoreman."

Ricky shook his head. "No one plays the girl, Bea. Get with it."

"I knew that," she said, snotty enough to dismiss the slightest hint of embarrassment. She regrouped, reminding herself why she was there—to have a drink with Ricky, one drink to relax without having to fend off the advances of horny college men, students and faculty alike.

Sneaking into Pixie's when she was a teenager was one thing, but being seen going into a gay bar now could have serious consequences. She would be graduating soon and beginning her search for a teaching position. What if the wrong person saw her in here? She could end up getting canned like Abby Gill and her high-school gym teacher before she was even hired. But as nervous as she was, Beatrice savored the placid sense of belonging as she followed Ricky to the bar.

"You're not going to be clinging to the back of my shirt all night, are you?" he asked. "They don't bite, you know. We homosexuals are very nice, docile people by nature."

"You don't have to pander to me, Ricky. I knew some homosexuals before I met you."

"Really? You have a secret past?" He sat on a barstool and signaled the bartender. "Suddenly, you're a lot more interesting than I thought."

"I'll have a Schlitz," Beatrice said.

"That's all you have to say for yourself, 'I'll have a Schlitz?' Start talking, sister."

Beatrice folded her arms across her chest like a plate of armor. Ricky was trying to get her to expose her secret, and she didn't like it one bit. Abby and Donna were the only ones who knew for sure, and she wasn't too keen on adding anybody else to the list. Sure, she'd known Ricky for about a year, but what if he opened his mouth and blabbed to everyone? What if he told their boss and Paul somehow found out? The fallout would be devastating. Paul would tell everyone at the university. She'd be expelled, and then nobody would hire her to teach.

"I just knew a woman—I used to work with her in New Haven. She was nice."

Ricky's knowing expression unsettled her. "It's okay, Trixie. Don't sweat it. I get it."

She propped her hands on her hips. "What do you get?"

"You want to keep it in the closet. I understand. You have a lot more to lose than some swishy little Puerto Rican kitchen worker like me. But I really thought we were friends."

"Of course, we're friends. But I'm not a lesbian. I have a boyfriend."

"You see that guy over there with the beard?" He pointed to a man at the end of the bar having a martini with a group of young leather- or denim-clad ruffians. "He's married."

"To a woman?"

"Who else would he be married to?" Ricky wrapped his small fingers around hers. "Look, if you don't want to talk about it, I won't pester you. I want you to know I'm a loyal friend, and if you want to tell me anything, I'll keep it in the strictest confidence."

She squeezed his hand in return, her eyes watering as she sipped her beer.

"Listen, you'll be okay if I take a walk around alone?"

She nodded and took a larger swig from her glass. "Good luck."

"You too," he said over his shoulder with a wink.

She grew restless sitting stock-still at the bar for nearly an hour as Ricky danced and socialized with numerous men. Clutching her third glass of beer and fondling peanuts in a bowl, she tried to stop staring at everyone. They seemed so free and at ease, like guests at a masquerade ball uninhibited in the anonymity of their disguises. How did they manage that? Didn't they have jobs, the fear of God? Or mothers?

"Are you gonna eat those or just play with them?" A woman sat beside her and gave her a playful smile.

"I guess I have to eat them now since I contaminated them." She piled a handful onto a napkin.

"So what's her name, if you don't mind me asking?"

"Huh? Who?" Beatrice asked, munching the peanuts.

"The girl that's doing this to you," the woman said, rubbing a rose tattoo on the outside of her bicep.

Beatrice cocked her head with a wry smile. "I have a boyfriend."

"Ah, that was my second guess. My name is Judy." She held out her hand.

"Beatrice."

She shook the woman's hand, captivated by her Rita Hayworth smile. Judy might have looked like a "butch," as Ricky would say, but those lips were uncompromisingly feminine.

"Does your boyfriend know where you are now, Beatrice?"

"My hope is that nobody knows where I am right now."

"I'll drink to that," Judy said, tapping her beer bottle into Beatrice's glass. "Is this your first time here?"

Beatrice nodded.

"Can I buy you your next drink?"

"I've already had three. I should slow down."

"What fun is that? When we slow down, we die. Maybe I can interest you in a dance?"

Beatrice's heart began to pound. She was sure the beers were getting to her when she almost said yes. Instead, she blurted, "I don't dance."

"Me neither, but I figured when in Rome." Judy offered a pack of cigarettes. "Smoke?"

Beatrice grinned, drawn into the flirtation. "Don't smoke either."

Judy lit a cigarette and exhaled a billow of smoke. "Don't dance, don't smoke. What do you do, Beatrice?"

"I think. I think an awful lot—sometimes too much."

"You never just let down that beautiful hair and act on impulse?"

"Yeah, I've done that a few times, too. But I've learned from my mistakes."

"For me, making mistakes is when I'm having the most fun—especially if they're made with the right person."

Beatrice's face grew warm. Judy's eyes were boring into hers. Straining to hear, she and Judy moved closer as they chatted. Seemingly out of nowhere, another beer slid before her.

"In case you get thirsty," Judy said, her lips touching Beatrice's ear.

Beatrice grabbed the fresh beer and displayed it like a prize on a game show. "Here's one thing I do." She grinned as she gulped it down, beginning to understand how everyone seemed so free.

Judy laced her arm through Beatrice's, and they clumsily drank. "You're adorable, you know that?"

Beatrice smirked. "No, I didn't know that, but thank you."

"Doesn't your boyfriend tell you?"

"Who cares?" she said in a drunken whisper.

At that, they broke into giggles, teetering on the bar stools, falling into each other.

Judy rested her hand on Beatrice's knee. "What do you say we get out of here?"

Although Beatrice was attracted to Judy, leaving the bar with her would be taking it to a dangerous level. Not that Judy was a dangerous woman, but Beatrice felt too willing to go with her.

"I don't think so," Beatrice said. "I actually came here with my friend, Ricky. I should go look for him." She stood and needed a moment to secure her land legs.

"Easy, girl." Judy braced her until she was steady. "Can I call you some time?"

"I don't know about that," Beatrice slurred. "I have a boyfriend."

"You said that before." Judy lightly rubbed Beatrice's back.

"But this time I mean it." Straining against the urge to kiss Judy, she shuffled through the crowd toward the ladies' room before she fell victim to her impulses, as she had so infamously done in the past. Ricky was nowhere to be found.

Inside the bathroom stall, Beatrice sucked in a deep breath, her heart still pounding. Judy was very attractive, but kissing those luscious lips would be a mistake. She was with Paul and at the moment was rather tipsy. Retreating to the ladies' room had been a smart move.

"Everything all right, Beatrice?" Judy's voice echoed off the tile.

Beatrice opened the stall door and found Judy blocking her path to the sink. "Yeah, everything's fine."

Judy pushed her inside the stall and shut the door. She trapped Beatrice against the wall and began kissing her. The thought of resisting might have occurred to Beatrice, but by that point, her hormones were taking charge of the situation. Judy's lips were soft and moist, a tangy residue of beer on her tongue as she flicked it around Beatrice's. Judy's hands touched, squeezed, and caressed her all over. In all the time she'd been dating Paul, her body had never responded like this in any situation. She could deny who she was to other people all she wanted, but not to herself. Suddenly, nothing else mattered as she threw her arms around Judy's neck, allowing the exquisite physical abandon to wash over her. When Judy reached under Beatrice's work skirt, it happened before she had a chance to stop it—not that she wanted to.

"Let's go have some privacy," Judy whispered in her ear. "My apartment's down the street."

Still shuddering and now enveloped in shame, she gently pushed Judy's hands off her. "I'm sorry, Judy. I can't," she said, looking down. "I'm sorry about all this."

"What are you sorry for?" Judy picked up Beatrice's chin. "Was this your first time?"

Beatrice nodded. Her beer buzz completely evaporated, she felt claustrophobic in the tight stall. "I'm sorry. I really have to go."

Judy attempted to kiss her, but Beatrice shoved past her. "Beatrice, wait. Why don't you calm down for a minute before you leave?"

But she was already out the door, sprinting down the sidewalk to her Irving Place apartment, the crisp night air never touching her skin. She slammed the door shut, fastened the deadbolt, and collapsed facedown in a pillow on her sofa. It was well after two a.m., and sleep couldn't have been further from her mind. As queasy as she felt, she didn't have the need to run into the shower and wash herself clean like she had after being with Paul. Her head was pulsating, her body still trembling as she came down from the adrenaline rush. She revisited the encounter now that she was safe at home. How could she enjoy an intimate experience like that with a stranger more than with her own boyfriend? The answer had been right in front of her. Judy was the final piece of the puzzle.

CHAPTER TEN

The next morning Beatrice was on the telephone with Ricky as soon as she got home from Sunday mass at Saint Patrick's cathedral. She had gone in there numerous times since moving to New York, mostly for the love of its hallowed silence and architectural brilliance, but that morning a different need had impelled her.

"You went to mass?" Ricky asked. "Wait one doggone minute. What happened last night?"

Beatrice attempted to laugh off his insinuation. "What do you mean? What's so unusual about a Catholic going to Sunday mass?"

"You and I have discussed our Catholicism before. Come on, Trix, spill the beans. You left without saying good-bye last night. Did you leave with someone, you lucky dog?"

She wanted desperately to confess her powder-room rendezvous in some vain hope that it might ease the burden of shame, but it was so hard to utter the words. Secrecy was an issue of concern, but Ricky had more or less proved that once classified information was deposited in his ear, his lips sealed like a bank vault. No, the roots of her reticence went much deeper. There was permanence in a confession, some part of herself she would lose. Once she revealed the truth in her own words, her own voice, she wouldn't be able to reclaim it.

"Hello?" he said. "Should I take your silence as an admission of guilt?"

"Oh, Ricky, do you swear you can keep a secret?"

"My whole life is a secret—of course I can. I'd pinky swear if we weren't on the phone, swear it in blood."

She exhaled deeply into the receiver and watched her fingers quiver. "I did something awful last night."

Ricky's brief pause startled her. "How exciting," he finally breathed. "What? What?"

"Oh, God, I can't even say it out loud."

"Look, honey, we're on the phone. You can't act it out in sock puppets."

"I don't know, Ricky. I have so much to lose."

"We all do, Bea, but you have to be able to trust someone. You'll go crazy if you don't."

As she processed his words, she glanced up at the small wooden crucifix nailed to the wall above her kitchen archway. Her mother had given it to her when she moved in, warning that if she didn't display it somewhere in her apartment, a world of untold misfortune would befall her.

"I suppose you're right."

"It's your dime," Ricky said impatiently.

"I had an encounter last night," she whispered.

"I knew it."

"How on earth could you have possibly known it? You disappeared."

"You're fresh meat, Bea, gorgeous meat at that. It was bound to happen. Your place or hers?"

"Oh, Ricky, that's what makes it even more awful. It wasn't at anyone's place. It was in the ladies' room." She made a distressed gurgling sound. "In a stall."

Ricky chuckled. "Did you enjoy it?"

"Yes," she replied, still distressed.

"Welcome to the club, Beatrice Darby."

"What, the pervert club? Ricky, what does this mean? I'm a lesbian, aren't I," she declared more than asked, whispering as though Hoover had a tap on her telephone.

"Seems that way to me. Think about it. You once described sex with your own boyfriend as feeling like having a primate on top of you, yet you enjoyed anonymous sex in a bathroom with a woman you just met."

"It wasn't anonymous," she protested. "I knew her name."

"Her last name?"

"Oh, my God, Ricky." She wound the telephone cord around her finger until it pulsed purple. "I am a pervert, just like they say. Decent girls don't do things like that. I mean, I didn't even resist when she made her move."

"Because it's something you've wanted for a long time and probably never thought you'd get. Look, you can cry about it all you want, but this is life."

"This is really what it's like to live a homosexual lifestyle?"

"Not always. Not if you can meet someone," he said, pausing as though searching for his own reassurance. "But sometimes it's the best we can do. They don't make it easy for us. I mean you either do what society expects you to or be who you are. You don't get to do both. Personally, I choose to be Ricky Rodriquez, flaming homosexual."

"I don't want to be a deviant or any of those other terrible things they call homosexuals. I just want to be me."

"If this is you, Beatrice Darby, I think you're nothing short of fabulous."

Beatrice sank into a chair at her kitchen table. "Ricky," she whispered. Tears flowed from the release in sharing with someone who truly understood.

❖

Beatrice and Paul's evening of soul food and poetry readings at a supper club in Harlem had ended too early for her to sneak away without a well-planned excuse. She usually hovered in a state of agitation whenever she went out with Paul, but this night her anxiety was higher than normal after her recent conversation with Ricky. Plus, it was their six-month anniversary. Excuse-making on anniversaries was at best in poor taste. One of her mother's famous quotes, never refuse your husband, haunted her all evening to the point that she couldn't remember any of the memorable poems they'd heard. Although they weren't even engaged, the same pressure still applied.

As she followed him into his apartment, the pungent scent of stale marijuana resin assaulted her nostrils.

"Have a seat, baby doll." He winked and extended his arm in a flourish toward the musty royal-blue velour sofa.

So anxious from anticipation, she resorted to her usual plan of faking yawns. "Oh, I could drop my head on my pillow right now and sleep till noon."

"That sounds like a fantastic idea," he said, approaching with two glasses of brandy. "That is after I make love to my beautiful girl on our anniversary." He leaned against the sofa pillows after handing her the brandy, which she guzzled like a shot. "Take it easy." He laughed as he gently kissed her neck. "You'll be out cold before I even get you out of your panties."

"Paul, don't talk like that. It's lewd."

"I'm sorry, baby. Just a little joke. I can't help it that you drive me to distraction."

Her shoulder muscles stiffened as the brandy burned her stomach. It was a futile situation really: either she submitted to his wishes against her own or refused and risked upsetting him.

"Paul, I'm really tired. Do you think we can just watch a little TV, and then you can take me home?"

"Take you home? Bea, it's our anniversary. Wouldn't you like to spend some time together and then wake up in my arms in the morning? I want to show you how much I love you."

She took his hand and held it when it started making its way across her breast. "Oh, Paul, you show me you love me all the time—like tonight. You bought me a lovely dinner and cocktails at the club."

"Yes, but darling, this is the best part." He tried kissing her lips, but she gave him her cheek.

"Paul, I told you I'm worried about getting pregnant."

"And I told you, I use protection. Don't worry about anything. All you have to do is lie back, relax, and enjoy it."

Beatrice's stomach tightened in dread. They'd made love several times since that dreadful first time in her apartment. She hadn't found it pleasurable then or on any occasion thereafter. For a while, she'd wondered what was wrong with her. Why didn't she enjoy it the way Paul did? At least she assumed he did. He sounded more like someone pushing a piano uphill by himself, but afterward he always seemed happy. She once overheard two girls talking enthusiastically about sex at the campus coffee shop but couldn't imagine what all the fuss was about—until Judy and the bar bathroom. She cringed at their animalistic behavior in the dingy stall, yet she couldn't stop replaying the encounter all week.

"Atta girl," he said, reaching behind her to unclasp her bra.

"No, Paul. I can't." She pushed at his chest to make him stop.

"Aw, do we have to go through this shy-girl routine every time I want to be with you? It's better when you relax and let it happen. How about some reefer?"

"No, I want to go home." Her eyes began filling with tears.

"What's the matter? Don't you feel well?"

She was tempted to grab his convenient excuse and run with it, blaming the collard greens at Ma Rainey's, but she realized that she simply couldn't go through with this act anymore.

"That's not it, Paul."

"*Paul*," he repeated. "Why don't you ever call me dear or sweetheart or anything? You sound so formal every time you say my name."

She hesitated, stared at the floor as his fingers laced between hers.

"Bea, what is it?" he asked gently.

"I'm sorry, Paul, but…"

"But what?"

"I don't think I want to see you anymore."

He unlaced his fingers and moved away from her on the couch as though she'd informed him she had a communicable disease.

"What are you talking about? Where did this come from?"

Despite the confidence in her feelings, this obscure, lingering sense of obligation to him, or to social conformity, held the words at bay until she finally forced them out.

"I don't want to marry you."

His eyes smiled with relief. "Is that all? All right, you don't want to talk about marriage. Then we won't discuss it until you're ready."

She summoned the courage to look him in the eye. "That's the thing, Paul. I don't know if I'll ever be ready."

"Isn't that a little extreme? Okay, so you're not ready now—understandable. You haven't even finished your degree yet. We'll put it on the shelf for a while and just focus on dating."

"You don't understand. That's not the life I want for myself."

He sloped forward, elbows on his knees, fingering the scruff on his chin. "Does this have anything to do with that woman, Donna, who came to the bistro?"

"What do you mean?"

"Well, obviously, she plays for the other team. Has she tried to influence you?"

A rush of indignation flooded in. "Oh, I get it. If she's a lesbian, she must be some sick predator trying to sink her claws into my young, innocent flesh, is that it? And I'm too stupid to figure it out."

"Christ, Bea, that's not what I meant at all." Hurt flickered in his boyish eyes. "All I meant was if you were questioning something in yourself, now would be the right time to explore it."

His sympathy stripped her anger down to self-consciousness. "Why do you think I'm questioning myself? What makes you say that?"

"Nothing, other than your vigorous opposition to the mere idea of marriage. And let's face it; you're not exactly warm toward me."

A quiet rage boiled below the surface. How she despised when people attempted to expose her, intentionally or otherwise. She was about to lash into him until she remembered the implication in Queen Gertrude's line from *Hamlet* about how the lady doth protest too much. She relaxed her rigid posture and softened her tone.

"I just don't think I'm good with relationships."

He scratched at his stubbly chin for a moment. "Perhaps an experience with a woman might clear up the confusion, show you which side your bread is really buttered on. Maybe we can arrange something together, so you'll feel more comfortable."

Beatrice was aghast at the suggestion—if he was, in fact, suggesting what she thought he was.

"Why are you looking at me like that?" he asked. "This is city life, Bea. The enlightened and the urbane aren't hung up on ideology and tradition that preclude us from exploring the beauty of what the natural world has to offer."

Beatrice sat quietly for a moment, absorbing his strange idea. She wanted to be urbane and enlightened, but if that was the way one became those things, she'd stick to being awkward and artless.

"If you're up for giving it a try," he said, "I'd prefer to find someone more feminine than Donna."

She studied him as though he were an alien life form. "I think I'm gonna stick with my original plan of breaking up with you."

Suddenly, she felt like the alien. As he regarded her in icy silence, she glanced around at the untidy bachelor pad, praying he'd hurry up and snap out of it so he could take her home.

After a moment, he let go a gust of breath and gazed straight ahead. "I can't believe you're serious about this."

"I'm sorry, Paul." The words fell out automatically, but in a way she was sorry. He was a decent man and probably would have made a good husband.

"Could you just…could you not say my name."

"I should go."

Beatrice got up and shuffled to the door, hoping his famous chivalry would kick in after all this, and he'd offer to escort her to the subway entrance at this late hour. No such luck.

Beatrice navigated the desolate streets to the number-four subway entrance alone. While breaking up with Paul felt like breaking free from invisible tethers, she couldn't help but wonder if Frost ever considered the isolation and fear of the unknown one encountered while wandering down that road less traveled.

❖

The trip home to New Haven for moral support and to regain some sense of normalcy turned out to be a huge miscalculation on Beatrice's part. She sat at the table with her chin resting on her knuckles as her mother ladled more split-pea soup into her bowl.

"I can't understand why Paul would break up with you." Her mother sat down next to her and watched her eat. "What did you do?"

Beatrice ignored the insinuation that was typically her mother. "I'm sure I didn't do anything other than be myself. Maybe I wasn't pretty enough or smart enough for him. He's a professor, you know."

"Oh, that's nonsense, Bea. There isn't a man in the world you're not pretty enough for."

Although Beatrice loathed the dishonesty, subterfuge was necessary to avoid the five-alarm lecture that would have ensued had she informed her mother she'd ended things with Paul.

She shrugged. "I think maybe he just wants to play the field."

Her mother nodded knowingly. "Well, if he wouldn't wait for sexual relations with you until you two were married, then good riddance. There's nothing I dislike more than low moral character."

Beatrice shook away a dark, steamy flashback of Judy and the bathroom stall. "You're so right, Mom."

"Are you going to see Gwen and Quentin today?"

"I don't think so. I'm only here for the day, and I'm sure they're busy."

"Why are you assuming? I'm sure Gwen would love to see you. She's just the loveliest pregnant woman I have ever seen."

Beatrice rolled her eyes.

"Did you even call and ask if she's free?" Her mother reached for the phone.

"No, don't," Beatrice blurted. "I, uh, I figured it would be nice if you and I could spend the day together, you know, shopping or something."

What the hell—what was one more lie?

Her mother clutched her hand to her chest. "Oh, Beatrice, you've never said you wanted to spend time with just me."

Beatrice was amazed at the depths to which a desperate person could sink. "Well, then it's long overdue." She forced a charming smile.

Her mother beamed. "Finish your soup, darling. Then we'll go downtown and look for a nice new dress for you." She began poking at her upswept hair in the hallway mirror. "Oh, I know. We'll call Mrs. Swanson and ask her to join us. Her son, Eric, recently passed the bar, and he's still single—but not for long you can bet."

"Mom, we just got through saying we'd spend the day together, just the two of us. Why would you call Mrs. Swanson?"

"Eric Swanson, a handsome, single lawyer, that's why."

Beatrice rose and took her bowl to the sink. "Then you and Mrs. Swanson can go shopping together. I'll head back to the city now."

"For heaven's sake, Bea, there's no need to get testy."

"I've good reason to be testy, Mother. I'm not here for matchmaking. Don't you think I'd like some time to get over my broken heart from Paul?"

Borrowing from her mother's playbook, Beatrice saw no reason not to run this Paul thing into the ground.

"I'm sorry, dear. I suppose that was rather insensitive."

Beatrice hoisted herself onto the counter, letting her feet dangle against the cabinets. "Are you proud of me?" The question took them both by surprise.

Mrs. Darby moved away from the mirror and poked her head around the corner. "What kind of question is that?"

"A simple one—at least I thought it was."

"Would you get down from there?"

"Can you just answer me?" Beatrice said before sliding off.

"Of course I am. You've stayed out of trouble, you're studious, and best of all, someday, you're going to make me a proud grandmother."

"I stay out of trouble." Beatrice pondered the statement. "That's my greatest achievement in your eyes?"

"It's nothing to sneeze at, Bea. A girl getting pregnant out of wedlock is a terrible thing. Oh, the shame it brings on the family. Things like that always get out, and no matter what the circumstances, it always reflects on the mother. How could I show my face in church or anywhere else in town after that?"

"How does having a daughter at New York University reflect on you?"

"Oh, it's a wonderful accomplishment, Bea, but like I've said before, once you marry and start a family, it won't matter." She smiled broadly. "I can hardly wait till you make me a grandmother."

"Gwen's going to make you a grandmother this summer."

"I know that, but it's different when your own daughter has a child. Gwen has a mother who'll probably be there during those first few weeks. I'd just be in the way."

"I wouldn't hold your breath waiting for me."

"Now don't be discouraged because things didn't pan out with Paul. Mr. Right is out there—you'll see."

Beatrice could almost feel her fingers wrapping around her mother's neck. "Mom, can we please drop this subject and go shopping?"

"If you insist, but one of these days you'll see I'm right. Anyhow, today I'd like to look at some new curtains for your room."

"Oh? Are you finally turning it into that sewing room you've always wanted?"

Her mother regarded her strangely. "No, darling, for when you finish this degree and come home. You know, I was thinking, you can get a job as a secretary at one of the law firms downtown. This way, you'll be close by, and what a marvelous way to meet a lawyer."

Beatrice recoiled from the maniacal gleam in her mother's eye. "Wait a minute. Rewind for a second. Who said I was moving back in here when I finish school?"

Her mother shot her that what-a-stupid-question look Beatrice had been raised on. "Well, of course, I just assumed—I mean where else would you live, now that you won't be bringing home a husband?" She straightened out the dish towel stuffed through the refrigerator handle and muttered, "Yet again."

"I'm staying in the city."

The announcement had Beatrice and her mother squaring off at opposite ends of the kitchen.

"Have you lost your mind?"

Beatrice arched an eyebrow in defiance. "No, but I do think I'm well on my way."

Her mother grabbed the dish towel and started waving it about.

"I have been worried sick about you living in that Godforsaken city, biting my tongue, trying to be supportive of these little endeavors of yours, and now, of all things, you say you're not coming home. What are you going to do, wait tables for the rest of your life?"

"I'm going to teach."

Her mother was too fired up on righteous indignation to be rational. "You'll be twenty-four years old this year. When are you going to grow up?"

Beatrice fought the tears as she always had, refusing to give her mother the satisfaction of knowing she still knew the right buttons to push.

"Since when do you bite your tongue about anything? And since when have you ever supported anything I wanted to do without a barrage of negative remarks to make me feel guilty?"

Her mother propped her hands on her hips. "How quickly you forget that I let you go to New York and pursue this master's degree."

"I was twenty-one years old," Beatrice shouted. "I didn't need your permission."

"Why, you little ingrate. I see you've forgotten how I let you run off to Salve Regina when you were only seventeen. Do you know how many other mothers make their daughters go to work right after high school? God knows we could've used the money in this household. But do you ever think of that when you're condemning me? Just like your father, God rest his soul—always putting himself first."

"Don't talk about my father like that," Beatrice said quietly. "The man is dead."

"Naturally, you stick up for him. What did I ever do to make you turn on me like this?"

"I never turned on you. I've just had it with you trying to control me. No matter what I accomplish, it's never good enough because it isn't what you want me to do. Quentin does whatever he wants, and whatever he does makes him a prince in your eyes. Do you think all I aspire to be is someone's wife and mother, so I could end up fifty years old, stuck in a four-room apartment with nothing better to do than make my kids miserable? That's not where I'm headed, Mom, so you might as well get used to it."

For a moment, Beatrice almost wished she could unsay her words as her mother stood stunned like a deer full of buckshot in the seconds before it fell.

"Well, I guess you told me," her mother said meekly. "You're all grown up now."

"Mom, I—"

"I don't think I feel like shopping today, Beatrice. I need to lie down for a little while."

Beatrice trailed her mother into the small living room, watching as she lowered herself on the couch like a store mannequin falling over in slow motion. Pangs of guilt were already gnawing at her insides. Should she apologize for what she'd said? It's not like what she said wasn't true—it was. That's what made her all the more sorry. Really, what else did her mother have in her life than to nitpick through Beatrice's?

"Do you want me to heat you up some of that soup?" Beatrice asked after a long while of standing like a sentinel by the couch.

"Not now. I'm too upset to eat."

"I didn't mean to upset you."

"Well, you did."

"You upset me, too."

"Apparently, that's what us mothers do, nag and upset our children, wanting everything for them that we never had ourselves. It's a constant struggle, but of course, you'll never know what it's like 'cause you won't be making that sacrifice."

Beatrice shook her head, swishing the words "I'm sorry" around in her mouth. She opted for principle instead. "Can I get you anything, a drink of water?"

"No, thank you. I wouldn't want to be perceived as controlling for asking you for a glass of water."

Without a word, just some cabinet slamming, Beatrice poured her mother a glass of water from the faucet and took it to her.

"I'm going to head home. If I leave now, I can pick up an extra shift at the bistro."

"Could I impose upon you to get my pills before you leave?"

Beatrice went into the kitchen and brought out one Valium for her mother. "Here you go."

"Why didn't you bring me the bottle?"

"Your prescription says to take one pill as needed."

"Now who's the controlling one?" her mother said, swallowing the pill dry. "Would you please get me the bottle, so I won't have to get up later?"

Or until tomorrow. She reluctantly handed her mother the prescription bottle.

"Are you going to be all right?"

"I'll manage. I always do." Her mother closed her eyes.

Beatrice descended the stairs to the street slowly, her body weight making each old wooden step creak. How come every time her mother insulted her, she was the one who ended up walking away remorseful? At least now she could walk away.

CHAPTER ELEVEN

During her shift at the bistro, Beatrice scurried about like a pigeon trying not to get kicked, straining to stay centered on her duties. Thanks to the recent tumult in her life, she mixed up an order, jumbled her recitation of the specials twice, and miscalculated a customer's check. As she headed into the kitchen, she flashed back to that psychology-class documentary, wondering if the old thousand-volt nightcap wasn't in her immediate future. When Antonio slapped the order-up bell, it was the final strike to her nerves, sending two dishes of raspberry cheesecake cascading to the floor.

"What the hell is the matter with you, Beatrice?" Antonio snapped.

"You could take it a little easier on that bell, Tony," Ricky said before addressing Beatrice. "Are you all right?"

She nodded in appreciation. "My head's a little out of whack."

"Honey, if it's only a little out of whack, you're ahead of the game. How about coming out for a drink tonight? You sure as hell look like you could use one."

"I don't think so, Ricky."

"Don't tell me you're still afraid of the big, bad dyke?"

Beatrice shushed him as she glanced around the kitchen. "What if Judy's there? Or someone else like her? I don't want to do that again."

"Then don't," he said. "Trix, nobody can seduce you without your permission. If you see a girl you like, get her telephone number and call her for a date."

Beatrice felt like she was turning the color of the raspberries she was wiping up from the floor. "Oh, my God, Ricky. I could never. And stop calling me Trixie. You make me sound like a tart."

"You should be so lucky. At the rate you're going, you'll be settling into dull, depressing spinsterhood in no time." He gave her his best Norma Desmond glare from *Sunset Boulevard* before retreating to his stack of dirty dishes.

"Why is everyone so convinced I'm destined for spinsterhood?" She huffed before departing for the dining room. But as she carried out the replacement desserts, the sting of Ricky's observation lingered. If she didn't want men and was afraid to set foot in that kind of bar again, how could she expect anything else? As fraught with complication as relationships seemed, she didn't want to be alone forever.

"Darby, table seven is waiting to order," snapped the maître d'.

As if her thoughts weren't scattered enough, she glanced over at table seven to see Donna sitting with a woman whose back was toward Beatrice—a brunette with shoulder-length hair, not the short, choppy hair that still won her attention on women she passed on the street.

Donna noticed and waved her over.

Slowly, she headed toward the table, her heart thrumming in her throat. Could it be? After all this time? Oh, please let it be.

"Beatrice." Abby jumped up to give her a hug.

"Hi," Beatrice said softly, distracted by the warmth of Abby's arms around her. Despite the moment's awkwardness, she melted into its familiar tenderness.

"How nice to see you again." Abby cupped Beatrice's shoulders and eyed her from head to toe. "You're all grown up."

Beatrice beamed at the highest of compliments from Abby. "Your hair is longer," she said, reaching to touch the ends, then retracting her hand. "I like it."

"Thank you." Abby casually fluffed up the sides. "You're as lovely as ever."

"I feel like I'm intruding," Donna said. "You two ought to find someplace a little quainter."

"Donna, she's working." She looked up at Beatrice with those eyes, two marigolds sparkling in the fluorescent sun. "I'm sorry, Bea. Don't let us keep you."

"You're not," she said with enthusiasm reminiscent of her library days. "Let me check the kitchen, and then I'll be right back to take your order."

Beatrice flew into the kitchen and braced herself against the large stainless-steel refrigerator, gasping for breath. Her hands were actually shaking as her mind reeled with possibilities. The restaurant was closing in an hour. Would Abby wait for her so they could talk? Should she take Ricky's advice and ask for her phone number? After all this time, could Abby have an interest in her?

It was all too much to consider at the moment. She needed to keep her mind on her job and save this conjecture for an appropriate time. But for the rest of her shift, Beatrice stole glances at Abby every chance she got and flattered herself to think Abby had been doing the same.

To Beatrice's delight, Abby and Donna finished their last cups of coffee as the restaurant was closing.

Donna signaled her over to the table. "No change needed," she said, folding her wallet and stuffing it into her chinos.

Beatrice thanked Donna effusively but never lifted her gaze from Abby for more than a second or two. "Well, it was nice seeing you both."

"You, too, Bea," Abby said, her eyes flaming with second chances.

Donna hesitated, then glanced conspiratorially at Abby. "Say, Bea, we'll be down the street at Dandy's for a bit. Why don't you stop in when you get done here?"

"That is if you're free," Abby added.

"Oh, I'm as free as a spinster," Beatrice replied with an awkward grin. "I don't know why I said that."

Abby giggled. "I don't know either, but I'm glad you are."

Beatrice wrung her trembling hands, scanning each face as she and Ricky walked into Dandy's smoky atmosphere simmering with energy. As they approached the bar, Donna and Abby waved at her from a corner table.

Over the din of chatter and Sam Cooke's "Twistin' the Night Away," Ricky smirked and shouted, "Boy, you're like flypaper in these joints."

"Shush," Beatrice said in his ear. "That's Abby."

"The famous library Abby?" Ricky bounced on his tiptoes around Beatrice's shoulders for a better view.

"Shut up, will you? Stop that! They're going to see you." She shook her hands out by her sides and groaned with nervousness.

"She's beautiful." He paused and wrinkled his forehead. "You are talking about the one that doesn't look like Brando, right?"

"Stop it. Oh, my goodness—they're coming over here." She grabbed his arm and pivoted his skinny frame toward the bar.

"Still drinking Coca-Colas?" Abby asked from behind.

Beatrice glanced over her shoulder. "Sure, but with rum in them."

"Atta girl." She clapped her hand on Beatrice's shoulder.

After the introductions, Beatrice and Abby found themselves alone in conversation at the bar. Beatrice studied every contour of Abby's familiar face awash in the neon from a Rheingold beer sign over the bar.

"What a delicious coincidence that you ended up in New York," Abby said, twirling a drink stirrer between her teeth.

Beatrice nodded and sipped her drink. "I'm surprised we haven't run into each other sooner. I've been here almost two years working on my master's at NYU." Her cool, fluid speech camouflaged her knees bobbing on the bar stool.

"Master's degree. Good for you. I'm not at all surprised." Abby sat on a stool next to Beatrice and signaled for the bartender. "What's it been, about six years now?"

Beatrice took another hearty sip for courage. "I'm not jail bait anymore."

"Yeah, I noticed. You've really blossomed into a beautiful young woman."

Beatrice had an urge to poke Abby in the arm to make sure this was real. Her first love, so fierce and unattainable, was sitting in front of her looking at her the way she'd dreamed she would a thousand times—with nothing standing in their way.

"When are you done? Are you going home to Connecticut when you finish?"

Beatrice shook her head. "I'll be done in May, but I'm planning to look for a teaching position here. There's nothing for me in Connecticut."

"Congratulations. And hey, since you're staying, we can be friends," Abby said excitedly. "I mean, if you want to, that is."

Beatrice felt her mouth twitch at the second part of her statement. "Of course I'd want to."

Abby smiled and draped her hand over Beatrice's. "I never forgot you, Bea—and not for lack of trying."

Beatrice gazed at her, savoring Abby's skin on hers.

"Did you forget about me?" With her narrowed eyelids and shimmering lavender lips dragging on her cigarette, Abby was something right off a movie screen.

Beatrice was struck with the same love-sickness that had moistened her palms and wrought mayhem on her digestion back in '57. "Out of sight, out of mind maybe, but you never left my heart."

Abby grinned as she tapped her pack of cigarettes on the bar. "You must explain how anyone hasn't snatched you up yet."

"I was seeing one of my professors for about a year, but it didn't work out."

"Unlucky her."

"It was a him."

Abby arched an eyebrow and grinned. "A him, huh?"

Beatrice sprang into defense. "It was so hard, Abby. First you left, and then my brother married my college roommate whom I was hopelessly in love with, and I had to face all the relentless questions about why such a pretty girl doesn't have a boyfriend."

"Take it easy, Bea. We've all veered off down that road at least once—all except Donna. She's been chasing skirts since she was in diapers."

The joke lightened the mood only for a moment.

"I couldn't do it anymore," Beatrice said. "It didn't feel right, and I knew it had nothing to do with Paul."

Abby listened intently, drawing on her cigarette.

"I mean I kept waiting to fall in love with him," Beatrice said, "but it never happened. I even thought letting him make love to me would change things, but it only made things worse. I really tried to get along, to be like a normal girl, but it didn't work."

"You are normal, Bea, just not in the eyes of all those square conformists." Abby reassured her with a pat on the hand. "Your life is just beginning. Don't waste your best years chasing illusions."

"I don't think I can tell the difference between reality and illusion anymore." She downed the last of her drink. "I mean isn't a woman's reality motherhood and being a wife? Is that really all we're born to be?"

"Not all of us."

"Yeah, the misfits."

Abby scoffed. "Misfits, oddballs. We are who we are. True, most people are offended by it, but I refuse to live my life apologizing to everyone."

"I wish I had your self-assurance."

"If you've decided you're going to be true to yourself, then it sounds like you do."

"So why don't I feel better about it?"

Abby sucked at the filter of her nearly finished cigarette and tilted her head to spew out the smoke. "Probably the futility of it all. Either you disappoint others or you disappoint yourself. No matter what you choose, someone's gonna be unhappy. Personally, as long as I have a say in who I disappoint, it won't be me."

"Do you tell people?"

Abby narrowed her eyes. "I'm self-assured, not self-destructive. My friends know, but we're all alike anyway. Nobody else needs to know."

"Isn't that the same thing as living a lie if you can't be honest with everyone?"

Abby was suddenly grave. "Marrying a man you're not in love with and faking orgasms the rest of your life to make your mother happy is living a lie. What I'm talking about is self-preservation. Do you want to have a job, Bea? A safe place to live?"

"Of course I do."

"Then you better learn the difference." Abby clutched Beatrice's hand and smiled. "Hey, this subject is so heavy. After all this time, don't we have something more interesting to talk about?"

Beatrice smiled and reached for her new rum and Coke. "You're right—like what?"

"Let's grab a table in the corner and talk about that kiss at the library."

Beatrice blushed as she followed Abby's still-firm and shapely figure as it danced under a snug wool skirt. She pushed Abby's chair in for her and added, "What do you say we talk about that one you planted on me in Pixie's?"

Now Abby was the one blushing. "I can't believe I did that. I was clearly intoxicated."

"Hey," Beatrice said through pouty lips. "You mean you didn't want to?"

"Are you kidding? I wanted to all right, but I should've had the self-control not to—and would have if I weren't so sloshed. That's why kids don't belong in joints like that."

"It's still the most exciting thing I've ever experienced," Beatrice said.

Abby grinned. "Can I take that to mean you've never made love with a woman?"

Beatrice blushed again, this time at visions of Judy's magnificent maneuvers in the toilet stall. "Well, uh, made love? No. I haven't even been on a date with a girl."

She felt comfortable with her omission since what she and Judy did had nothing to do with love.

"I'm sorry," Abby said. "I didn't mean to embarrass you."

"You didn't. My track record with girls speaks for itself."

"Oh, I'm sure you only think so."

"Really? Hmm, let's see—there was that time when I was a teenager and lunged at you outside a public library. And then, of course, two years ago when I made a pass at my sister-in-law."

"The college roommate?"

Beatrice nodded with a trace of a smile.

"Oh, Bea." Abby couldn't help laughing. "You shared a room with her at school but waited until after she was married to make a pass at her? Whatever possessed you?"

"Clearly, my unrequited love for her got away from me."

"Clearly," Abby said, trying not to smile.

"I was so humiliated." Suddenly, Beatrice's smile was gone. "It ruined our friendship."

"I'm sorry, Bea." Abby shook her head as she crushed out her cigarette. "Oh, the whole goddamn game is so awkward. Chalk it up to growing pains."

Beatrice raised her glass in a mock toast.

"I have a confession," Abby said, her bare toes wandering over Beatrice's foot. "Your smooch in the library is still the best kiss I've ever had."

"Oh, Abby," she said in a breathy whisper.

Abby leaned over the table, and they formed a delicate arch, kissing over the collection of empty drink glasses and overflowing ashtray. Beatrice closed her eyes, transported by the rapture of her first kiss not stolen but given freely from the heart.

"My apartment's over on Tenth," Abby said. "We can have a cup of tea and talk more in private."

"I'd like that," Beatrice replied.

❖

Sitting on a plush burgundy sofa, Beatrice glanced around Abby's apartment cramped with antique furniture, and shelves crowded with books and a variety of porcelain dolls. She crossed and uncrossed her legs, cradling her teacup in her lap. Abby sat next to her sipping her tea, one leg thrown over the other, and air-tapping her toe as the Drifters crooned "Up on the Roof" from a transistor radio.

Beatrice held her breath as Abby's eyes took a slow tour around her face.

"If it makes you feel any better," Abby said, "I'm as nervous as you are."

Remembering to exhale, Beatrice slid her palms up and down her thighs. "It does a little. I don't know why I'm like this. It feels like we've just met and known each other forever all at the same time."

"It's the first time we've ever been alone, not in some dusty corner of a library hoping no one comes in." Abby smiled as she replaced her cup in its saucer. "I know what we should do."

Beatrice's heart fluttered in her throat. "What?"

Abby reached for her hand and wound her fingers through Beatrice's, holding them gently. "This is what I meant, silly. Better?"

Beatrice nodded and smiled. Her body trembled, her throat was dry, yet she'd never felt more alive as Abby's soft palm fell into hers.

"I keep looking at you," Abby said, "but I still can't believe you're sitting here."

"You?" Beatrice said. "Imagine what I'm thinking. I had the biggest crush on you. My God, to think I'd actually be next to you holding your hand all these years later."

Abby smiled and began tracing figure eights with her index finger on the inside of Beatrice's forearm. "Looking back, I had a little crush on you, too. Of course, with the age difference..." She punctuated her sentence with a frown.

"You don't have to remind me. I remember that day you walked away from the library with your box of belongings like it was yesterday. I never thought I'd see you again. My heart was broken."

"I thought about writing you at college, to see how you were doing, but something told me I should leave you to discover yourself on your own."

Beatrice nodded. "I guess it was a good thing you didn't—although you might've saved me from falling in love with my best friend."

Abby grinned. "Show me a lesbian who hasn't fallen in love with one of her friends, and I'll show you a woman whose friends are all men."

"Boy, I've done some stupid things in the name of love."

"Stupid or hopelessly romantic? You were so adorable asking me to come to Newport with you."

Beatrice blushed. "I hoped you would've forgotten that. God, that was so embarrassing."

Abby smiled warmly. "Aw, don't be embarrassed. Life is so complicated when you're a teenager. Then you grow up, and it gets even more complicated."

Beatrice laughed. "It can also surprise you in the most amazing ways. Being with you tonight, this is magical."

"We're just having tea in my tiny apartment," Abby said. "But yeah, it is pretty magical."

"It feels so right, so easy. I don't know how to describe it other than..." She searched for the precise word. "Natural."

Abby kissed Beatrice's cheek, pecking slowly across until she reached her lips. Beatrice shuddered as Abby's fingers crawled under her ponytail and gently pulled it free from the elastic. Trying to divest herself of her empty cup and saucer, Beatrice missed as she reached for the coffee table and sent the dishes crashing to the hardwood floor.

"I'm sorry, Abby. I think I broke the handle."

"Forget it, honey," Abby whispered, smothering her neck with kisses. She nudged Beatrice down on the couch.

How different this felt with Abby. With Paul, her body would automatically tense in response to his touch as she waited for it to be over. But with Abby, she couldn't get close enough. As hard as she clutched her, she wanted to sense Abby more deeply, to crawl inside of her and feel her beating heart. Her desire was overwhelming, alarming. Good girls weren't supposed to want sex—they did it because it was their wifely duty. But with no husband or man in the mix, where did that leave her? She'd always heard that only loose women loved sex, but this feeling Abby gave her was more intense than anything she'd experienced.

"I want to make love to you," Abby whispered.

Beatrice opened her eyes. "I want that, too, but isn't it too soon? We haven't even gone on our first date."

"Oh, Bea," Abby said, laughing. "You're delightful, such an old-fashioned girl."

Beatrice bristled at the remark. She felt silly, like she was still that goofy teenager too immature for this kind of experience—that is until Abby began tracing her bottom lip with her finger.

"We can wait if you want to," Abby whispered seductively.

Beatrice nuzzled her face in Abby's neck. "I don't want to wait. I'm just a little nervous."

Abby hugged her tightly. "There's nothing to be nervous about. The first time isn't uncomfortable like it is with a man. It feels marvelous."

"That's not why I'm nervous."

Abby stroked Beatrice's cheek and smiled tenderly. "Tell me what you want."

While her body screamed for Abby's touch, Beatrice struggled to make sense of her feelings—fear of falling too hard, shame at having no self-control, anxiety knowing once she allowed it to happen she couldn't turn back.

"I have to go to the powder room."

"Sure, baby. Take your time." Abby kissed her on the nose and sat up to light a cigarette.

In the bathroom, Beatrice examined her reflection. Her hair was mussed, her lips puffy and smeared with Abby's lipstick. Pushing her cheeks together with her fingers, she still couldn't erase the smile lines on her face. She'd made Paul wait several months before she went to bed with him and then broke it off with him a month later. Could that happen with Abby if she had sex with her? A voice inside said no—this situation was unlike any other.

She smeared a dollop of Abby's Gleem toothpaste across her teeth, took a deep breath, and started toward the couch where Abby lay reclined, launching smoke rings into the air. On her way back, Beatrice stopped at the bookshelf when she recognized Abby as one of two women in a photo nestled among the porcelain dolls.

She picked up the frame. "Who is this girl with you, Abby?"

Abby poked her head up over the back of the couch. "Who?"

"This girl." Beatrice showed her the photo.

"Uh, she's just a friend."

"Oh," Beatrice said, unconvinced. She strolled to the sofa and sat down at the far end. "Just a friend," she said after a moment. "You look awfully cozy for just friends."

"Bea, let's not make a big deal out of this," Abby said.

Beatrice eyed her for a moment. "Well, what kind of deal is it?"

Abby exhaled and reached for Beatrice's hand. "I was going tell you. I just didn't know how to work it into the conversation."

Beatrice yanked her hand away and stood up, furrowing her brows in shock. "You have a girlfriend? Did you figure you'd work it into the conversation after you made love to me?"

"I'm sorry. I didn't mean to deceive you. It's a very complicated situation."

"Yes, I'm sure two-timing is quite complicated. How could you make love to me when you're in love with someone else? You know how I've always felt about you."

"See, that's the thing, Bea. I'm not in love with her. You don't understand the—"

"What's to understand? You're a lousy cheat." Beatrice's eyes pooled as she marched toward the door.

Abby went after her, pressing her hand against the door to stop Beatrice from storming out. "Bea, listen to me. Janice and I aren't happy."

Janice. Hearing Abby say her name churned her stomach.

"I've wanted to break it off with her," Abby said, "but it's been easier to keep putting it off. And right now is the absolute worst time."

"Oh, I'm such a fool. I can't believe I let you break my heart *again*." She tried to shove Abby away from the door, but Abby held her footing.

"Bea, you've got to believe me. If I thought there was any chance I'd run into you some day here in New York and we'd rekindle our old flame, I would've broken up with Janice months ago. But things are so complex right now. If you'd only let me explain."

Beatrice looked into Abby's eyes, desperately wanting to believe her.

"I've never felt with anyone what I felt from our first kiss at the library," Abby said. "I was so ashamed at the time because you were still a kid, but that doesn't change the facts. I truly never thought I'd ever see you again."

"Does she live with you?"

Abby looked away and nodded.

"Where is she?"

"Up in Albany. Her mother's sick."

"Shouldn't you be with her?"

"Oh, sure. How's she supposed to explain me to her dying mother?" Abby sighed and stepped away from the door. "If you want to leave, I understand."

"I should leave."

"Go ahead if you want to." Abby's expression was stoic at first but gave way to an irresistible pout. "Do you?"

"Yes. I mean, no. I mean I don't know what I mean."

Abby caressed her cheek. "Then stay."

"I can't," Beatrice said, staring at Abby's lips.

Abby pushed her against the door and kissed her passionately. When it came down to it, some things weren't complicated at all.

❖

The rising sun seeped around the window shade, casting a glow across their feet tangled under the bedsheet. Beatrice opened her eyes with a start. She hoped that when she glanced down at the face still cuddled in the crook of her armpit, it would be Abby's smiling up at her. The night before flashed through her mind like a slide show— nothing like she feared and more passionate than her imagination had the talent to conjure.

"Good morning." Abby's voice was sleepy as she kissed Beatrice's shoulder.

"Good morning," Beatrice whispered.

"How do you feel?"

"Like I'm floating on air. Is this what it's like every morning after?"

Abby giggled. "Only for the lucky ones. I'm surprised you're not still exhausted. I thought you'd never want to go to sleep."

Beatrice blushed. "I'm sorry. Did I do okay?"

"Oh, you were more than okay," Abby purred as she rolled on top of her. "You've spoiled me for everyone else," she added, nibbling Beatrice's earlobe.

"Even Janice?"

Abby buried her face in Beatrice's pillow. "I told you I'm going to take care of that."

"I'm not trying to tell you your business. I mean I can't force you to, but I know I wouldn't feel comfortable continuing to see you if you're taken."

Abby's head snapped up. "You still want to see me?"

Beatrice rolled her eyes. "Of course I do."

Abby pecked at her lips. "I could see myself really falling for you, Bea."

"Me too. In fact, I think I already have." She hugged Abby close to her. "When do you think you'll talk to her?"

"I will tonight, but I'm not sure when I'll talk to her about breaking up."

Beatrice gently pushed Abby off her and sat up, covering her chest with the bedsheet. "Why not?"

Abby propped herself up on her elbows. "How exactly do you propose I handle this? Give her the gate over the phone while she's sitting at her mother's deathbed? This is going to take a little time and a lot of finesse."

Beatrice got up and fumbled to put on last night's clothes bunched on the floor. "I think I should just go."

She pushed past Abby, who trailed her to the door.

"Bea, I thought you understood. I mean we had such a special night together."

"We did, but the more I think about it, the more this whole thing stinks. Why didn't you break it off when you realized you weren't in love with her? It's pretty cowardly to string someone along."

"Boy, everything is so cut and dried with you, isn't it, Miss Young and Independent? This may come as a shock to you, but it's a lonely world out there, especially if you're waiting around for Miss Right to come knocking on your door."

Beatrice scoffed. "Like I don't know anything about being lonely. You can spare me the condescension."

"I'm sorry, but wait till you're alone in your mid-thirties and then tell me about it. It's damn hard to find a decent girl, Bea. You have to play a thousand guessing games to figure out who is and who isn't, who you can approach and who you can't. When you do learn about joints like Dandy's, then you have to wade through the lot of them to find the ones who aren't drunks or aren't running so scared from themselves, they can't stop long enough to let someone love them."

As Abby paused to regain her composure, Beatrice studied the lines around her mouth and eyes, reminders of how loneliness cast an even darker shadow in their world.

"Janice is a nice girl. It felt good and safe to be with a decent woman." She slipped both of Beatrice's hands in hers. "But she never made me feel like you do."

Beatrice's mind swirled with confusion.

"I'll call her later and find out when she's coming home," Abby said.

Her hands still captive, Beatrice nodded, fighting the allure of Abby's eyes.

"Say something, Bea. Tell me you understand. Tell me to call you later or tell me to fuck off—anything."

"I don't want you to fuck off, Abby." Beatrice closed her eyes as Abby cupped her cheeks and gently kissed her lips.

As Beatrice walked home through the tranquility of Sunday morning in the Village, she could still smell Abby on her skin, traces of Evening in Paris and faded cigarette smoke. She wrapped her arms around herself against the early chill, recalling the physical sensation of rolling and twisting together in Abby's sheets, Abby's lips discovering parts of her body it seemed she hadn't known existed before last night. Best of all was the completeness in waking up in Abby's arms after not even remembering falling asleep. How could this feeling be wrong? If God is love and love is natural, how could anyone believe this unnatural?

Her reverie halted when she remembered Janice. She found no moral ambiguity to play with in that. This woman, an apparition smiling at her from a photo, was sheltered away somewhere in upstate New York awaiting her mother's demise, completely unaware that her lover was betraying her.

Suddenly, as Beatrice's guilt built momentum, her mind flashed with grotesque carnival side-show images of how their breakup would transpire: a casket draped in roses, a preacher throwing dirt on Janice's mother as Abby broke the news to Janice graveside. As Janice collapsed in heartbreak, her dead mother would pop open the lid of her casket, shake her head, and wag a reproachful finger at Beatrice. Soon a chorus of others would join in the upbraiding: the preacher, Janice herself, and the rest of the gathered mourners, all of them closing in on her with menacing features.

Beatrice leaned against the cold brick of the coffee shop around the corner from her apartment and squeezed her eyes shut to block out the horrible images. Although her night with Abby felt like stepping into the most romantic of dreams, how could she have allowed herself to do that? Her mother's face flashed before her with the same contemptuous glare as the ones from the funeral. Did this make her an adulterer? At the very least, she must have been an accomplice to adultery.

"Holy shit," she said out loud. "I broke one of the big commandments."

She immediately thought of turning around and attending Sunday mass, but with only fifteen minutes till it started, she'd never make it home to shower first. She couldn't possibly sit in a church pew with the magnificent stink of Abby and sin all over her. That would be downright mocking God. She closed her eyes and propped her head against the building's façade, sucking in a long, deep breath before going inside and searching for redemption in a cup of espresso.

CHAPTER TWELVE

The day Beatrice had dreaded for weeks had arrived. With less than a month until its due date, she was to meet with Paul to discuss the final draft of her research thesis on Emily Dickinson. She loitered in the hall around the corner from his campus office, trying to dispel the awkward scene of the night she broke up with him. Why was she feeling so guilty about it now that they were to meet professionally?

She simply didn't love him, and it was better to let him down now than after they were unhappily married. If anything, she'd done him a huge favor, freeing him for a girl who would love him the way he wanted to be loved. Still, for some reason, she couldn't shake the unsettling feeling that she'd again disappointed someone. Inching toward his office like the floor was a sheet of ice, she braced herself before rapping on his open door.

"Good afternoon, Miss Darby." He barely made eye contact from behind his desk. "Please have a seat."

"Thank you." Beatrice sat, absently lifting her books to form a shield in front of her chest.

"I've completed my review of your final draft and made a few grammar corrections, so after you've addressed those, you're ready to submit it to the grad office." He tossed her the sixty pages, and they landed with a slap on the edge of his desk.

Beatrice flipped through the thesis, her eyes bulging at the bloody streaks of red ink scrawled throughout. "How about the content? I'm still not sure if my interpretation for "I Could Not Stop for Death" is thorough enough. Did you look it over?"

Paul nodded. "It's okay. I wouldn't worry about it."

"I don't want it to be just okay, Paul. Do you think I have enough analysis to support my argument?"

"Professor Wainwright, if you don't mind, Miss Darby."

She rolled her eyes.

"You do a fine job using it to support your morbid obsession argument," he said, "but then that's a rather obvious point. However, the part about emotional weakness leaves something to be desired."

"Why? What else does it need?"

He smirked. "How about a whole new argument?"

"You know I won't have time to formulate a new argument. Why didn't you tell me this sooner?"

"First off, you handed in the draft to me late, and secondly, you've been a bit difficult to get ahold of."

Beatrice's blood surged into her temples. "You told me it would be okay to hand it in late that night we went to the Whitman reading at Fordham, remember?"

"No, I'm sorry, I don't."

"Paul, you can't do this to me. You know I can't graduate on time without that grade."

"Bea, stop playing this game. Why don't we go for a cup of coffee tonight and talk things over—the thesis and us."

"Clearly, I'm not the one playing games."

"All right, maybe I was a bit harsh in my assessment, but have a heart. I'm still a wounded man." He tried an endearing smile on her.

"You can't penalize me because our personal relationship didn't work out. It's unethical."

"This whole thing is very disappointing, Miss Darby. I don't want to think the only reason you dated me was for an A in my class and an edge on your thesis."

Beatrice skewered him with her gaze. "How dare you suggest I prostituted myself for grades? Have you seen my transcripts? I've hardly dated every professor and teacher I've had since high school."

"A moment of honesty here, Beatrice," he said, chewing on the end of his pen. "I can't stop thinking about you."

She shifted uncomfortably in her chair.

"We were such a perfect couple," he added. "It doesn't make sense for us to be apart."

"Look, Paul, it didn't work out, and I'm sorry. I didn't intend to hurt your feelings. On the bright side, there's no shortage of eager replacements around here."

He removed his eyeglasses and reclined in his chair. "So you're graduating. Then what? The next logical step is to get married, isn't it?"

"Since I'll have an MA in English, the next logical step for me is to teach and write. I don't see how I'm supposed to do that while I'm baking cookies, changing diapers, and fetching my husband's slippers before dinner each night."

"Bea, you've got it all wrong. That's not the marriage I want. I don't need kids. But I am thirty years old. It's time to grow up and settle down with a nice girl. I'm ready for the quiet life of a henpecked husband." He smiled broadly, seeming honored to offer himself as a sacrifice for the good of humanity.

"I'm not interested in henpecking anyone. I have my own plans, and marriage doesn't fit in with them now."

"You know I was only kidding when I said I couldn't wait. I don't mind putting it off for another year or two."

She shifted again in her seat. "Paul, you're not hearing me. My first priority is getting a teaching position."

He rose from his chair and moved toward her. "Say no more, Bea. I know people. A few phone calls and I'll have you all set up."

"Thank you, but I'd rather do it on my own."

He grinned. "Don't be droll. It won't be so easy doing it on your own. There are only so many positions available for women adjuncts. But I'm happy to lend a hand."

"I don't want your help or the obligation that would go along with it. I'm not in love with you. Now please understand that."

She stood, surprised by her directness. As she reached for the doorknob, his outstretched arm pushed the door closed.

"How about a kiss?" He pressed his body against hers. "It won't do any harm, and it might even change your mind."

"I'm going to be late for class," she said, backing away.

"Come on, just one." He held her shoulders and kissed her lips.

She thrust her three-ring notebook into his stomach. "I couldn't even count on you to review my thesis draft properly. Now you expect me to rely on you to find me a job? Good-bye, Paul."

She flung open the office door, and he grabbed her arm.

"A word of advice, Bea. This attitude isn't going to serve you very well in your career. Men don't like working with women who try to act like them, even in the liberal world of academia."

"Thanks for the advice, Professor."

She left his office without another word, deciding not to press her luck before her degree was in hand. After apologizing to the instructor for arriving late to her next lecture, she spent the rest of the class trying to forget her encounter with Paul and stop stewing over the fact that it had been nearly three weeks, and she still hadn't heard from Abby.

❖

In the restaurant's steamy kitchen, Beatrice dabbed her forehead with the back of her hand. Ricky tried to attract her attention through the crowd of wait staff clamoring at the counter. She finally looked up and saw him mouth the word, anything? She shook her head as she filled her serving tray with entrees. What did she need Abby for anyway? Or the guilt that had taunted her into insomnia for having had sex with someone who belonged to someone else?

If Abby didn't want to leave her unhappy relationship with Janice, that was her business, but Beatrice didn't plan to wither away, pining for her like she had six years earlier. She needed a love triangle like she needed a hole in her thesis theory. And since Paul had all but abandoned her, she spent any free time she had working even harder to put the appropriate finishing touches on her manuscript. She was determined to complete her academic career with the same standard of excellence she'd always maintained, with or without his help.

In the dining room, she noticed Donna sitting by herself at her preferred corner table, reading the menu. Beatrice approached her with a manner too indifferent to be convincing.

"Hi, Donna, has anyone taken your order?"

Donna folded her menu closed. "Nope. Waiting on you, cutie. Scotch and soda, and the chicken cordon bleu." She paused as Beatrice scribbled on her pad. "Has Abby called you?"

"No. Should I expect her to?"

"I would think so. Janice is all moved out."

Beatrice drummed her pencil on the pad. "Is that so? Well, I wouldn't know that since she hasn't called."

Donna tried not to smirk. "Don't worry, kid. You'll be hearing from her—soon."

"Who said I was worried?"

"Not me." Donna yielded a smile as she unfurled a *New York Times*.

"Beatrice." Abby waved tentatively from the maître d's podium.

As Abby approached, every word of warning Beatrice had with herself ran off like a con artist ditching the check. What was it about this woman that reduced her to a jumble of emotional contradiction?

"Look, I know you're busy and probably can't talk," Abby said, "but I just want you to know Janice and I are over. She picked up the last of her stuff a few days ago."

Beatrice stopped herself from jumping into Abby's arms, given the somber nature of the circumstances. Her heart actually ached for Janice at that moment as she gazed into Abby's eyes, vulnerable and full of mystery. Losing Abby after having her had to be far worse than the mere pang of missed opportunity.

"Are you doing okay?"

"Sure," Abby said with a shrug. "I know in my heart it was the right thing."

A shrug? Not exactly the demeanor Beatrice was expecting. "Well, um, I'm happy for you—I guess. I mean is that how I should feel right now?"

Abby looked at her quizzically. "What do you mean?"

"You don't seem very happy about it."

"It's bittersweet, Bea, not something I feel like rejoicing about. It's just, well, I don't know."

Beatrice didn't know either. Now that Abby was free to be with her, she expected her to come charging into the restaurant to proclaim her love. But then that's what she could've expected in a Deborah Kerr movie. Abby had waited so long to contact her, and now she wasn't even enthusiastic about it. Was she having second thoughts?

"Congratulations," Beatrice said icily. "I have to get these orders into the kitchen."

"Bea, hang on." Abby grabbed her arm. "Is something wrong?"

"Nothing's wrong." Beatrice glared at her. "In fact, everything's peachy."

"Good," Abby said, searching her eyes for confirmation. "I'll take a 7 and 7 when you get a chance."

"Coming right up." Beatrice stormed off toward the kitchen grumbling, "Good. I'll take a 7 and 7 when you get a chance." Of all the lousy nerve. That was all Abby had to say for herself?

She broadsided Ricky at the sink. "Can you believe this? After hanging me out to dry for the last three weeks, she's out there acting cooler than James Bond."

"Who?"

"Who? Abby, that's who."

"Did she break up with Janice?"

"Oh, she broke up with Janice, all right. Now she's acting like we're nothing more than casual acquaintances. I could just scream, Ricky."

Ricky's eyes indicated Chef Antonio eyeing them. "Pipe down. The walls have eyes and ears."

"I knew I never should've slept with her."

Ricky's jaw hung to his Adam's apple.

"Oh my God, I can't believe I said that," she blurted, and covered her lips with her hand.

He started chuckling once he regained his breath.

"Ricky, stop laughing. Tony is really looking over here now. Oh, crap, do you think he heard me?"

Ricky shook his head. "I think I'm offended about this. Something this juicy happens, and you didn't even tell me."

"I couldn't bring myself to let you know I was a co-conspirator to adultery." Beatrice rubbed her forehead. "God, I can't imagine what you must think of me. In spite of how it seems, I'm really not a tramp, honestly."

"I know you're not a tramp. Believe me, I know tramps."

Antonio's voice bellowed across the kitchen. "Ay, are you still on the clock, Darby, or what?"

"Yes, Antonio, but I don't recall hearing the order-up bell."

Antonio's fat hand slapped the bell frenetically.

Beatrice glared at him and then deferred to Ricky. "What should I do about Abby?"

He threw a hand on his hip and gave it careful consideration. "If you want to land yourself James Bond, you'll have to play it as cool she is. If she doesn't jump on your bandwagon, remember there are plenty of fish in the sea. You're too pretty to flop around on the deck waiting for some crazy broad to see the light."

Beatrice smiled. "Even though you mix your metaphors, you always manage to make me feel better."

Ricky smiled. "It's a gift."

Beatrice loaded her serving tray and headed into the dining room. Once out there, however, following Ricky's advice to remain cool was easier said than done. Despite her vow to elude Abby's penetrating eyes, she was losing the fight with her heart, especially when Abby waved her over to the table.

"Do you think you could take my food order?"

"Oh, I'm sorry. I thought you were only here to drink," Beatrice drawled, grinning with satisfaction at Abby's expression of surprise.

"No," Abby replied. "Strangely enough, I'd like something to wash down my whiskey with. How's the trout?"

"It leaves a little to be desired, I'm afraid."

"Oh? How so?"

"Well, you'll spend an awful lot of time waiting for it to come around, and then when it finally does, it won't be nearly as wonderful as you expected."

Abby and Donna exchanged looks.

"Maybe that's because the person waiting for it has overly idealized expectations," Abby said.

"What's that supposed to mean?"

"You have to admit, even the best trout isn't perfect. No fish is."

"Then maybe the menu shouldn't advertise more about the trout than the trout is able to deliver. Then the customers wouldn't be disillusioned."

"Maybe the menu did give an accurate description of the trout, but the customer was too naive about trout to understand what it is she was getting."

Donna rolled her eyes. "Enough about the trout. Can't you two just talk?"

"I'm working," Beatrice said stubbornly.

"Perhaps we can finish discussing the trout at Dandy's when you get off," Abby said, yanking her napkin off the table and spreading it across her lap. "Would that be all right with you, Beatrice?"

Beatrice shrugged and marched into the kitchen, still indignant. Making her way toward Ricky, she mumbled half to him, half to herself. "How could she leave me languishing on the vine for weeks and then be so blasé about the whole situation now that we're actually free to be together?"

Ricky wiped the steam from his chin. "You're making my head spin. Do you want her or don't you? I have to know so I can either hate her or smack some sense into you so you don't blow it with this Princess Charming."

Beatrice scoffed. "Do I want her? Oh, I can't stand her. She's so smug, I just want to…ugh."

Ricky nodded and wiped his hands on a towel. "You want her."

"I want her, but it doesn't seem like she wants me."

"How do you figure that? She broke up with someone for you."

"I don't know. She seems so strange about it, almost like she regrets the decision. I don't want to be hurt by her again."

"Again? You can't blame her for leaving you blubbering on the steps of the library. You were seventeen years old."

"That's not funny, Ricky. I was almost eighteen, and it really hurt."

He smiled sympathetically. "You know what? I think since Abby didn't react exactly the way you expected her to, you've decided the whole thing is a bust."

Beatrice stewed over the temerity of his suggestion, tapping her shoe on the kitchen tile.

"You do that sometimes, you know," he went on. "If things don't go exactly the way you think they should, you get yourself all in a dither. Life isn't a romance novel, no matter how we try to convince ourselves."

She folded her arms stubbornly before conceding. "I suppose you make a sensible point."

"How did you two leave it?"

"She wants me to meet her at Dandy's after work."

"Are you going to?"

"I don't know. I want to, but I'm afraid. Whenever I've let my heart have free rein, it's ended up in a million pieces."

"Speaking in defense of love, you haven't exactly picked the most promising candidates to fall for—a thirty-year-old woman when you were a teenager and your hetero college roommate? Those are some pretty tall orders, even for Cupid."

"I get the picture, Ricky. I'm just afraid of getting hurt."

"When you figure out a way to fall in love without that risk, please let me in on it." He brushed her disheveled bangs out of her eyes. "Go to Dandy's and be brave, my friend, be brave."

Following her friend's advice, Beatrice entered Dandy's with her shoulders squared, determined to win Abby. She grabbed a beer for herself and a 7 and 7 for Abby and made her way to the intimate corner of their reunion weeks earlier.

"I was starting to think you weren't coming," Abby said, standing and gazing into Beatrice's eyes.

"I almost didn't." She handed Abby her drink. "But I have to know one thing."

"What?" Abby sat and gestured for Beatrice to join her.

"Why did you take so long to call me?"

Abby sipped her drink pensively. "You scare me, Bea. Well, not you but my feelings for you. I needed time to straighten out my head after I broke up with Janice."

"You seemed like you regretted the decision."

"Not at all," Abby said, grabbing Beatrice's hand. "You have to understand I was feeling an awful lot for you in a short time, but you're much younger than I am. You're just starting out. I was afraid I was going to move too fast for you."

Beatrice smiled. "You're not moving fast enough."

CHAPTER THIRTEEN

Beatrice stretched her limbs in their bed, roused from sleep by the clanking of spoons and cups and saucers in the kitchen. As Abby cooked breakfast, a Sunday tradition since Beatrice had moved in nearly three years earlier, the aroma of sausage links, pancakes, and brewing coffee drew her from her linen cocoon.

Sundays were their favorite day of the week. If they weren't taking in the city's arts-and-culture scene, they would take out the Packard and drive over the Tappan Zee in search of a rural hamlet for some shopping and, later, a bistro for a light dinner. This Sunday was different, however. The Packard was going to squire them to Connecticut for dinner with Beatrice's mother, a visit both were anticipating with the enthusiasm one usually reserves for a tooth extraction.

Beatrice padded into the kitchen, crept up behind Abby at the stove, and wrapped her arms around her stomach with a squeeze.

"Good morning." Abby twisted to give Beatrice a peck on the lips and then popped a strawberry into her mouth.

"You spoil me," Beatrice said, chewing.

"I love spoiling you." She placed Beatrice's plate of pancakes smothered in fresh strawberries on the table.

Beatrice smiled and sat, deciding to approach the touchy subject that always made Abby squirm after Abby had started on her second cup of coffee. "These strawberries are so sweet," she said with a smile to match the berries.

"I'm glad you're enjoying them," Abby said. "Should we take the rest to your mother's for shortcake?"

"I'm sure she'll have dessert, but sure, we can." Beatrice sipped her coffee, watching Abby cut a piece of sausage with her fork while scanning the Lifestyles section of the newspaper.

After a few minutes, Abby looked up. "What's going on, Bea?"

"Why do you assume something's going on?"

"I can feel you staring at me."

"Maybe I'm admiring your beauty."

"Okay." Abby grinned knowingly and sipped her coffee. "Does this have anything to do with visiting your mother today?"

"No." Beatrice casually swirled a triangle of pancake around in a pool of syrup before eating it. "But as long as we're on awkward subjects."

"I knew it. What is it?"

"I was just wondering how much longer you want to pay someone else's rent."

Abby crunched the paper down into her lap. "Unless you've inherited a building from a long-lost uncle, I don't see how we can avoid paying someone to live somewhere."

"You know that's not what I'm talking about, Abby. Doesn't it make more sense to pay a mortgage company for something in our names?"

"You know, along with the mortgage in our names comes all the responsibility of keeping it up, too—mowing the lawn, broken pipes, leaky roof. Here, if something goes wrong, we just call the super."

"But it's not our place, Abby. You lived here with Janice a long time before I moved in."

Abby's expression relaxed. "Oh, well, if that's what's bothering you, we'll find another apartment. We don't have to stay here. That's another good thing about not owning. We can pack up and go whenever the place no longer suits us."

"I don't want to keep packing up and going. If we buy the right place, we won't have to worry about it not suiting us. I want a garden, a place to have friends over for barbecues, a place we can call ours."

"Like your brother and Gwen?" Abby got up to refill her coffee cup. "Now look, Bea, we're not them, far from it, so I wouldn't go getting carried away in some *Ozzy and Harriet* daydream."

"Daydream? Abby, we're a couple, aren't we?"

"Sure, we're a couple. We don't need to own something together to make it real. It is real."

Beatrice studied her. "If I didn't know any better, I might think all this opposition to a house was part of a ruse to hide your fear of commitment."

Abby's mouth hung open for a moment. "What?"

"Maybe you like the idea of being able to pack up and move on from me if the notion strikes you. Nice and easy, a clean break."

Abby took her plate to the sink and leaned against the counter. "How could you say that? These last three years have been the happiest of my life. I've never been more content with anyone. As far as I'm concerned, this is ever after."

"Me too, baby." Beatrice approached her and threw her arms around Abby's neck. "That's why I don't see why we can't have what other couples have. We both have good jobs. We can afford a mortgage."

"Sure, we can afford a mortgage, but who's going to hand one over to two women? What are we supposed to tell the realtor is the reason why we're buying a house together?"

Beatrice released her grip and countered her, leaning against the stove.

"First of all, we may have to search around, but we will find a bank that'll give us a mortgage. Secondly, who cares about what the realtor thinks? All he needs to know is that we qualify and that he's getting his commission."

"What world do you live in that says homosexuals can just go about life doing everything that normal couples do?"

"What world do you live in that says we can't?"

Abby flung her arms out dramatically. "Uh, this one."

"Oh, right." Beatrice glared at her. "Boy, has your tune changed since you gave me that pep talk back in New Haven. 'There's nothing wrong with us, Bea. We're not the freaks everyone thinks we are.'

Oh, really, Abby? I guess that was a nice speech so long as you were hiding out in an underground bar."

Abby ran her hands through her messy hair. "I don't know what to do with you, Bea. Do you realize once everyone knows we bought a house together, our secret will be out. What excuse can we possibly give then?"

"Maybe I'm tired of making excuses."

"Well, go ahead then, drop a bomb on everyone we know, and see who's still standing by us when the smoke clears."

"Our gay friends will be. So will anyone else who matters."

"Oh, good. Hopefully they'll be the ones who'll put us up, because when we both get fired from our jobs, the whole mortgage debate will be a moot point. Is that what you want?"

"No, Abby, that's not what I want. I want what everyone else wants."

After a long silence, Abby shook her head. "We'll have to talk about this later. I have to get in the shower, or we'll never make it to your mother's on time.

❖

Beatrice tightened her grip on the steering wheel as she and Abby drove on Interstate 95 toward New Haven. A preoccupation with the untold horrors that might arise during dinner with her mother had temporarily eclipsed her desire to further campaign for a house in the suburbs. She stared straight ahead squinting in the glare of an unmerciful afternoon sun. Abby leaned over and flipped down the visor for her.

"Thanks," Beatrice said, ending the stretch of uncomfortable silence.

"Sure."

"I really tried to come up with an excuse to get out of this visit. But I've used up all the plausible ones."

Abby smirked and patted Beatrice's knee. "I know you did. I also know you're sick of making excuses. That's why I don't know why you insisted on bringing me."

"It's important to me that we don't live separate lives."

"It's dinner with your mother," Abby said. "It wouldn't be a big deal to leave me home if having me come along is going to make us both nervous wrecks."

"I wanted you to come," she said in a whisper, and grasped Abby's hand. "Abby, I want to tell her about us. I think it's the right time."

Abby withdrew her hand like she'd unwittingly stuck it into a viper's nest. "Oh, Bea, not this again."

Beatrice dug her fingers into the hot steering wheel.

"Abby, she should know. You're as important to me as Gwen is to Quentin. Frankly, I've had it with all the deception."

"That's a lovely thought, dear, but she'll never accept me like she does Gwen because she'll never view us as a couple like them. In this society, a couple consists of a man and a woman. Two women are just close friends, even if they are screwing each other."

"What makes you so sure?"

"My God, you can't be that naive."

"It's a matter of principle. You're my family, like Gwen is Quentin's."

"You're taking a huge risk to stand on principle."

"What exactly am I risking? The warm, affectionate relationship she and I've always shared?"

"Sarcasm noted, Bea. This is what I don't understand about you. Your relationship with her is already strained. Why would you want to reveal something that'll only widen the chasm?"

"She's my mother. She should know who I really am. Besides, this business of always having to make up lies is degrading. I feel like a naughty child."

"Can't you have this conversation over the phone, when I'm not around?"

"Oh, I see what's going on here. You don't want to be caught in the crossfire. I thought I could always count on you to stand by me."

"Don't be ridiculous, Bea. Of course you can, but sometimes you can't tell the difference between a battle worth fighting and a lost cause. You seem to have forgotten I've already been through one of these horrid family confessionals. It was a disaster."

"But—"

Abby gently pinched her lips shut. "Look, I used to think honesty was the best policy, too, until I learned that most people don't want honesty. They want to preserve the delusions they've created for themselves in their own little insulated worlds. When you mess with that, Bea, that's when the problems start."

"I'm twenty-six years old, Abby. I shouldn't be sneaking around anymore, afraid I'll be caught doing something wrong, feeling guilty just for being me. I don't like how it feels. I'd rather take what comes with being true to myself."

"I'm thirty-nine years old, Bea—too old to be undermined by people's ignorance or scorned by someone's mother because I'm not the lawyer husband she always dreamed of for her daughter. I don't need it, and after my own family fiasco, I decided I wouldn't take it anymore."

"*Someone's* mother?"

"Oh, Bea, you know what I mean."

"I feel like you're not even trying to understand where I'm coming from."

"How can you possibly say that? I know exactly where you're coming from. I was there myself fifteen years ago. I used to be idealistic, too, but it's amazing how fast your father telling you you're dead to him can wipe the luster right off that idealism. Don't you remember the story?"

Beatrice was quiet for a moment.

As Abby continued, her face became an unfamiliar sculpture of stone. "When my father found out about me, he said, 'Get out of my house, you sick bitch. You disgust me.' When I tried to walk toward my mother, tears streaming down my cheeks, he slapped me across my face, pulled me by the arm, and literally pushed me out the door, the back door so the neighbors on the street wouldn't see the ugliness of our family's dirty laundry." Her eyes pooled as she recounted the haunting scene. "I felt so dirty, so ashamed. After I finally stopped bawling, I swore to myself that I'd never let anyone make me feel like that again. Personally, I don't think anything's worth serving yourself up for that kind of judgment."

"I still can't believe he actually said that to you and meant it. How could any father say something so awful to one of his children? I know my father never would."

"You think he wouldn't, like I used to. But then my parents thought they knew me until I revealed this dark, sinister side of myself. It changes the game. You become a stranger to them, and suddenly disowning you isn't so far-fetched."

"There's nothing dark or sinister about either one of us."

"Preaching to the choir, doll." Abby shrugged. "My father has two other daughters who are carbon copies of my mother. He could afford to toss one of us into the ash heap."

Beatrice drifted back to being six years old, watching her father yank Quentin's arm when he shoved her down on the wet lawn after a summer downpour. Quentin had run crying to their mother, sparking a bonfire of anger in the kitchen between her parents.

"Even if my father had ten daughters, he never would've felt that way."

"Look, if you're hell-bent on going through with this, you better prepare yourself for the same reaction from your mother. She sounds as self-righteous as my father."

Beatrice shook her head in resignation as she negotiated the exit ramp into downtown New Haven. "Does this mean I have your support today?"

"Well, there isn't a lot I can do about it now that we're a few blocks away, is there?"

Beatrice smiled in spite of herself. "I'm not just doing this for me, you know. It's for us and for my three-year-old niece, whom I've seen only twice since she was born. I want her to know the real me."

Abby nodded impatiently. "That's great, Joan of Arc. You know, I can only carry so many buckets of water."

"Every movement requires its martyrs." She reached over and tickled Abby's stomach.

"Can we please discuss something else?"

"Like what, the cocktail menu for Ricky's party next week?"

Abby beamed. "Now you're talking."

Beatrice groaned.

"Oh, Bea," Abby said, squeezing her knee, "you take life too seriously."

"You don't take it seriously enough."

"What's more important than having fun and enjoying life?"

"Living an authentic life."

"I happen to think it's pretty darn authentic finding happiness in a world custom-designed for your misery."

"Not if you're finding it by pretending to be something you're not."

"Now you're splitting hairs." Abby rolled her eyes.

"I've decided I'll tell her after dinner but before dessert," Beatrice said, nodding her resolve. "Seems like an appropriate time for something of this nature."

Abby grabbed Beatrice's hand and squeezed. "You're a dreamer, Bea, a hopeless dreamer. I think I love that about you."

Beatrice smiled. "A perfect match for your incurable pessimism."

"I think so, too."

Abby was about to lean over and kiss her on the cheek but stopped when a flood of pedestrian traffic flowed into the intersection.

CHAPTER FOURTEEN

A fter dinner, Beatrice and Abby exchanged tentative smiles once Mrs. Darby had gone into the kitchen to prepare dessert. Beatrice even risked a playful tickle on the nape of Abby's neck as she gathered the glasses and crumpled napkins her mother left behind.

"My lip finally stopped twitching," she whispered. "How are you doing?"

"Not bad, but let's hold off on the celebration till the Packard hits the pavement," Abby replied in a whisper. "Does your mother have Bromo-Seltzer? Anxiety is bad for the digestion."

"Welcome to dinner at the Darbys'."

In the kitchen, Mrs. Darby stood at the sink filling the coffee percolator with water. She seemed shorter to Beatrice, a little wider and a lot grayer. She was only in her mid-fifties, but her perpetually distressed face created the illusion that she was older. How bitterness had its way of strangling youth and beauty like a weed. Beatrice scrubbed the dishes with a soapy rag, knowing her effort would inevitably fall short, and her mother would rewash them later. It was merely a stall tactic anyway.

"What do you think of Abby?" she inquired without turning around.

"Nice girl. Pleasant mannered," her mother replied.

Beatrice stared at her mother's back as she spooned coffee into the percolator basket. "That's it? Pleasant mannered?"

"What else shall I say about her? It's not like you've introduced me to my future son-in-law."

By now, Beatrice could almost recite her mother's responses in unison with her. "Well, I'm sorry to disappoint you yet again."

"It's all right. I'm getting used to it." Her mother added in a whisper, "But I'll tell you one thing. Spending all your time with your friend out there isn't going to help your cause any."

Beatrice reached for another pot and a scouring pad so her mother wouldn't see her teeth gnashing. Although she was moments away from enlightening her once and for all, she couldn't suppress the urge to strike back.

"You're contradicting yourself, Mom. First you tell me I shouldn't settle for any old boy who proposes to me, and now you're suggesting I better get on the ball because time's running out. Which is it?"

"Oh, Beatrice, you're exasperating sometimes. I can't for the life of me understand why you broke it off with that handsome salesman, James. What a catch."

Beatrice recalled with dejection how she'd used Ricky's boyfriend, James, as a beard at last year's family picnic, an obligation she'd fulfilled only two months ago by posing as his date for his sister's dreary wedding.

"I told you why I had to dump him. He fooled around on me."

"Oh, they all do that before they get married. He's a young man. You're lucky if you get one who's sown his wild oats before he marries you instead of after."

"Sowing his oats. What a charming euphemism for cheating."

"Your problem, Beatrice, is that you're unreasonably picky. If you're waiting for some knight on a white horse to knock on your door and sweep you away like they do in the movies, I can save you the trouble. He doesn't exist."

Beatrice took a deep breath and stepped out on the ledge. "Um, about that, Mom, look, there's something I'd like to talk to you about."

"Bea, don't bother drying those." Her mother plucked the plate and dish towel out of her hands. "I'll have to rinse them again myself."

"Mom, did you hear me? I need to talk to you about something. It's important."

"Of course, dear, but let's get the table set for dessert first."

Beatrice rubbed her palms on her pants as a film of sweat blanketed her body. "All right, then. Do you want me to take out the apple cobbler?"

"Yes, please. I'll bring out the coffee in a minute. Oh, by the way, I have a little surprise for you."

Beatrice stopped short, nearly smashing the plate of cobbler into the swinging door. "Don't tell me Mrs. Keebler's bringing over her club-footed son, Warren."

"Honestly, Bea. Warren is a gentleman and very smart. But no, that's not the surprise."

Beatrice pushed through the door and grumbled, "Forget Bromo-Seltzer. I need a Valium."

Before Abby could react, the doorbell rang. Quentin walked in holding three-year-old Joanne in a flowery pinafore, followed by a very pregnant Gwen, her skin more peachy and radiant than ever. The air in the room stopped moving as Gwen and Beatrice noticed each other.

"Beatrice." Gwen finally breathed. "You look wonderful."

"Hi, Gwen." Beatrice smiled warmly. She glanced toward her beautiful niece now clinging to her father's side, clutching his finger as they exchanged gazes.

In strode Mrs. Darby brandishing the percolator and a Donna Reed grin. "Surprise," she exclaimed. The only thing that could have surprised everyone more would have been one of Castro's missiles sailing in through the parlor window and landing in the apple cobbler. "Finally, the whole family together." She glanced over at Abby as though she were an intruder. "Bea, why don't you introduce your friend?"

"Gwen, Quentin, this is my fr...uh, my roommate, well, my friend and roommate, Abby." She withered in defeat.

"How do you do, Abby," Gwen said, shaking her hand.

Beatrice disliked Quentin's expression. "You look familiar," he said as he approached to shake her hand. "Abby what?"

"Gill, Abby Gill."

"You used to work at the New Haven Public Library," he said.

"That's right." Abby maintained eye contact. "Bea and I worked there together for almost a year."

"This is Joanne," Beatrice interjected, looking back and forth between Abby and her brother.

As Beatrice crouched to touch Joanne's small hand, Quentin pulled the girl away and shuffled her over to an exhausted-looking Gwen. "She needs to go to the potty."

Gwen took Joanne's hand in hers. "She's just learned to use the potty," she said, offering Beatrice a plaintive glance before taking her daughter to the bathroom.

Beatrice and Abby read Quentin's body language fluently.

"Mother, can we get to dessert now? We need to get back to the city." She then paused to glare at her brother. "Traffic into the city's going to be predictably obnoxious soon."

The coffee and apple cobbler neutralized tensions somewhat, enabling all parties attending the dessert summit to communicate in stilted pleasantries. As Quentin regaled everyone about his lightning-fast rise to northeast sales manager and his twelve percent pay increase, Joanne wandered over to Beatrice and fingered the chunky bracelet shining on her wrist.

"You like my bracelet?" she asked, smiling down at the girl. Joanne looked up with Gwen's breathtaking marble-brown eyes. Beatrice hadn't known it was possible to feel so much love for someone she barely knew.

"Jo Jo, don't pester Auntie Bea now," Gwen said kindly.

Beatrice smiled warmly at Gwen as her niece attempted to climb into her lap.

"Joanne," Quentin said sternly. "Get down. We have to go bye-bye now."

The girl started to whine as Quentin snatched her off Beatrice's lap.

"Quent, darling, we don't need to rush off right this minute, do we?" Gwen glanced helplessly at Beatrice.

"Yes, we do. You need your rest. Mother, thank you for dessert. We'll see you for dinner Wednesday night, all right?"

Mrs. Darby appeared confused as Quentin and Gwen hastened to gather their things. "Yes, dear. I'll bake a nice strawberry-rhubarb pie."

As Beatrice swirled the coffee grounds around the bottom of her cup, she felt the gentle touch of Abby's foot on hers.

"So long everyone. Don't be a stranger, Bea," Quentin said for his mother's benefit before ushering his family out the door.

"Bea, you didn't even say good-bye to your brother," her mother said. "I raised you with better manners than that."

Beatrice slumped in her chair, feeling every bit as dirty as her brother's manner had insinuated. She couldn't bear to look at Abby at that moment or respond to her mother. What a disaster. After spending days mustering up the courage to have the conversation with her mother, all it took was the challenge of her brother's judgmental eyes and all that bravado had deserted her. Clearly, Abby was right. Her family would never accept the truth. Quentin already had his suspicions about them, and all the play with semantics in the world wouldn't convince him otherwise.

In the car, Beatrice clung to Abby's hand as she lay reclined in the passenger seat relishing the warmth of the setting sun on her face.

"I'm glad we went today. Now I won't have to feel guilty about avoiding them until next year."

"It wasn't so bad," Abby said, clutching the steering wheel. "Comparatively speaking, of course."

"It was hideous and dreadful, thanks to my asshole brother, and if I ever get stupid enough to entertain another visit, I'm going to make my mother sign an affidavit swearing they won't be there."

"Hmm, and I thought I was the dramatic one in this pair. It was pretty awkward, but it could've been worse."

"I can't believe that bastard. What does he think I'm going to do to my own niece? Does he think it's contagious? Does he think my depravity is going to rub off on her?"

"Don't say that, Bea."

"What? That we're depraved? That's what they think about us."

"Now do you understand why I've been trying to discourage this mission of masochism you've been on?" Abby said softly.

Beatrice was too riled for reason. "Can you believe that Gwen? She didn't say one word about his behavior."

"She looked like she wanted to."

"But she didn't."

"She's his wife, Bea. What did you expect?"

"Gwen was never a follower. She would always tell you exactly what was on her mind. That's what I loved about her. So this is what married life's done to her? Besides, she was my best friend before she was his wife. That should count for something."

"Sorry, but husband trumps girlfriend—it's the law of the land. It's one of the things we have to accept."

Beatrice's voice rose with indignation. "You always say that, Abby. 'It's one of those things we have to accept.' Well, you know what? I'm sick of accepting things that aren't right. I've only seen my niece three times in three years, and I wasn't even allowed to hold her in my lap. I'm supposed to accept that?"

"If you don't, it'll eat you alive."

"Abby, it baffles me how you can accept things that are so fundamentally wrong. In my book, doing nothing about injustice is what eats you alive."

"Oh boy. I thought you were joking when you mentioned being martyrs before. What do you propose we do, Bea? Tell your brother and your mother to fuck off sideways? Then you'll never see your niece or the new baby. On the upside, we won't ever have to schlep up here on a Sunday again."

Beatrice let go of her frustration in a quiet stream of tears. She lifted her and Abby's interlocked hands. "Why is this wrong?"

Abby squeezed her hand tighter and shook her head.

"She's a beautiful little girl," she said after a few moments. "She has your smile."

Beatrice wiped her cheeks as a smile flitted across her lips. "Yeah, I thought so, too."

"Someday she'll be old enough to make her own judgments—hopefully she'll make the right ones. Then you can tell Quentin to fuck off."

"Maybe I just won't answer any phone calls from Connecticut anymore."

"There's that, too."

❖

The birth of Quentin and Gwen's second daughter, Janie, two months later, came and went with little fanfare extended to Beatrice. A simple notice arrived in the mail, a photo of the scrunched-faced infant, her vital statistics, and tiny images of pink rattles, bottles, and bows scattered across the background. When Janie's christening invitation arrived in the mail without the words "and guest," Beatrice went ahead with her "will not attend" act of protest in spite of Abby's objections.

"You're cutting off your nose to spite your face."

Beatrice waved the invitation in Abby's face. "This isn't right. I've a good mind to call my mother and tell her."

"What do you think she'll say? She's going to side with them. They all think you're single, so why would they put 'and guest'?"

"They think I'm single thanks to me chickening out. Besides, if they knew for sure, they probably wouldn't have even invited me. Just what every parent wants, a homosexual couple at their child's christening."

Abby brushed a hand across Beatrice's back. "Don't be so hard on yourself. You planned to tell your mother the last time we were there. It's not your fault you were ambushed by a living Norman Rockwell painting."

"I should've made the announcement when we were all there together, killed everyone's hopes and dreams with one stone."

Abby grimaced. "I think you handled it the right way. If I were you, I'd go to the christening and leave everything else alone."

"I'm not going. I'll send my gift, but I'm not going."

Abby grabbed Beatrice's wrists and swung them affectionately. "Bea, honey, you're making an awfully big deal out of this."

Beatrice choked down her emotions. "It is a big deal, Abby, to me. They didn't even ask me to be a godmother."

"You knew Gwen's sister was going to be Joanne's."

"What about Janie's? It's probably going to be one of Gwen's snooty cousins."

"What did you expect? You've hardly spoken to them in the last five years."

"And whose fault is that?"

"Mostly yours for being so stubborn, always standing on principle."

"My principles matter to me."

"More than knowing your nieces?"

"I don't want them knowing me as someone I'm not," Beatrice said. "Do you remember the look in Joanne's eyes when Quentin pulled her away from me?"

"She was just confused."

"I'd rather have them not know me at all than be humiliated like that again."

Although she'd been disappointed to see the invitation to Janie's first birthday party also left off "and guest," Beatrice accepted and took Abby anyway. The curious ache to see Joanne, now four, and meet Janie had won out over righteousness. Besides, another year away from her family had altered Beatrice's perspective enough that she slowly began to view people's ignorance and prejudice toward her as their problem, not hers.

Late September at the Connecticut shore was as close to heaven as Beatrice would ever get. The leaves on the maple trees boasted golden highlights, while the faint aroma of a salty breeze made its way into Quentin and Gwen's yard. Abby and Beatrice sat in the afternoon sun sipping lemonade, amused at the antics of Joanne and Janie scampering around the yard with two of their cousins on Gwen's side and several neighborhood children.

"Is there any way I can persuade you to get me a refill," Abby whispered, shaking her glass of ice cubes.

Beatrice smiled when she noticed her mother hovering around the refreshment table. "I'm going to cash in on your fear of my mother tonight," she whispered lasciviously. "And not even feel guilty about it."

"You're so fresh," Abby said with a wink. "I hope that's a promise."

Beatrice approached the refreshment table draped in a tablecloth of country red-and-white checks. Her mother stood rearranging bowls of macaroni salad, baked beans, and a gelatin mold Gwen had set out earlier.

"You should be relaxing, Mom, enjoying your grandkids," Beatrice said as she refilled Abby's glass with lemonade.

"Oh, I'm fine helping Gwen tidy up. I'm happy you could make it to Janie's party, what with being busy grading all those papers."

Beatrice offered a cool smile. "I'm also a contributor to several academic and literary journals, and working on my own collection of short stories."

Mrs. Darby replied with a clueless nod. "Did you have enough to eat? You're getting too thin. Maybe Gwen will give you a plate to take home."

"No, thank you. I've eaten plenty and will probably need a Brioschi before bed." She stifled a belch.

Mrs. Darby glanced over at Abby lighting a cigarette. "I'm wondering, dear. Does your friend have to go everywhere you go?"

"No, she doesn't have to go everywhere with me. I want her to come with me. If you're offended by her presence, we don't have to stay."

"Don't be so touchy, Bea. She's anything but offensive."

"Then there should be no problem with her coming to our family gatherings."

"She's not family."

The suggestion scorched her insides like the briquettes in Quentin's new, custom-made stone barbecue pit. But Beatrice remained cool, challenging her mother with a pointed stare. "She's my family."

Her mother blinked rapidly as she tried to regard Beatrice patiently. "She's not. You should be here with your husband," she whispered, "not some *woman* in her forties. And your children should be playing with your brother's."

Beatrice glanced around the yard at the oblivious party guests. "Jesus Christ, Mom, is me finding a husband really all you ever think about? With all that's going on in the world, is that the most pressing issue of the time?"

"Now what are you raving about?"

"Boys are dying over in that jungle in a war we don't even belong in, and the country is still so divided over civil rights. That hasn't shifted your focus out of the kitchen for even a minute?"

"Oh, Bea, you and your causes. The war is a necessary evil to keep those commies from coming over here. As for that Reverend

King, he should know better than to be so brash and outspoken down South. Everyone knows how they feel about coloreds."

"That's sort of the whole point of all his speeches—that we should all see each other as people, regardless of color, religion, or who they love."

Mrs. Darby rubbed her eyes as though bored with the discussion. "I've told you before, Beatrice, you're never going to change the way people think. Instead of wasting your energy trying to fix the world, use it to spruce yourself up so you can attract a nice man."

Beatrice gently pushed her mother's hand away as it attempted to tuck Beatrice's hair behind her ears and away from her face. "Honest to God, you're a broken record."

"Pardon me for wanting what every mother wants for her daughter."

"What about what I want? In all your plans and schemes, hasn't it ever occurred to you to ask me?"

Her mother folded her arms and sighed impatiently. "Okay, Beatrice. What do you want?"

"I want my life the way it is. I may not be the girl next door with a picket fence, Simplicity patterns, and my own Brownie troop, but I'm happy—just the way I am."

"Oh, Beatrice. You can't possibly be happy living alone. A woman needs a family and children to care for."

"I don't live alone. I live with Abby and you know that."

After a disapproving scowl, her mother glanced around and lowered her voice. "Don't you worry about what your neighbors will think? I mean living with another girl was fine while you were in college, but at your age? It just isn't normal."

No matter how often she heard them, reminders of how abnormal she and Abby were never lost their bite. "Truth is I don't give a rat's ass what my neighbors think, or anyone else for that matter. And I don't need a goddamn husband to make me feel normal."

The ambrosia Mrs. Darby was piling into a bowl plopped onto the tablecloth. "Please don't use such vulgar language around me, and stop using the Lord's name in vain. If you keep up with these disrespectful outbursts, you won't be welcome here."

"I haven't felt welcome here in years."

"Now you're being absurd. Of course you've been welcome. You're the one who's chosen to stay away."

"Because I can't stand coming here and listening to you gripe about the numerous ways in which I've let you down. What about what I have accomplished? I'm a college professor, a published essayist, and a volunteer with several charitable organizations. Why is it so hard for you to be proud of who I am?"

"Because I don't know who you are—aside from being the spitting image of your father. Boy, the acorn didn't fall far from the tree in your case. Always had to be contrary, your father, always insisted on marching to a different drummer. I can clearly see you're exactly like him."

Beatrice smiled, dipped her finger in her mother's bowl of ambrosia and licked it. "That's the nicest thing you've ever said to me."

She trudged over to the picnic table where Abby was observing a heated debate between two of Gwen's girlfriends over fabric softener. She grabbed Abby's arm, barely slowing to allow her to crush out her cigarette butt.

"Is something wrong?" Abby asked, looking confused.

"Yeah, you might say that." Beatrice finally released her when they arrived at their car parked on the elm-lined street.

"Beatrice," Gwen called out from the veranda that stretched across the front of the house. "Are you leaving?"

"Yes," she barked. "Thank you for your hospitality."

"Wait. Can I talk to you?"

"Go ahead," Abby said. "I'll be in the car."

Gwen descended the steps and met her halfway down the stone sidewalk lined with fluffy purple petunias. "Were you going to leave without saying good-bye?"

"I'm sorry, but my mother got to me—again."

Gwen grinned through the tension. "Mothers are good for that. God, I hope I won't be that way with Joanne and Janie."

"I'm sure you will," Beatrice said dryly, trying to be lighthearted.

"Bea." Gwen fumbled for words. "It's been a long time since we've spent any time together. You know, what happened in my kitchen, that's water under the bridge. You were upset about our friendship changing. It was an emotional time for both of us. That shouldn't keep us estranged anymore."

All these years later, and Gwen was still clinging to an innocent rationale for the kiss. Beatrice couldn't blame her, really. A solution that everyone could live with was impossible. All Beatrice would have to do was go along with it and everything could be normal again. She could have her friend back and even have relationships with her nieces—so long as she consented to her part in the sham, pretended she never had feelings for Gwen and that Abby was just her roommate. She remembered that night at Pixie's in the fifties and Peggy's explanation of *Passing*, how Clare Kendry denied her ethnicity to be accepted by the white community. Was this situation any different? On the other hand, if people preferred their delusions, who was Beatrice to force the truth on them?

"I'd love to have a cup of coffee with you and be friends again," Beatrice said.

Gwen's eyes brightened. "Oh, I'm so glad, Bea. I was afraid city life had spoiled you for quiet afternoons in Madison."

"Are you kidding? Look at this place. It's breathtaking and right down the street from the water. I'm delighted that my brother's been able to provide so nicely for you and the girls. And a little shocked."

"Don't be. Quentin is capable and very well-regarded by the company. He was recently promoted to head of the Northeast sales division."

Beatrice smiled, her steely reserve no longer necessary. "Your daughters are just gorgeous."

"They're the loves of my life," Gwen said, beaming. "Oh, Bea." She threw her arms around her and gave her a quick, tight squeeze like she did when they were girls. "Let's have coffee soon."

"I'd like that." Although the warm familiarity of the hug and the promise of reconciliation tugged at her heart, she couldn't help considering the ultimate cost of Gwen's easy way out. She glanced at two squirrels chasing each other round and round a thick tree trunk. "But we can't go back to the friendship we used to have."

"Oh, I know. Our lives are different now, but we can still be close. After all, we used to be best friends."

Beatrice shielded her eyes from the late-afternoon sun. "Gwen, when I kissed you, it was because I wanted to—I was..."

"Hey, you don't owe me an explanation," Gwen said.

Beatrice shrank from the discomfort on Gwen's face and forced a smile. "I'll call you, Gwen. We'll get together soon."

"I hope so, Bea. I'd love to have...Well, I don't want us to be strangers anymore."

As long as Gwen couldn't hear the truth, that was exactly what they would stay at the heart of it all. Beatrice glanced over at Abby in the passenger seat reading a cheap paperback, sunglasses resting in her raven-black hair. She loved Abby and couldn't pass her off as a friend to Gwen, not if they were ever to have an authentic friendship.

"Abby's an amazing woman, Gwen. I just want you to know."

Gwen nodded and smiled, but her awkwardness was palpable. A lump rose in Beatrice's throat. No matter how sincere Gwen was in her effort to rekindle their friendship, she wasn't ready to have it with the woman Beatrice had become.

"I'll give you a call," Beatrice said, and waved once more before getting into the car.

CHAPTER FIFTEEN

Beatrice sat on the front stoop of their brownstone, sipping a glass of chardonnay, lulled by the scurry of dead leaves trapped in a wind swirl. She closed her sweater tighter as the October evening air sent a shiver through her. If she thought life at seventeen was confusing, this whole mess with her lover, her family, and her self-respect was quite the enigma to sort out.

"It's getting dark and cold, love," Abby said, poking her head out their living-room window.

"I know," Beatrice replied pensively. "It's keeping my wine nice and chilled."

"Why don't you come in and sit with me."

Beatrice dragged herself off the steps and padded into their apartment. After downing the last sip of wine, she plopped on the couch and wrapped herself like a mummy in an afghan.

"What's on your mind, love?" Abby asked.

"I don't know," Beatrice said. "It's this whole thing with Gwen and my mother and brother. Everything feels so disconnected, so unsettled."

"I hate to admit this, Bea, but your mother was right. You're never going to change people's mind when they feel strongly about something."

Beatrice raised an eyebrow. "Tell me about it. I live with one of those people."

"What are you talking about?"

"The house."

"Oh, Bea." Abby sighed. "I know how bad you want this, but the whole idea of it makes me so uncomfortable."

"Why do you care so much about what other people think?"

"This isn't a matter of keeping up with the Joneses. We have jobs we can be fired from, reputations that can be tarnished. We could get blacklisted here and never find new jobs. Don't you remember what happened in *The Children's Hour*?"

"You can't be serious, Abby. That was a movie. We live in New York City, not some little dust bowl of a town."

"I know it's a movie, but you're fooling yourself if you think it can't happen."

"I'm not that naive, Abby. I've tried so hard not to let the opinions of others define me, but the contempt for us is so pervasive. By not buying a house because society says we shouldn't, we're feeding right into that. I don't want to be ashamed of myself or our love."

"Bea, don't you see what you're doing? You're deciding that we're not okay the way we are by forcing us to fit into a mold we don't belong in. Society says couples have to have a house with a yard and all the trappings that go along with it, or they're not legitimate. You perpetuate that myth by wanting to conform. I love you, and I'm committed to you no matter where we live."

"Maybe you're not as committed as you think. Not having our names on something together makes it as easy to get rid of me as it was Janice."

Hurt emanated from Abby's eyes like a sad song. "Stop saying that, Bea. It's not true, and you make it sound like I put her out like garbage. I never loved her the way I love you. If that's a crime, then I guess I'm a criminal." Abby got up from the couch and started for their bedroom. "By the way, if you want to pick a fight with me because you're not getting your way, you're doing a good job of it."

Beatrice disentangled herself from the afghan and flung it on the couch. "Pick your battles," her father used to say. Was she standing too tall on principle by reaching for something unattainable? Was Abby right that it didn't matter where they lived as long as they lived together? Maybe she was too easily sold on the *Ozzie and Harriet* dream of backyard barbecues and apple pies on windowsills. Who knew if it was real for anyone? It seemed to be for Gwen.

She went in the bedroom, crawled into bed, and curled up next to Abby, resting her head on her chest.

"I'm sorry, love. I didn't want to fight. I just go a little batty whenever I hear the words *you can't*."

Abby kissed her head. "I know. Maybe someday."

Beatrice let that idea sink in over the eleven o'clock news droning from the small black-and-white TV on their dresser. Maybe someday. That seemed to be the resolution for everything in her life. Reuniting with her first love had happened through a divine act of serendipity. But what about owning their own home someday? Resolving her friendship with Gwen? Was she supposed to sit back and let chance resolve those, too?

The spirit of the Christmas season inspired Beatrice to make good on her word back in early fall to give Gwen a call. She favored starting each New Year fresh, with any and all loose ends from the year before tied neatly and stored away for posterity. Their get-together was strategically designed to include neither Abby nor Quentin, although both would have to be brought in eventually if she was to feel true resolution.

Beatrice observed the frenetic scene in Gwen's kitchen as she sat at the table. Joanne and Janie had finally settled down in the middle of the linoleum floor playing with their new baby dolls, two presents from the armful of early Christmas gifts Beatrice had brought them. Joanne carefully cradled and doted on her baby, wrapping it in a small pink blanket, while little Janie tossed hers carelessly around the floor.

"Jane Elizabeth Darby, if you break that doll, Auntie Bea's going take back the other toys she brought you. Is that what you want?"

The toddler's round brown eyes looked up at her mother with only partial understanding, and then she threw the doll at Joanne, who took protective custody of it along with hers.

Beatrice grinned. "She's fifteen months. I don't expect the toy-death toll to stop at one."

Gwen grinned, too. "I'm afraid of what I can expect from Janie when she actually hits the terrible twos."

Looking somewhat harried yet still radiantly attractive, she brought a tray of coffee, cream, and sugar cubes to the table.

"Sorry. She gets that from me. I was murder on my toys." Beatrice chuckled to herself. "I'll never forget my eighth Christmas. My mother didn't give me any toys because I'd destroyed the dolls I already had with haircuts and brain surgery."

"Oh, she didn't really do that," Gwen said, looking surprised. She sat and cut into the cinnamon bunt cake she'd baked that morning.

"She most certainly did. It didn't matter. I had more fun with Quentin's train set anyway. Then a week later my dad slipped me a new doll on the sly, this funny-looking thing with braids and a plaid dress. It was hideous, but I loved it because he gave it to me."

"Now I know where your brother gets it from. He spoils those girls to no end."

Breaking off a piece of her cake, Beatrice smiled and tried not to feel envious of the charming family scene her brother was lucky enough to live each day.

"I'm so glad you called, Bea. I honestly didn't think you would."

The essence of a finely aged awkwardness still hovered between them.

"I didn't know if I should," Beatrice said. "So much time has passed and our lives are so different now."

"I would hope no amount of time or difference would prevent us from speaking, or being friends, especially since we're family now."

Suddenly queasy, Beatrice put down her dessert fork. "There's quite a difference, Gwen, a huge one."

"Lord knows we were never clones of each other in college, but we still managed to get along famously. Don't you remember?"

"I remember." To her surprise, Beatrice began to tear up.

Janie let out a piercing screech, angry at Joanne for shoving her away after she stomped like Godzilla all over the pretend nursery.

"Mommy, tell her to stop," Joanne whined.

"Janie, come here and have some cake." Gwen scooped the child up and into the high chair, quelling her crankiness with a piece of bunt cake. "I'm sorry," Gwen said, flustered. "Where were we?"

"I was just saying I remember how we used to be."

Beatrice smiled at Janie smashing small bits of cake into her mouth.

"I don't care about what happened in the past. I'd like to think we could be close again," Gwen said ruefully. "The girls barely know you."

"Gwen, I have to clear the air with you about something—Quentin, too," Beatrice said slowly, but the rest of the words stuck in her throat.

After a long pause, Gwen said, "I think I already know."

Beatrice's eyes welled again. "I'm a lesbian," she said in a whisper. "God, why is it still so hard to say it out loud?"

Gwen nodded and patted her hand. "You don't have to say it. I know."

"I do have to, Gwen. I have to know it's all right with you." She wiped away a tear and straightened her back.

"It's who you are. It has to be all right."

"You have to know I'm not crazy or dangerous."

Before Gwen could respond, Joanne brought her new baby doll over and placed it in Beatrice's lap, looking up with a twin set of Gwen's voluminous eyelashes. Beatrice laughed in relief. "Thank you," she said, and brushed her fingers under the girl's chin.

"Give Aunty Bea a big hug, Jo Jo."

Joanne climbed up into Beatrice's lap and hugged her, resting her head on Beatrice's shoulder for a moment. Then she was back to attending to her baby business on the floor.

"If you can stay for supper," Gwen said, "we can sort this out with Quentin, too. He knows you're coming today."

After a tense dinner filled with stilted conversation and much diversion toward the girls' mealtime antics, Beatrice and Gwen stood at the sink washing and drying the dishes, pots, and pans. An afternoon of sharing conversation and confidences had rethreaded some of the tattered bond between them.

"I want you to talk to Quentin while I put the girls to bed," Gwen said firmly.

"All right already," Beatrice said, clutching her stomach against some indigestion.

"I'm going to make him a Manhattan. You can take it to him."

"Does he really need it to have this conversation?"

Gwen paused pensively. "I better make it a double."

"Thanks," Beatrice drawled.

"Buck up, Darby," Gwen said with a smirk. "It can't be any worse than facing Claire Billingsley."

Beatrice chuckled at the memory. "That was the night I knew you were a woman among women."

"Oh, it was awful what they did to those girls. I wonder whatever became of Shirley Dandridge."

"Hopefully, she didn't end up in the booby hatch," Beatrice said, and they broke into giggles.

Later, she took the cocktail from Gwen and walked into the living room, handing it to Quentin, who was deeply engrossed in the latest episode of *Mannix*.

"Oh, thanks," he said, sitting up in his leather chair.

Beatrice dropped down on the sofa. Quentin took a long sip of his drink and expressed his satisfaction with a resounding *ahhhh* and something about Gwen making one hell of a bartender if they ever needed another paycheck.

"So, Gwen and I had a nice talk this afternoon." It took quite an effort for Beatrice to sound casual.

"Oh?" Quentin's attention was still fixed on the television.

"Yep. She suggested I have the same conversation with you—if you can tear yourself away from Mike Connors for a minute."

He slowly tilted his head toward her. "What's on your mind?"

"You know what I'm going to say, don't you?"

"Although I'm a man of many talents, I can't read minds."

Beatrice took a deep breath. "You were right about me—what you said years ago."

"What did I say years ago?"

"That I'm a lesbian. I believe the word you used was *queer*."

As Quentin sipped his drink, the ice cubes made a clicking sound against the glass. He looked toward the television, but Beatrice could see he wasn't looking at the screen.

"When you regain the ability to speak, you can skip over all the classic responses, you know, *freak, deviant, sinner.* I've heard them all before, and they don't move me much anymore."

She sounded convincing, but in truth, those words still cut through stone and would even more so coming from her brother.

"Well, it is a sin," he finally replied with an eerie calm.

"Yeah, and I also know how you and I both feel about the church."

"I'm still a Catholic, Bea, even though I disagree with *some* things."

"I don't know what I believe about Catholicism anymore, but I do know this is the way God made me."

"God doesn't make homosexuals. He made man to be with woman so they can procreate and prevent the human race from going extinct."

"Well, obviously He made a few exceptions to the rule. Not every heterosexual human being procreates either."

He shook his head with obvious disdain. "If that's what you tell yourself to feel better about your decision—"

"Decision?" Beatrice scoffed. She leapt off the sofa and paced by the side of his chair. "You think I *decided* this? To be different from everyone I know? To be the object of scorn and derision from every ignoramus who believes homosexuals are monsters? Oh, sure, Quentin. It was the smartest *decision* I ever made."

Quentin took a moment to comprehend her sarcasm. "So what then? People are just born that way?"

"I don't know how it happens. But I know it's part of who I am, and when I tried to deny it to myself and live a normal life, as it were, I was miserable. Being with Abby is the first thing in my life that feels right."

"Look, I don't know what to tell you, Bea. It's your life. If this is how you're going to live it, I can't do anything about it. But I sure hope you don't expect my approval."

Beatrice smirked, her heart racing with an inexplicable sense of victory.

"I don't need your approval. But what I do feel entitled to as your sister is your acceptance. I happen to love your wife as a friend and adore your daughters, as little as I know about them. We don't have much family, Quent. You, me, and Mom—that's it. But I can just as easily go back to New York and never show my face here again, if that's what you want."

Quentin tilted his glass back until the ice cubes hit his lips, his molars crunching into a melting cube.

"That's not what I want, Bea. You're my sister, and Gwen misses your friendship. But I have to admit, I have more than a few reservations about the girls growing up around you and Abby. Wouldn't want them picking up any bad habits."

Beatrice sat on the arm of the sofa and laced her fingers in a stretch, suddenly bored with the conversation.

"Hey, if I didn't pick up any bad heterosexual habits from Aunt Josephine and Uncle Phil, I'm sure your girls will be safe around us."

Gwen popped her head around the corner from the kitchen. "Sorry to interrupt, but would you like another Manhattan, darling?"

"You're not interrupting, Gwen," Beatrice said, her voice clearer and stronger than it had sounded in a while. "We're through talking."

"I know. I heard most of it," she replied with an impish smile and then turned grave. "The next time you come for dinner, I expect you to bring Abby—right, Quentin?"

A barely audible "*mmm*" served as his begrudging agreement.

"Sure I will."

"Say, what are you going to do about your mother?"

Beatrice offered a half smile. "I'll tell her eventually, once I stop trying to avoid her for simply being her."

"Now I really know you're crazy," Quentin said.

"Quentin." Gwen stared at him.

"I honestly don't think anything will change my relationship with my mother one way or another. The next time she guilts me into visiting her, she'll learn the truth."

"Forget one Manhattan," Quentin said. "You better prime her for that with a pitcher of them."

"Can you take me to the train station now?" Beatrice asked Gwen.

"Sure. While I make him one last drink, Joanne wants you to kiss her good night." She shut down Quentin's anxious expression with a stern glare. "Down the hall to the left."

CHAPTER SIXTEEN

Inspired by the hope from her peace mission to Gwen and Quentin's house, Beatrice had decided that the next morning she'd approach the subject of buying a house with Abby again. Despite Abby's interpretation, it wasn't all about political grandstanding. It was about the promise of the American dream: a space to call one's own, and the stability and security found only where seeds could be planted and roots take hold. It had always been important to Beatrice to stand up for what she believed in. Shouldn't she do it in her relationship as well?

She sat at the table brooding over her coffee and toast, waiting for Abby to emerge from the shower. She was determined to resolve the issue once and for all that morning. She had bargained with herself into believing Abby would be reasonable and see that she was right, but what if she wasn't? They'd be caught in a standoff. Then what? An ultimatum? If so, was she prepared to follow through? The alternative was relinquishing something deeply meaningful to her. And that wouldn't do either.

Abby padded into the kitchen and poured a cup of coffee. "If we don't have anything planned today, I'd like to go a pottery class."

"That's fine. I have some papers to grade," Beatrice said listlessly.

"What's the matter?"

Beatrice braced herself with a sip of coffee. "I'm going house hunting tomorrow," she said, fixing her eyes on her cup as she anticipated the fallout.

"What are you talking about?"

"I'm tired of living in an apartment. I want a house, and I'm going to make it happen."

"Just like that?"

Beatrice finally looked into Abby's eyes. "Yeah, just like that."

"What about me?"

"I hope it's with you."

"What if I say that's not what I want?"

Beatrice shrugged. "Then I guess we won't be living together anymore." The words sounded like someone else had said them.

"Are you serious?"

"Abby, this means a lot to me, obviously more than you know. I can't make this sacrifice anymore, not for the reason you gave me."

"How dare you give me an ultimatum? This has to be the most immature stunt you've ever pulled."

"You know something? I'm sick of you calling me immature whenever I challenge your word because I'm younger than you. There's nothing immature about feeling passionate about something that's extremely important to me. I didn't want to give you an ultimatum, but there didn't seem to be any negotiating with you on this."

Abby glared at her. "All right, you're not being immature—just extremely selfish."

"You're being selfish and cowardly. I want this for us, not just me. All you can think about is what other people will think and how your life will be inconvenienced."

"Bea, a hell of a lot more than convenience is at stake."

"Yes, I know. The sheriff and his posse are fixin' to ride us out on a rail as we speak. Hey, maybe our new neighbors will be so eager to get rid of us, they'll offer to buy us out at a profit like in *A Raisin in the Sun*."

"Keep making stupid jokes. That'll solve everything."

Abby walked out of the kitchen with Beatrice trailing her down the hall.

"Where are you going?"

Abby stopped and spun around. "Please, don't let me stand in the way of you freeing yourself from this den of oppression any longer. Happy house hunting."

With that, she grabbed her purse and slammed the door on her way out.

Beatrice slumped in a chair, a pit in her stomach growing as she feared she'd pushed Abby too far. Is this what she truly wanted, to own a home alone?

❖

By seven p.m. Abby still hadn't returned home or called. Beatrice had grown increasingly frantic as the hours ticked away. She'd placed a couple of calls to Donna, who denied knowing her whereabouts, but, of course, she was lying. Unable to stay home and watch the clock any longer, she sought refuge in Ricky's company at Dandy's.

"You should cut her some slack," Ricky said, sipping a daiquiri.

"You're a traitor, Ricky. Since when do you advocate hiding?"

"Yes, I'm out, but look at me. I couldn't pass if I tried."

Beatrice watched his hand flamboyantly poke at his hair.

"Oh, please don't tell me you would pass if you could. I can't take being disillusioned by another person I respect."

"All I'm saying is I understand why people do. I'm sure it makes life a lot easier."

Beatrice grimaced.

"Do you know what it was like growing up gay with two older brothers?" He paused dramatically. "They smacked me around regularly, thinking the solution to my femininity was to beat the faggot out of me. The only fruits Latinos can deal with are the ones on top of Carmen Miranda's head. I had to move more than a thousand miles from south Florida to feel comfortable with myself. So no, I don't blame Abby if she isn't beating down everyone's door singing, 'Take a Look at Me.'"

This was all too familiar to Beatrice, a broken record skipping over a nasty refrain. "Okay, okay. I can see I picked the wrong audience to seek sympathy from."

"I don't mean to sound like I'm taking sides, Bea. I just know what it's like to be afraid. I work in a kitchen. If I get canned, my job is a dime a dozen. Yours aren't. Once people find out you two are shacking up in a house you bought together, that's it, the jig is up.

Your brother and Gwen accepting you is definitely an exception to the rule."

"My brother doesn't accept me. He tolerates me for Gwen's sake."

"Then consider yourself among the fortunate few."

"Abby doesn't even see her family. She talks to her sisters on the phone occasionally, but her father disowned her years ago when he found out."

"That doesn't help you see her point of view?"

Beatrice slumped in her seat. "You're making me feel like a first-class heel."

"I don't mean to, but we're not all as courageous as you are, Bea. Some of us have more to lose. When you walk down the street, nobody shouts 'queer' or 'faggot' and throws rocks or empty beer bottles at you."

"That happened to you?"

Ricky nodded and stirred his cocktail.

"That's awful." She shook her head with indignation and sympathy. "But I'm not trying to pass. This is just how I look."

"I know, and it insulates you from some of the shit the rest of us have had to take."

"I get scared, too, you know. Do you know how nervous I was telling Gwen face to face? When I was with Paul and realized I could never have a normal life with a man, I was absolutely terrified. But I knew I couldn't be happy if I kept trying to fool myself so I could fit in."

"Like I said, some people don't have your courage."

"So you're saying I should just surrender my dream and stay in that apartment for the rest of my life?"

"I'm saying give her more time."

"I've already given her four years. How much more time does she need?"

"How much do you love her?"

Beatrice sighed. She couldn't possibly quantify the depth of her love for Abby.

She left Dandy's prepared to apologize to Abby for the ultimatum but determined to let her know it was something she wanted in the future. As she walked up the steps to their building, she checked her watch. It was nearly eleven p.m., but their apartment was still dark. Unlocking the door, she assumed Abby had gone to bed already. She flicked on the light and walked toward the bedroom, rehearsing her words so they wouldn't sound like a complete surrender.

"Abby," she said in a raspy whisper. "Are you asleep?"

No answer.

When she entered their room, the undisturbed quilt and pillows startled her. Where had Abby been all night? She had to come home eventually, hadn't she? When she did, how would she react? Would she accept Beatrice's apology, or had the ultimatum done irreparable damage?

Beatrice was disoriented when the jingle of the key in the door woke her from a fitful sleep. She looked at the clock. Six forty a.m. She'd fallen asleep on top of the bed in her clothes waiting for Abby, and at last, she was finally home. She smoothed her wild hair as she padded into the living room.

"Hi," Abby said tentatively.

"Hi," Beatrice said, inching closer. "Where were you?"

"Donna's."

"Remind me to thank her for lying to me."

"It's not her fault. I asked her to."

"I was worried about you. I never even changed out of my clothes in case the police called."

"I'm sorry. I needed some time to think." Abby kept her distance at the credenza where she tossed her keys in a decorative bowl.

"Abby, I just want—"

"Bea, I don't want to lose you."

Beatrice charged at her and bound her in an embrace. "I don't want to lose you either. I'm sorry about the ultimatum."

After a moment, Abby pulled back to look at her. "You have a right to want what you want. But I'm a private person, Bea, not an activist. I'm extremely uncomfortable opening myself up to that kind of scrutiny if it's not necessary."

"I never asked you to be an activist, just to share my dreams."

Beatrice walked into the kitchen, bristling at the bitter taste of defeat. As she made a pot of coffee, she cried quietly, confronted with the choice of either letting Abby or her convictions go. As much as she wanted to win this debate for all the right reasons, she could never savor any victory if it meant losing Abby. She quickly dried her eyes in the crooks of her arms as Abby came up behind her.

"You know, um," Abby began, clearing her throat, "I don't suppose there's any harm in taking in an open house or two in West Chester some Sunday."

Beatrice grabbed Abby's hands and pulled her close, scooping her up in a hug. "Do you mean it?"

Abby smiled. "It wouldn't hurt to look."

❖

Gazing out at downtown New Haven's skyline of office towers, Beatrice simmered in frustration from the chair beside her mother's hospital bed. She drove all the way up to New Haven for the third health scare in as many months, and there her mother sat, propped up with pillows, reading *National Enquirer* as though she were under a dryer at the salon. She murmured her disapproval at Liz Taylor's romantic escapades and her relief at the distant locations of the latest UFO sightings. Beatrice cleared her throat in an effort to win her mother's attention.

"Beatrice, you don't have to sit here all afternoon," her mother finally said without an upward glance from the paper. "I'm going to be fine. They're releasing me tomorrow."

"Mom, you have to start taking better care of your blood pressure. You're in here again, and this time for a heart attack, not indigestion."

Mrs. Darby flattened the paper in her lap and rolled her eyes. "It was a mild heart attack, and I do take care of myself."

That wasn't exactly true. Since developing high blood pressure, her mother had neglected to take her medication regularly and follow a proper diet.

"I think you should give serious thought to Gwen and Quentin's offer to live with them. You shouldn't be by yourself all the time."

"Beatrice, I'm only fifty-nine. That's hardly ancient."

"But you're not a healthy fifty-nine. Something could happen to you, and you could die before anyone got to you."

"Well, maybe if you called me more often." She picked up the paper again and peeked over the top for Beatrice's reaction.

"I could call you every day, but that's not going to make you any safer. I really think you ought to move in with Quent."

"Don't be ridiculous, Bea. They have two wild little girls over there. Their house is a free-for-all."

Beatrice groaned as her conscience needled her to pose the dreaded question. "Do you want to stay with me?"

Her mother chuckled. "How would moving to that filthy city be better for my health?"

"Abby and I are closing on a house in a few weeks. It's a nice place in a quiet suburb of Queens."

She dropped the paper in her lap. "Closing? What does that mean?"

"Abby and I are buying a house."

"Together? Is it a two-family?"

"No, Mom, it's a one-family, a three-bedroom ranch."

Mrs. Darby shifted in bed and poked the tabloid with contempt. "Can you believe what this Hollywood has come to? None of them have any morals anymore, everyone sleeping with everyone else."

Beatrice grew anxious for her mother to finish processing the news.

"It's distasteful is what it is."

"Don't I even get a congratulations?" Beatrice said with a wan smile.

Her mother closed the paper in her lap and folded her hands over it. "You want me to congratulate you for buying a house with another woman? I don't even know what to say about that."

"This can't come as a surprise to you. I've been with Abby for five years now."

"What do you mean you've 'been' with her?"

"God, Mom, you really don't know?" Beatrice scratched her head, beyond flustered. "Abby and I are a, I mean, I'm a, I'm gay, Mom. I'm a lesbian."

Had Mrs. Darby's doctor seen the look on her face then, he would've undoubtedly reconsidered her discharge.

"Beatrice Ann Darby, tell me you're joking."

"This isn't something to joke about."

"I should say not. Homosexuality is a sin, a sickness."

"Sin, yes, in an abstract way, but it's not a sickness. In fact, I know a few straight people with more screws loose than my gay friends."

"Gay friends? Good Lord, Beatrice, don't you know you're judged by the company you keep? People are going to start assuming you are."

"I am," Beatrice shouted. "I am, and I'm tired of caring what other people think."

She clutched the window ledge to steady herself. After an eleven-year journey to feel comfortable in her own skin, one singular glare from her mother threatened to derail the entire process. Out of nowhere tears began streaming down her cheeks.

She thought she'd stopped needing her mother's approval long ago and now this? After encountering glowers and whispers during her five years with Abby, including the recent remark by a real-estate broker about being unable to land men as they house hunted, Beatrice believed the experiences had cultivated a skin so thick a knife literally couldn't cut her. But now she stood in front of her ailing mother, a frightened child wishing for a bed to hide under until the storm of judgment blew out to sea.

Mrs. Darby exhaled a choked-off breath and stared at her as though Beatrice were a cold-war spy.

Beatrice finally released her own breath, still unable to look her mother in the eye. She reached for a tissue on the nightstand and patted her wet eyelashes. "You have nothing else to say?"

Her mother casually flipped through the gossip rag. "So, this is it, huh? This is the life you've chosen for yourself? All my carrying on about a husband and family year in and year out was a waste of my breath."

"I wouldn't exactly call it a choice," Beatrice replied.

"No? Then what would you call it?

"It's who I am, Mom. I'm happy with Abby, so the only choice I've made is to be with the person who makes me happy."

"This is ridiculous. This isn't who you are. It isn't how God made you, and it's certainly not how I raised you."

"How do you know this isn't the way God made me?"

"Because it's a sin. It says so right in the Bible. It's unnatural. God made Adam and Eve so they could procreate. End of story."

"It's not the end of the story. It's where the narrow-minded think it ends."

"I am not narrow-minded."

"You never had sex without intending to procreate? You never once had sex and waited on pins and needles for days afterward hoping the rabbit didn't die?"

Her mother tossed the magazine at the foot of her bed. "I don't need to explain to you the personal details of my marriage to your father."

"Then why do I have to explain the personal details of my relationship with Abby?"

"You can't compare your fling with this woman to a marriage."

"Sure I can. Abby and I have a committed relationship."

"It's abnormal, an abomination in God's eyes."

Beatrice gripped the bed's metal foot rail. "Would you just shut up about it being abnormal and sinful. Just shut up about it. Loving someone is not a sin."

"I'd love to know what Bible you're reading."

"I'm not reading any Bible, and if the one you're reading is telling you that loving and caring about someone is an abomination, you should stick to *National Enquirer*."

Mrs. Darby shook her head. "You don't have children, so you can't possibly understand how it feels knowing your own flesh and blood is going to burn in hell. You ought to have counsel with Father Perrelli before you go home. I've always felt guilty about not being stricter with you kids about church. And now look—I'm being punished for it."

Beatrice smirked. "*You're* being punished."

"You don't go around telling everyone about this, do you?"

"I don't have to. The billboard I took out on Fifth Avenue reaches a wide audience."

"I can do without your sarcasm, Beatrice. Obviously, you have no use for social traditions, but I am still your mother and deserve respect."

"I think everyone deserves to be treated with respect."

Mrs. Darby closed her eyes and folded her hands across her chest. "I'm very tired, Beatrice. Thank you for coming by."

Her mouth open, armed for a war of words, Beatrice stared dumbly at her mother's eyeballs twitching under her eyelids. No matter how convincing her logic was, clearly, she would never change her mother's opinion.

"Sure," she said after a long silence. She shuffled across the green-and-white tile floor and stopped at the door. "I hope my news didn't upset you."

"Not at all. It's what every mother longs to hear."

Beatrice stewed in the elevator all the way down to the lobby, disappointed with herself for not only letting her mother have the last word again but for allowing her to see that she'd got to her, *again*. The train ride home had softened her enough to smile when she saw Abby waiting in the car outside the station.

"Hi." Abby pulled away from public view before leaning to the side to receive Beatrice's peck on her cheek. "How is she?"

"I almost gave her a second heart attack telling her about us."

"Oh, Bea, you didn't," Abby said, shaking her head. "I guess that means she's not moving in with us."

"After hearing the news, she'd prefer dying alone in her apartment to our cozy digs in the suburbs."

"You sure picked a fine time to spring it on her."

"No time like the present."

Abby smiled and grabbed Beatrice's hand. "If she's still speaking to you, it turned out better than I'd expected."

Beatrice closed her eyes and reclined her seat, exhausted from the exchange. "I'm twenty-eight years old. I really thought I'd gotten over my need for her acceptance."

"She's your mother. We all want our parents' approval, no matter how old we are."

"You've done all right without it."

Abby shrugged. "So have you. And you never know. She may just need a little time to digest the news."

Beatrice laced her fingers through Abby's. "Oh, you really think so?"

"No," Abby said, and squeezed Beatrice's hand playfully. "Hey, how about I run you a nice, hot bath when we get home? With a glass of chardonnay, too?"

"Only if you'll join me."

"In the wine or the bath?"

"Both."

Beatrice glanced at Abby's profile, warmed by the laugh lines around her mouth and the familiar curves of her face. She smiled to herself, grateful that for every leap of faith she took in life, Abby's love and loyalty were constants.

Although Beatrice had hoped her mother would eventually come to terms with her identity, she never did. After six months of dodging the issue in conversation altogether, Mrs. Darby died of a heart attack.

CHAPTER SEVENTEEN

Gwen had delivered the news by phone two days earlier, but seeing her mother's name arranged on the sign in white peg letters stopped Beatrice cold in the funeral home's foyer.

"Are you ready?" Abby asked after a moment.

Beatrice stared at the letters until they blurred.

Abby's comforting caress on her back finally encouraged Beatrice to step toward the viewing room. As the instrumental to "Nearer My Heart to Thee" filled the room, she and Abby walked toward Quentin, Gwen, and their daughters hovering by the flower-lined casket twenty minutes before calling hours began. Her eyes pooled when she recognized the heart-shaped rose bouquet draped with a *Mother* sash that she and Abby had selected from a florist's catalog. She let her eyes slowly drift to the body lying in the casket. Her mother looked so peaceful, as though she were simply asleep, her gray hair arranged in the neat bun she'd always worn, her head cradled in a pillow.

Beatrice knelt before the casket, signed the Trinity, and mouthed a perfunctory prayer, her insides tangled in a knot of regret. Had she made an awful mistake all these years? Was it her fault they'd never developed the warm mother-daughter relationship she'd always longed for, especially after her father died? If she was honest with herself, she'd never been very good at agreeing to disagree. She'd never given up hope, though, that her mother would somehow find a way to accept and be proud of the woman she'd become. Now, that hope was hours away from being sealed forever inside silk and mahogany. As she rested her hand on her mother's, cold and draped in rosary beads, her tears flowed without restraint.

Toward the end of the wake, in the fluorescent light of the ladies' room, Beatrice leaned over the sink and blotted the mascara streaks from under her vacant eyes. The mixed aroma of roses and tiger lilies lingering in her nostrils reminded her of her father's funeral two decades earlier. She pictured her mother shaking her head at the drunken Darby uncles and her father's cronies from the bar carrying on at O'Shaughnessy's Pub after the burial. It had been the worst day of her life, and they were all laughing as though his death was the social event of the season. As punishment, she'd licked her fingers and run them across the platter of corned beef at their table while they were lost in slurred storytelling.

It wasn't until much later that she realized they seemed happy because they were celebrating their beloved friend, a man who loved life and brought such joy to theirs. She reveled in the memory of her father convincing her she was skilled enough to play outfield for the Yankees, teaching her how to deal with stage fright at the spelling bee, and taking her out in the yard to show her how to box like Sonny Liston so when her brother or anyone else bullied her, she could defend herself. She'd never thrown a punch in her life, though, honoring her father's belief that if she couldn't win an argument with words, it couldn't be won.

Then she thought of her mother's legacy. She was such a bitter woman, always blaming others for her unhappiness, expending so much energy wishing for things that would never be. Who would be celebrating her life after she was laid to rest? Softly, the tears fell again.

"You okay?" Abby said as she crept in.

Beatrice nodded with a wry smile. "I'm a real head case, huh? Who da thunk it?"

"She's your mom, no matter how difficult she was." Abby squeezed her shoulder. "She loved you, you know that. She only wanted the best for you."

"Why didn't I try harder to understand that?" Beatrice whimpered, taking Abby into her arms.

Abby tucked her head under Beatrice's chin and held on tightly. "Because you were trying so hard to understand yourself."

❖

After the funeral service, Beatrice crossed the restaurant's red-and-black swirled wall-to-wall carpet toward the bar to get much-needed cocktails for Abby and her. Cigarette smoke clouded the rectangular stream of early afternoon sunlight pouring into the dusky room. She planted her elbows on the bar and smiled to herself, relieved to be on cordial terms with Gwen and Quentin and uplifted at the thought of slowly building relationships with them and her nieces.

"Hope you're not still tryin' to dodge me, Darby."

She smirked at the voice. Turning to its owner, she gave him a playful punch on his chest. "Rob, so glad you could join us here."

Her old friend, Robert, clasped her hands in his. "How ya' doing?"

"I'm all right. God, it's been so long. What's going on with you?"

"Oh, you know, can't complain. Got a great wife, a couple of kids, a house in East Haven, the whole deal." He handed her a picture from his wallet.

"Your wife's beautiful," she said, "and your boy looks just like you."

"She wanted to come meet you, but she had to take Debbie to the doctor's. She got strep or something."

"That's awfully nice of her. And nice of you to come, too, Rob. It means a lot."

"It's nothing, Bea. I've always thought of you as a good friend, you know? A pal." Robert looked down, his shyness still as charming as when he was a teenager. "Jill and me, we'd like to have you and your friend over for dinner some time, you know, to catch up under happier circumstances."

"Abby and I would like that." She smiled awkwardly, adding, "You know, she's more than just my friend."

He nodded bashfully. "Yeah, I kinda figured. You did all right there, Darby."

"How come you're not falling over in shock or disappointment or horror?" she asked playfully.

"Eh, what for? It all makes perfect sense. What other reason would you have to turn down a mug like this?" He guided his chin to a profile with his index finger and laughed.

Beatrice grinned, pleased that neither time nor age had diminished his goofy appeal.

"So, how about tomorrow night? Or do you have to hurry home to the Big Apple and your big-shot writing and professor jobs?"

"How do you know that about me?"

"I ran into your mom downtown not too long ago, and she told me." His gestures became animated as he relayed the encounter. "All I says to her is 'hello, Mrs. Darby,' and the next thing you know, she takes me by the arm, telling me all about how you're a college professor and had stuff published in magazines. So I says to her, 'Sure, rub it in my face that I let her get away.'"

"She said that?" Her eyes began to pool from a strange twist of vindication and sorrow. How little she had truly known about her mother.

"Jeez, you okay, Bea?" Robert's face grew somber as he patted her arm. "Sure, it's a tough thing. Boy, was she proud of you."

Beatrice stood up straight and wiped under her eyes. "I'm really glad you came," she said, clinging to him.

As Beatrice approached the table with their drinks, she was awed by the natural beauty of Gwen and Abby sitting together, immersed in conversation as her nieces wriggled around in their laps. She handed Abby her 7 and 7 as she sat and entertained Janie by making her Raggedy Ann doll dance on the tablecloth.

After finishing her discussion with Abby, Gwen glanced around Joanne's head toward Beatrice. "How are you doing?"

As Beatrice admired their four faces, a collage of unconditional love, she experienced a sense of peace she'd always longed for.

"I'm doing okay," she said with a smile.

About the Author

Jean Copeland is a writer and English/language arts teacher at an alternative high school in Connecticut. Taking a chance on a second career in her thirties, Jean graduated summa cum laude from Southern Connecticut State University with a BS in English education and an MS in English/creative writing. She has published numerous short fiction and essays online and in print anthologies.

In addition to the thrill of watching her students discover their talents in creative writing and poetry, she enjoys the escape of writing, summer decompression by the shore, and good wine and conversation with friends. Organ donation and shelter animal adoption are causes dear to her heart. *The Revelation of Beatrice Darby* is Jean's debut novel.

Books Available from Bold Strokes Books

Love's Bounty by Yolanda Wallace. Lobster boat captain Jake Myers stopped living the day she cheated death, but meeting greenhorn Shy Silva stirs her back to life. (978-1-62639334-9)

Just Three Words by Melissa Brayden. Sometimes the one you want is the one you least suspect. Accountant Samantha Ennis has her ordered life disrupted when heartbreaker Hunter Blair moves into her trendy Soho loft. (978-1-62639-335-6)

Lay Down the Law by Carsen Taite. Attorney Peyton Davis returns to her Texas roots to take on big oil and the Mexican Mafia, but will her investigation thwart her chance at true love? (978-1-62639-336-3)

Playing in Shadow by Lesley Davis. Survivor's guilt threatens to keep Bryce trapped in her nightmare world unless Scarlet's love can pull her out of the darkness back into the light. (978-1-62639-337-0)

Soul Selecta by Gill McKnight. Soul mates are hell to work with. (978-1-62639-338-7)

The Revelation of Beatrice Darby by Jean Copeland. Adolescence is complicated, but Beatrice Darby is about to discover how impossible it can seem to a lesbian coming of age in conservative 1950s New England. (978-1-62639-339-4)

Twice Lucky by Mardi Alexander. For firefighter Mackenzie James and Dr. Sarah Macarthur, there's suddenly a whole lot more in life to understand, to consider, to risk…someone will need to fight for her life. (978-1-62639-325-7)

Shadow Hunt by L.L. Raand. With young to raise and her Pack under attack, Sylvan, Alpha of the wolf Weres, takes on her greatest challenge when she determines to uncover the faceless enemies known as the Shadow Lords. A Midnight Hunters novel. (978-1-62639-326-4)

Heart of the Game by Rachel Spangler. A baseball writer falls for a single mom, but can she ever love anything as much as she loves the game? (978-1-62639-327-1)

Getting Lost by Michelle Grubb. Twenty-eight days, thirteen European countries, a tour manager fighting attraction, and an accused murderer: Stella and Phoebe's journey of a lifetime begins here. (978-1-62639-328-8)

Prayer of the Handmaiden by Merry Shannon. Celibate priestess Kadrian must defend the kingdom of Ithyria from a dangerous enemy and ultimately choose between her duty to the Goddess and the love of her childhood sweetheart, Erinda. (978-1-62639-329-5)

The Witch of Stalingrad by Justine Saracen. A Soviet "night witch" pilot and American journalist meet on the Eastern Front in WW II and struggle through carnage, conflicting politics, and the deadly Russian winter. (978-1-62639-330-1)

Pedal to the Metal by Jesse J. Thoma. When unreformed thief Dubs Williams is released from prison to help Max Winters bust a car theft ring, Max learns that to catch a thief, get in bed with one. (978-1-62639-239-7)

Dragon Horse War by D. Jackson Leigh. A priestess of peace and a fiery warrior must defeat a vicious uprising that entwines their destinies and ultimately their hearts. (978-1-62639-240-3)

For the Love of Cake by Erin Dutton. When everything is on the line, and one taste can break a heart, will pastry chefs Maya and Shannon take a chance on reality? (978-1-62639-241-0)

Betting on Love by Alyssa Linn Palmer. A quiet country-girl-at-heart and a live-life-to-the-fullest biker take a risk at offering each other their hearts. (978-1-62639-242-7)

The Deadening by Yvonne Heidt. The lines between good and evil, right and wrong, have always been blurry for Shade. When Raven's actions force her to choose, which side will she come out on? (978-1-62639-243-4)

Ordinary Mayhem by Victoria A. Brownworth. Faye Blakemore has been taking photographs since she was ten, but those same photographs threaten to destroy everything she knows and everything she loves. (978-1-62639-315-8)

One Last Thing by Kim Baldwin & Xenia Alexiou. Blood is thicker than pride. The final book in the Elite Operative Series brings together foes, family, and friends to start a new order. (978-1-62639-230-4)

Songs Unfinished by Holly Stratimore. Two aspiring rock stars learn that falling in love while pursuing their dreams can be harmonious— if they can only keep their pasts from throwing them out of tune. (978-1-62639-231-1)

Beyond the Ridge by L.T. Marie. Will a contractor and a horse rancher overcome their family differences and find common ground to build a life together? (978-1-62639-232-8)

Swordfish by Andrea Bramhall. Four women battle the demons from their pasts. Will they learn to let go, or will happiness be forever beyond their grasp? (978-1-62639-233-5)

The Fiend Queen by Barbara Ann Wright. Princess Katya and her consort Starbride must turn evil against evil in order to banish Fiendish power from their kingdom, and only love will pull them back from the brink. (978-1-62639-234-2)

Up the Ante by PJ Trebelhorn. When Jordan Stryker and Ashley Noble meet again fifteen years after a short-lived affair, are either of them prepared to gamble on a chance at love? (978-1-62639-237-3)

Speakeasy by MJ Williamz. When mob leader Helen Byrne sets her sights on the girlfriend of Al Capone's right-hand man, passion and tempers flare on the streets of Chicago. (978-1-62639-238-0)

Venus in Love by Tina Michele. Morgan Blake can't afford any distractions and Ainsley Dencourt can't afford to lose control—but the beauty of life and art usually lies in the unpredictable strokes of the artist's brush. (978-1-62639-220-5)

Rules of Revenge by AJ Quinn. When a lethal operative on a collision course with her past agrees to help a CIA analyst on a critical assignment, the encounter proves explosive in ways neither woman anticipated. (978-1-62639-221-2)

The Romance Vote by Ali Vali. Chili Alexander is a sought-after campaign consultant who isn't prepared when her boss's daughter, Samantha Pellegrin, comes to work at the firm and shakes up Chili's life from the first day. (978-1-62639-222-9)

Advance: Exodus Book One by Gun Brooke. Admiral Dael Caydoc's mission to find a new homeworld for the Oconodian people is hazardous, but working with the infuriating Commander Aniwyn "Spinner" Seclan endangers her heart and soul. (978-1-62639-224-3)

UnCatholic Conduct by Stevie Mikayne. Jil Kidd goes undercover to investigate fraud at St. Marguerite's Catholic School, but life gets complicated when her student is killed—and she begins to fall for her prime target. (978-1-62639-304-2)

Season's Meetings by Amy Dunne. Catherine Birch reluctantly ventures on the festive road trip from hell with beautiful stranger Holly Daniels only to discover the road to true love has its own obstacles to maneuver. (978-1-62639-227-4)

Myth and Magic: Queer Fairy Tales edited by Radclyffe and Stacia Seaman. Myth, magic, and monsters—the stuff of childhood dreams (or nightmares) and adult fantasies. (978-1-62639-225-0)

Nine Nights on the Windy Tree by Martha Miller. Recovering drug addict, Bertha Brannon, is an attorney who is trying to stay clean when a murder sends her back to the bad end of town. (978-1-62639-179-6)

Driving Lessons by Annameekee Hesik. Dive into Abbey Brooks's sophomore year as she attempts to figure out the amazing, but sometimes complicated, life of a you-know-who girl at Gila High School. (978-1-62639-228-1)

Asher's Shot by Elizabeth Wheeler. Asher Price's candid photographs capture the truth, but when his success requires exposing an enemy, Asher discovers his only shot at happiness involves revealing secrets of his own. (978-1-62639-229-8)

Courtship by Carsen Taite. Love and justice—a lethal mix or a perfect match? (978-1-62639-210-6)

Against Doctor's Orders by Radclyffe. Corporate financier Presley Worth wants to shut down Argyle Community Hospital, but Dr. Harper Rivers will fight her every step of the way, if she can also fight their growing attraction. (978-1-62639-211-3)

A Spark of Heavenly Fire by Kathleen Knowles. Kerry and Beth are building their life together, but unexpected circumstances could destroy their happiness. (978-1-62639-212-0)

Never Too Late by Julie Blair. When Dr. Jamie Hammond is forced to hire a new office manager, she's shocked to come face to face with Carla Grant and memories from her past. (978-1-62639-213-7)

Widow by Martha Miller. Judge Bertha Brannon must solve the murder of her lover, a policewoman she thought she'd grow old with. As more bodies pile up, the murderer starts coming for her. (978-1-62639-214-4)

Twisted Echoes by Sheri Lewis Wohl. What's a woman to do when she realizes the voices in her head are real? (978-1-62639-215-1)

Criminal Gold by Ann Aptaker. Through a dangerous night in New York in 1949, Cantor Gold, dapper dyke-about-town, smuggler of fine art, is forced by a crime lord to be his instrument of vengeance. (978-1-62639-216-8)

The Melody of Light by M.L. Rice. After surviving abuse and loss, will Riley Gordon be able to navigate her first year of college and accept true love and family? (978-1-62639-219-9)

Because of You by Julie Cannon. What would you do for the woman you were forced to leave behind? (978-1-62639-199-4)

The Job by Jove Belle. Sera always dreamed that she would one day reunite with Tor. She just didn't think it would involve terrorists, firearms, and hostages. (978-1-62639-200-7)

Making Time by C.J. Harte. Two women going in different directions meet after fifteen years and struggle to reconnect in spite of the past that separated them. (978-1-62639-201-4)

Once The Clouds Have Gone by KE Payne. Overwhelmed by the dark clouds of her past, Tag Grainger is lost until the intriguing and spirited Freddie Metcalfe unexpectedly forces her to reevaluate her life. (978-1-62639-202-1)